"The slow build of Winter and Cade's relationship is satisfying and real. Walsh's debut raises the bar for NA books and will leave readers hungry for more."   —*Booklist* (starred review)

"This is why I love New Adult! Everything about *Caged in Winter* felt real. And Cade? Perfect book boyfriend."

—Jennifer L. Armentrout, #1 *New York Times* and
USA Today bestselling author

"Delicious! Captivating, sexy, and empowering, Walsh has created the perfect recipe for an unforgettable romance. Cade Maxwell is the best kind of hero—strong yet gentle, ambitious yet selfless. And Winter is a heroine to cheer for. A fabulous debut!"

—Rachel Harris, bestselling author

"With characters so real I feel like I've known them all my life, *Caged in Winter* is pure, sweet, hot romance. It's a must-read!"

—M. Leighton, *New York Times* bestselling author

Berkley titles by Brighton Walsh

CAGED IN WINTER
TESSA EVER AFTER

Tessa
EVER AFTER

BRIGHTON WALSH

BERKLEY BOOKS, NEW YORK

THE BERKLEY PUBLISHING GROUP
Published by the Penguin Group
Penguin Group (USA) LLC
375 Hudson Street, New York, New York 10014

USA • Canada • UK • Ireland • Australia • New Zealand • India • South Africa • China

penguin.com

A Penguin Random House Company

This book is an original publication of The Berkley Publishing Group.

Library of Congress Cataloging-in-Publication Data

Walsh, Brighton.
Tessa ever after / Brighton Walsh.—Berkley trade paperback edition.
pages ; cm
ISBN 978-0-425-27649-5 (paperback)
I. Title.
PS3623.A4454T47 2015
813'.6—dc23
2014046278

PUBLISHING HISTORY
Berkley trade paperback edition / May 2015

PRINTED IN THE UNITED STATES OF AMERICA

10 9 8 7 6 5 4 3 2 1

Cover photo: *Woman Portrait* by Sheftsoff/Shutterstock.
Cover design by Rita Frangie.
Interior text design by Kristin del Rosario.

To my husband,
because even though you lucked out
by getting to play Jedis instead of tea parties,
I know you would totally don
a bright yellow hat and pink feather boa,
because that's the kind of dad you are.

ACKNOWLEDGMENTS

I'm so lucky to have a wonderful team of people on my side to help me along the way when I'm sure I can't do this on my own. Thank you goes out to all the usual suspects for their help in making *Tessa Ever After* what it is today:

To Mandy for suggesting snippets of scenes to include and for a breakneck brainstorming session that set me at ease and let me breathe a little easier.

To Leis for digging deep, asking the tough questions, and coaxing the very best for these characters from my brain.

To Christina for being my sounding board and my Plot Whisperer and my ever-present, always-willing cheerleader. If I've said it once, I've said it a million times: You are a sanity saver.

To my BFF, Jaime, for being the first to set eyes on this baby in its entirety, for brainstorming with me when I had no idea what to do, and for loving Jason as much as I do.

To Amanda for giving me the idea of a non-cheesy-but-still-swoony non-grand grand gesture. I think it was a success.

To the readers who enjoyed Cade and Winter's story and were clamoring for Jason and Tessa's book while I was still working on it. It still amazes me people besides my friends read my books.

To my 4EvNo peeps who sprinted with me while I wrote this baby in a blur of shower-free days and evenings of takeout. Thank you for not judging my lack of hygiene/housekeeping.

To all the girls in Brighton's Brigade over on Facebook for being excited to get Jason and Tessa's story, and for giving me rec after rec for heroes that meet my, ahem, discerning tastes.

And, finally, to my guys. My little ones, who gave me the inspiration for blipstick, pamcakes, and zoomeums. So much of Haley's mannerisms, ideas, and speech patterns came from remembered times from when you were her age. And my big one, who teaches the important things to our kids . . . like how to do a flawless maniacal laugh. You all make my world bright, just being in it.

ONE

tessa

Some days I feel like I'm running forever on a treadmill that won't get me anywhere. Constantly behind, yet always moving.

I glance at my phone, noting the time, and try to rush my client out the door without being obvious about the fact that I'm doing it. It's not that I don't love her, because I do. She's a regular, someone who took a chance on a girl barely out of cosmetology school, and has stuck with me for the last three years, referring dozens upon dozens of friends my way while she was at it. But tonight, when I'm already running late getting Haley from day care, I just want her to stop talking and *leave*. I stayed late as a favor to her, and I'm paying for it now. I should've known I could never squeeze her in, not when she likes to stick around to chat after her appointment.

Once I've finally ushered her out the door and I've cleaned up my station, I wave good-bye to the other girls working tonight and head out into the bitter fall air. I stuff my hands in my pockets and rush to the car, not waiting for it to warm up before I'm speeding down the streets, hoping to get to Haley before her day care officially closes for the day. But as the clock creeps toward six and then slowly ticks past, I know that hope is futile.

I pull in the driveway at quarter after and jog up the front walk, opening the handle to the door and pushing through the threshold.

"Mama!" Haley runs at me full force, her smile as bright as the sun, and I squat to catch her in my arms.

"Hey, baby. How was your day?"

"Good! Miss Melinda had us make our own turkeys for crafts today. Lookit! Mine has all kinds of colored feathers and one of those gobbler things."

I laugh at her description. "I love it! We'll have to put him on the fridge when we get home. Why don't you go grab your coat so we can go."

She spins and runs off without a second glance, and I stand to my full height and see Melinda leaning against the wall next to the door Haley just disappeared behind. "Hi, Tessa."

"Hey. I'm sorry I'm late again, but I ran behind with a client."

"Tessa . . ." And from the look on her face and the soft tone of her words, I know what's coming. I've been bracing for it for the last five months, wondering when it would finally come. "You know how much I love Haley, and I realize what an adjustment period this has been since your brother moved away. These last few months can't have been easy for you. But I have a family, too, and six o'clock is the start of their time."

"I know. God, I'm so sorry, Melinda." I glance to the door Haley is hidden behind and lower my voice so she doesn't over-hear. "It's taking me longer to get into the swing of things than I thought it would since Cade left. I can't apologize enough."

"I know you don't do it on purpose, honey, but the fact remains that it keeps happening. I think I've been more than understanding, considering how long it's been. I wanted to give you some leeway, since Cade helped so much with pickups. I haven't implemented the tardy fees, but going forward, I'm going to have to."

I nod my head, my lips pressed in a thin line. It's not the fees—while they're exorbitant to dissuade parents from being late, I could swing it if I needed to—it's the fact that she even has to have this conversation with me. I feel like a kid in the principal's office, and whether or not I'm barely twenty-two, I haven't been a child in a long, long time.

"I understand."

She pauses and shifts her weight from foot to foot. "I hate to even suggest this, but maybe you can find something closer to your work? Make it a bit easier to get there before closing? I could give you some referrals . . ."

I'm shaking my head before she can even finish, knowing I will do anything—*anything*—to keep Haley here. It's the only day care she's been in since she started going when she was only a baby. And after all the upheaval—her uncle leaving in the summer, and then starting pre-K this year—I don't want to force any other changes on her.

"I'm not going to do that. I'll make it work."

Just then, Haley comes running out of the walk-in coat closet where all the kids' cubbies and coat hooks are, her long, dark hair flying behind her, her eyes sparkling as she smiles. She's . . . remarkable. The best thing I've ever done in my entire life, and ever since Cade left, ever since I've been truly on my own, I feel like I'm failing her.

I always thought I had a good grip on the majority of things in her life, shouldered the bulk of it, but since my brother moved away, I've become blatantly aware of exactly how much he was helping, how much slack he was picking up. It sent me into a tailspin.

And I'm still trying to find my way out.

jason

It's nights like these that make me want to shoot myself in the face.

Smells from the kitchen waft into the formal dining room where my mother, father, and I sit, our conversation stilted as it is every Tuesday evening. The clank of silverware on dishes is the only sound in this too-big room, filled with knickknacks you can't touch, paintings that cost more than some people make in a year, and furniture you feel like you shouldn't even sit on. My childhood home. If you can call a museum a home.

As if my mother has a bell under the table signaling when we're finished with the first course, the newest maid comes sweeping into the room to clear our soup bowls, only to return moments later with salad plates. I hate Tuesday nights. Having to come back here and listen to the two people who view me as merely a means to an end . . . well, I think I'd rather get kicked in the balls repeatedly than be forced to suffer through this week after week.

Alas, they pay the bills . . .

"I saw Sheila at the club yesterday," my mother says, her voice dripping with disdain.

Dad hums, briefly looking up from the *Wall Street Journal* spread out in front of him. Bastard can't even spare twenty minutes without his attention focused elsewhere. No wonder my mom had a fling with the gardener.

My father doesn't say anything, but Mom takes it as a cue to continue. "It's obvious she got Botox. And, if I'm not mistaken, she got those saline lip injections, too. Honestly, if you're going to have work done, at least be a little more discreet about it. She could—"

And just like that, I zone out, filling my mind with a hundred different things, just so I can get through the next half hour with my sanity intact.

It's not until the main dish is in front of me—duck confit, I'm told—that I register my father clearing his throat, the room otherwise silent. I glance up, finding both my parents staring at me.

"What?"

My mom tsks, shaking her head. "Hardly the way to speak to your parents, Jason."

I roll my eyes, because they've been a lot of things to me in my twenty-four years, but parents haven't been one of them, despite how desperately I crave them to be—though I'd never admit that aloud.

"Your mother's right. You'd think you've forgotten just who pays your bills."

"Oh, believe me, I haven't forgotten. How can I when you remind me every week?"

My father's eyes don't leave mine as he takes a sip of his bourbon before placing the glass back on the table. That stare has been known to make both women and men weep. Having been on the receiving end of it more times than I can fathom, I'm unmoved, so I simply stare back.

"I think we've been very lenient and understanding about your . . . *education.*" The way he says it, the way the word almost seems to get stuck in his throat, like he has to spit it out, makes my shoulders tense. He doesn't believe an art school—despite its being one of the top art schools in the country—could ever provide me with the kind of education I walked away from when I left his alma mater, a well-regarded university I had absolutely no desire to attend. Not that he had much of a choice . . . I left after less than a semester, ready to get loans if I needed to, when my grandfather stepped in and paid for my first year at the art institute. He always told me I should do what I loved, despite what my father wanted. Despite what my parents wanted *for* me.

One could say he and my parents had slightly different outlooks on life. And family.

Unaware, or just uncaring, of my stiffened posture, he continues, "We allowed you to take a year off after high school to do God knows what while living off our money. And since that little break, we've given you five years to complete your degree, which is laughable, quite frankly, especially for someone who ranked in the top five percent of their high school graduating class. We've allowed you to switch schools from a prominent and distinguished university to something . . . better suited to your tastes. And in doing so, we've been on the receiving end of judgmental whispers at the club."

"Oh Jesus. Not *the club.* How did you survive?" After my grandpa passed away a few years ago, those judgmental whispers at the club were the exact reason my parents decided to foot the bill for the rest of my education at the school they deemed inappropriate. How would it look to have a *Montgomery* taking out loans for school?

"Jason Daniel, that's enough," my mother snaps.

As if I never spoke, my father continues, "We're done, Jason. You've screwed around long enough."

I wait for a moment for him to say something more, to clue me in on what he's threatening this time. We've been here before, too many times to count, and I'm not in the mood to play games. "You're going to have to spell it out for me, Dad, because I'm not sure what, exactly, you mean."

"What I mean is we will allow you this semester. I had our lawyer do some digging and check your records at school—"

"Oh, that's nice. Who'd you pay off to do that?"

"—and you have more than enough credits to graduate, if you'd just declare your major and apply for graduation." He sits back, dropping his napkin on the table before he folds his hands over his stomach. He's like an older version of me—dark hair with only a hint of gray at the temples, dark eyes that can turn cold in an instant, and enough height to feel prominent when walking into a room. I can only hope our similarities end at our appearance.

I'm doing everything I can to make sure of it. To make sure I turn out more like the man my grandfather was than the man my father is. And the fact that I'm striving to be as good of a man as the one my father loathed is just icing on the cake, really.

I try to see him through the eyes of someone else, someone who might look up to him, might even fear him, but no matter what I do, he's still the same guy I've known my whole life. The same guy who paid more attention to the newspaper or his phone or his computer than he did to his only son. The same guy who was always too busy to attend even one of his son's Little League games. The same guy who pushed for only the best out of his child—not for his happiness, but for how it would be perceived by others.

And the sad thing is, I forgave him for all of it. I looked past it all and accepted it. I didn't *like* it, but I accepted it. And then after my grandpa passed away, my father shut down the foundation my grandfather built from the ground up—one that provided homes for lower-class families—just so he could pocket more money, and that was it for me. I knew then he'd never be someone I could look up to.

When he's sure I'm not going to say anything, he puts it bluntly, "Tuition will be paid through this semester. Your allowance for rent and necessities will continue until you've earned your master's in architectural design. The paperwork has already been submitted; the . . . persuasions needed to admit you without a portfolio have been taken care of. While you're completing your degree, I expect you to be at the firm, shadowing me and learning the ropes. I'm not getting any younger, and I'd like to retire sometime in the next decade. God knows it'll take that long just for you to figure out what the hell you're doing and not fuck everything up."

"Lawrence . . ."

With a careless hand, my father waves off my mother's rebuke, not sparing her a glance. "January second, Jason. Not a day longer. I'm tired of waiting for you to come around and stop this bullshit of playing computer games or whatever the hell it is they have you do at that arts and crafts school. It's time you stopped acting like a spoiled child and stepped up to take your place at the company."

TWO

jason

I stalk out the front door of my parents' house, letting it slam shut behind me, muttering every swear word I can think of as I head straight to my car. Really, their ultimatum doesn't come as a shock. In fact, I'm surprised it's taken them this long to institute some sort of deadline. After all, it doesn't look good in their circles to have a twenty-four-year-old son still in college—not unless he's getting his MBA or doctorate.

And even now, even with them pushing me to get my master's, they'll still be embarrassed of everything I've done . . . of the path I've taken to get where I am.

While I know I've got it good—parents paying for my degree, as well as all my bills—it's not what I'd pick if I were given a choice. Growing up, I'd have given anything to be part of either of my best friends' families. Both Cade's and Adam's parents made it a point to be involved in the lives of their kids. Made it a point to talk about more than getting straight A's, college prep courses, what the stock of the company was doing . . . I can't even remember the last time either one of my parents asked me a question that actually gave them insight into my life. Or asked a question and waited for an honest reply. The only time I got even a semblance of that kind of affection was with my grandfather before he passed away—a man my father couldn't stand because he thought he was weak. Weak because he wasn't running a multimillion-dollar firm. Because he "threw away" his profits to help others. Because he was an honest and decent man, something my father knows nothing about.

I peel out of my parents' long, circular drive, uncaring of the tire marks I no doubt left, and I don't even realize where I'm heading until I see the familiar streets. For as long as I can remember, this place has always felt like home, much more than mine ever did. It's different now that Cade's gone, but a sense of relief still settles over me whenever I walk through the door.

It's not too late—the clock on my dash showing just before eight—and I hope I'm early enough to catch Haley before she goes to bed. If anyone can make me smile, it's that little girl. While it's a bit jarring to realize just how much I've grown attached to her in the months since Cade left, I can't argue with the truth.

Tessa's car is out front, and I head for the back door, twisting the knob like always, only to find it's locked. Since Cade's been gone, Tessa's been more diligent about locking up—something her brother probably beat into her head before he went. I knock softly in case Haley is sleeping, but after a few minutes with no answer, I dig out my keys, using the spare I've had for years to let myself in.

The scent of fried food greets me, and a glance in the kitchen shows leftover chicken nuggets and a few fries on a small princess plate. Definitely a change of pace from the days when Cade was living here. He'd have a coronary if he knew what Tess has been feeding his niece.

I walk through the dark hallway to get to the living room, stopping short at what I see. Haley's in front of the TV, markers spread out around her as she draws some pictures. When she turns around to look at me, I jolt in surprise at the state of her face, but I don't have time to say anything before she rushes me.

"Jay!" Her mouth splits into a full smile as she hops up from the floor and barrels straight into me. I catch her and scoop her into my arms, careful to not get whatever the hell she has all over her face on my clothes.

"Hey, shorty. What's, uh, what's all this?" I ask, gesturing to her eyelids and cheeks and lips painted in too many colors to count.

Instead of answering, she looks down, avoiding my eyes.

"Haley . . ."

She leans in and whispers in my ear, "I found Mama's makeup."

Oh shit. If there's one thing I've learned in the many years I've known Tessa, it's that her makeup and whatever hair product shit she brings home are off-limits. And anyone who touches them is taking their lives into their own hands. She's been like that since she was a teenager, and it's only gotten worse since she went to cosmetology school. Haley clearly did this without permission.

"Okay," I say, my voice even. "And where is your mom?"

She twists in my arms and points to the couch. I walk to it and peer over the back, finding a passed-out Tessa lying there, still in her all-black clothes from the salon, one arm covering her eyes, the other hanging off the side of the couch.

"How long's your mom been asleep?"

"Since *Doc McStuffins* started." Her eyes well up as she looks at me, her bottom lip quivering. Her voice is shaky as she asks, "You're not gonna tell her, are ya?"

I probably should. Grown-up solidarity and all that, but I have a soft spot for Haley. And I'm not much for being a grown-up. "Nah, it can be our little secret. Let's get you cleaned up and to bed. It's late and you have school tomorrow."

If Tessa fell asleep and managed to stay that way through the blare of some of the most obnoxious cartoons known to man, as well as Haley's and my conversation, she must be tired. I'll let her catch a bit more sleep while I get the munchkin ready for bed. I carry Haley down the hall, grabbing a washcloth out of the linen closet before heading into the bathroom. When she's perched on the counter, I turn on the water to warm it up, then start the daunting task of getting this shit off her face. She looks like a goddamn clown, her cheeks bright pink, her lips covered in red lipstick spread down to her chin, green crap all around her eyes.

I shake my head. "How long did this take you?"

"I dunno."

"You know you're not supposed to get into your mom's stuff, right?"

Head hanging, she pouts. "Yeah."

"Have you ever done this before?"

"Just once."

"I bet you got in trouble, too, didn't you?"

"Please don't tell her, Jay." Her bottom lip quivers, and this time the tears roll, fat and plentiful, down her rosy cheeks. One look into those dark brown eyes and I'm a goner. I always thought she was a cool kid, but that was about it—a cool kid I saw every once in a while. Ever since Cade left, though, she's clung to me, and in the process gotten me wrapped around her little finger.

"I won't, but only if you promise me something."

"I promise."

I laugh, wiping at the mess over her eyes. "I haven't even told you what it is yet."

"I still promise."

"Are you sure? Because I was going to make you promise to play Transformers with me every day for a week instead of your tea parties."

Her mouth drops open, her eyes comically wide.

"Just kidding. But you can't do this again."

"Okay."

"I mean it, shorty. Not again."

"Promise." She holds out her pinky for me to shake—some girlie thing that apparently means it's serious business—and I hook mine in hers.

"All right. Now, let's get you changed and then I'll read a story."

"*Two* stories."

"One, but nice try."

She looks off to the side, clearly thinking about how she can get something extra out of me. "'Kay, one, but with funny voices."

"Deal."

ONCE HALEY IS in her pajamas and I've read a story and tucked her into bed, I head back into the living room, finding a still-sleeping Tessa curled up on the couch. Her mouth is parted, her lower lip pouty and full and taunting the hell out of me. Her breaths are even and deep and, though I try to stop it, though I try to tell myself not to look, the movement draws my eyes right to her chest. I glance away quickly, though not before getting an eyeful, frustrated and irritated with myself that I can't seem to get past this sudden, overwhelming attraction to her. Though *sudden* isn't entirely accurate. It's been building for longer than I'd care to admit, even before Cade left. And in the months since he's been gone, it's only grown, as much as I've tried to stop it.

Feeling guilty that this is Cade's little sister—the same girl I've known since I was nine years old . . . the same girl Cade asked me to look after like she was *my* sister—I force myself to turn around and then start cleaning up the small mess Haley left, capping her markers and putting her drawing station where it belongs. Once that's done, I go into the kitchen and put the leftovers away. I see only Haley's plate and wonder if Tessa got anything to eat. And then I wonder why I'm even thinking about it in the first place.

When everything's put away, I make my way over to the couch to try and rouse Tessa. She sleeps like the dead—always has. I should be ashamed of some of the shit Cade, Adam, and I did to her when we were younger. Basically every practical joke you could play on a sleeping person was in our weekend repertoires for too many years to count. I don't think she's ever forgiven us for making her wet the bed when she was fourteen. And thinking that only reiterates how much more like a sister she *should* be to me than a girl I fantasize about when I jack off.

I squat beside the couch so I'm eye-level with her. Once I'm close enough, I notice the faint bruises under her eyes, the exhaustion cloaking her face, even in sleep. Her short, dark hair is falling over one of her eyes, and I have to physically restrain myself from reaching out and pushing it behind her ear. I scrub a hand over my face, forcing myself to get a fucking grip. What in the hell is wrong with me?

Dropping my hand, I grab hers and give it a little squeeze. She doesn't move, her eyelids not even fluttering. Knowing I won't be able to wake her, short of tossing ice water on her face, I bend and lift her easily from the couch. As I walk down the hallway toward her bedroom, I force myself to think of a thousand different things other than how her body feels pressed against mine. How her thighs feel under my arm, under my hand. How sweet the scent of her shampoo is and how she presses her face into my chest, trying to get closer.

Though it's not *me* she's trying to get closer to. She's subconsciously reaching for something—or someone—and it's definitely not me.

Once I get her set on the bed, I turn on her bedside lamp, then take her shoes off and toss them to the side. Even that simple act has me thinking of all the other items I'd like to remove from her body, and just like that I'm hard as a rock. Closing my eyes, I hiss out a curse and shake my head, pissed at myself for thinking this shit and pissed at my dick for being happy about it.

When I've talked my cock down and have myself under control, I try to shift her so I can get the covers out from underneath her. I jostle her enough that she finally rouses and turns toward me, her eyes fluttering once before she bolts upright, her forehead knocking me right in the chin.

"*Jesusfuck!*"

"Ow!" she groans as she presses her fingers to her forehead. "Jason? God, you scared the shit out of me! What are you doing in here?" She glances around the room, then down at her clothes before she checks the time. "It's almost nine? Shit, I have to get Haley ready for bed. I must've fallen asleep." She moves to get up, but I stop her, dropping on the end of her bed as I rub my chin where she whacked me.

"It's all right. I took care of it."

She snaps her head toward me, her eyebrows raised. "You did?" At my nod, she asks, "How long have you been here?"

"About an hour."

Her mouth drops open. "An *hour*? Why didn't you wake me up?"

"*Could* I have woken you up? Besides, I figured there was a reason you were passed out on the couch, so I thought I'd let you sleep. It wasn't a big deal."

"God, I am failing left and right today," she says as she falls back on the bed, her head on her pillow. The defeat bleeding into her voice is unmistakable.

"What do you mean you're failing left and right today?"

"It's nothing."

I raise an eyebrow, staying silent as I stare her down. We've played this game before, and I always win.

With a huff, she says, "I was late getting Haley from day care . . . *again*. Melinda says if it happens anymore, she's going to start charging me the tardy fees. And it's not even the money, you know? It's that I can't even get there to pick Haley up in the first place." She shakes her head, her arm going over her eyes. "I just feel like such a failure since Cade left. And I love that he went—hell, I *pushed* him to go. I didn't want him here anymore, not when he had that amazing opportunity. But . . . it's hard. I mean, I fed Haley frozen chicken nuggets for dinner tonight because I didn't have time to cook anything decent. Last night was boxed mac and cheese. The night before, Spaghettios. Meanwhile, Cade always had dinner worthy of a five-star restaurant ready for us every night."

"Cade's a chef, Tess."

She drops her arm to the bed as she looks at me again. "Doesn't matter. Every day, I feel a little worse about how I've been handling—or not handling—everything since he left. One of these days I'm going to wake up with a World's Shittiest Mom trophy next to my bed."

"Oh Jesus."

"Don't 'oh Jesus' me." She shoves her foot into my thigh, kicking me lightly. "I'm telling you how I feel. You don't get to poke and prod and push me to open up and then roll your eyes when I finally do. You wanted it, so you get the full brunt of it now."

I concede with a nod. "Fine. What else?"

She blows out a deep breath, her eyes on the ceiling. "I was just blind to everything he did for us, I guess. Which makes me a shitty sister on top of everything else. I feel like such an ass."

I roll my eyes—can't help it. She always was one for dramatics. "You're not an ass, Tess, or a shitty sister. And you're sure as hell not a shitty mom. Yeah, Cade did a lot when he was here, but you had one hundred percent of the responsibility heaped on you in a week when he was suddenly gone. Give yourself some time to acclimate."

"I maybe could've bought that back in June or even July, but it's been five months, Jason. Five *months*. I should have my shit together by now."

"Don't be so hard on yourself. You do a hell of a lot more than I ever could. It took me forty-five damn minutes just to get Haley in her pajamas and get her teeth brushed."

That finally pulls a smile from her. "Yeah, she needs a lot of direction at bedtime," she says with a laugh. "Thanks, by the way. She didn't give you any trouble, did she?"

"Nah, she's a good kid."

Her smile grows into the kind that lights up her whole face, and once again I'm struck by how fucking *gorgeous* she is. I don't know when she went from being annoying Tess, younger sister to my best friend, to being this . . . hot, amazing woman who I'd prefer wasn't related to any of my friends. It would sure make these near-constant and almost always inappropriate thoughts easier to handle.

"Thanks, I think so, too." She yawns, stretching out as she tucks her feet between my thigh and the mattress, and the easy physical affection between us is just another reminder of why I need to get my shit together and stop thinking about her under me in my bed. "Why'd you come over, anyway?"

The reminder of what happened before I came here is like a bucket of ice water down my pants. Closing my eyes, I groan and scrub a hand over my face.

"Uh-oh . . . only one thing gets the always-unshakable Jason that frustrated. Dinner at your parents', huh?"

"Yep."

"What happened now?"

I lie back on the bed and prop myself up on my elbows, turning my head to her. "They gave me an ultimatum. I have till the end of the semester to finish up my undergrad, then it's off to get my master's in architecture or they're cutting me off."

Her mouth pops open as she stares at me. "Seriously?"

I nod. "They found out I've got enough credits to graduate if I'd just declare a major, so they're not buying my bullshit anymore. No more putting off the inevitable. But, hey, I had a good solid five years of avoidance. Time to pay my dues, right?"

She's quiet long enough for me to raise my eyebrow at her in question. When she still doesn't say anything, I ask, "What's with the silence?"

"I don't know . . ." she says, hesitancy in her voice, then waves her hand while shaking her head. "Nothing, never mind."

"Jesus, Tess, just spit it out."

"I just . . . I don't get you. I mean, you've got this amazing job waiting for you after graduation, one most people fresh out of college—even after getting their master's—would kill for, where you'll probably make three times what I could ever even *hope* to make, and you're moping around like a petulant child. *And* it was your grandpa's firm . . . I thought working there would make you happy. What gives?"

I snap my mouth shut, clenching my jaw and blowing a deep breath through my nose. "Look, I know how good I have it, okay? And I feel like a selfish asshole for not being grateful for it. But how would you like it if your whole future had already been mapped out for you from before you could even walk? It's a lot of pressure. And not only that . . . Yeah, working for my grandpa's firm would be awesome, if I could do it on my terms, but my dad won't be satisfied with that. He won't accept me working in their web division. More than that, though, the firm stopped being my grandpa's when my dad got his claws in it, added a bunch of partners to boost revenue, and conveniently forgot about ethics. My grandpa is probably turning over in his grave at the shitshow my father has turned Montgomery International into."

"Have you actually *talked* to your dad about doing a different job within the company? Maybe he'd be okay with you taking on a lesser role in another department."

I shake my head. "Nope. No way he'd go for it. It's all or nothing with him. He doesn't know the meaning of the word *compromise*."

"So you're total opposites, then, huh?"

"When you start comparing me to my father, that's my cue to leave." I move to get up, but Tessa laughs, pressing both her feet on top of my thigh to get me to stay put.

"I'm just kidding; don't be so touchy. You're nothing like him, not really. But you *are* stubborn. Which is why I'm so surprised you're taking this lying down. Just try it. What have you got to lose? He might surprise you."

Or he might prove every thought I've ever had of him right, and I'd be back at square one.

THREE

tessa

Being on top of everything is *exhausting*. I got up thirty minutes earlier than usual just so I could have Haley's clothes set out for her and be able to make her something for breakfast other than cold cereal. It was only oatmeal, but hey . . . it's a step. I diligently stayed on schedule all day, moving faster when my clients showed up late, working my ass off to make sure I was out of the door of the salon by five thirty so I could get to Melinda's with time to spare.

Dinner still isn't up to Cade's standards, but I figure with everything else I managed to do today, I'd cut myself a little slack. I pick at the broiled chicken breast and salad I made for myself while Haley retells every second of her day in between bites of her food.

"... then we had snack. Apples and peanut butter. That's my favorite, huh?"

"Mhmm, I know, baby."

"And then we practiced our letters. We're on *j* this week. Like jump and jelly bean and jog and Jay! And then—"

And I try so hard to pay attention. To listen to her and stay involved, but the fact is I've been up since five o'clock this morning, and after getting Haley and myself ready, rushing her to preschool then myself to work, followed by eight hours on my feet at the salon, and another hour standing at the stove prepping dinner when I got home, I'm bone-deep tired. I want to fall face-first into my bed and not move for twelve hours. In reality, I'll get to bed at nearly eleven and barely manage to squeak in six hours of sleep.

"Mama!"

Haley's voice snaps me back to attention, and I lift my eyes to her. "What?"

"Can I have a treat?"

I should say no. She doesn't need a treat, especially after the shit I've been feeding her, but the truth is, I don't have the fight in me tonight. With a sigh, I relent. "Eat your green beans first."

She scoops up a giant bite on her fork and shoves it in her mouth, like there's a time limit on my offer. And for a minute, I let myself just watch her, get lost in her deep, dark eyes as she tells me more stories from her day, in the way she purses her lips when she's thinking of what to say next. Her hair is tangled, and she keeps pushing it out of her face. I've needed to give her a trim for a month but haven't found the time. She's amazing and gorgeous, and she's *mine*. And no matter what happens, what goes on in my life, I know at the end of the day, she's there with me.

She's a force of nature, this wild, crazy, vivacious little girl, and I love her more than anything in the world. She makes me laugh harder than anyone in my life. She's kind and compassion-ate and the best part of my life.

But sometimes . . . sometimes on nights like tonight when I've had a rough and exhausting day, I wish it weren't just the two of us. That there was someone else here to take some of the burden from my shoulders. To help in the mornings, to take her to the park, to read her bedtime stories in funny voices. Someone to keep me company while I'm cooking dinner. To have a glass of wine with me after Haley's in bed. To warm me up during the cold winter nights.

And just like every time I have this thought—every single time—a crushing wave of guilt immediately follows it, and I regret thinking about it in the first place. Because what we have is pretty great, and thinking about filling our lives with some-thing else, something more, feels like I don't think she's enough. Like *we're* not enough, together.

But that's not it at all. I love her and would give my life for her. The times we spend together are my favorite in the world. But at the end of the day, when she's in bed, it's just me.

It's just me, and I can't help but want something more.

jason

I should've gone out tonight. Should've called up Sean or Kyle and had them meet me at Shooters or, hell, anywhere. At least then I'd have the interference of noise and people to distract me from what my brain won't stop gravitating toward, what it won't stop focusing on—namely a girl with dark brown hair and a personality too large for her petite frame.

But I'm just lying to myself if I think any of that would help. Because in the last nine months, I've done everything in my power to try and get Tessa out of my head, to stop this interest before it even started, and she just keeps working her way back in.

I've tried to distract myself with women who are the exact opposite of her—leggy and blond and reserved. Hell, I've tried to distract myself with women who are seemingly just like her. Same build, same hair, same eyes. But it doesn't matter. It doesn't help. Because, at the end of the night, they're *not* her, and my mind still snaps right back to her every single time.

Every. Single. Fucking. Time.

Groaning, I grab the remote and flip through the channels until I get to the football game on tonight. Taking a pull of my beer, I lean back on the couch, the leather creaking under me, and try to focus on the game, but my mind's going a million miles an hour. Where Tessa's not overwhelming my thoughts, the shit from my parents fills the void. There's no avoiding it. No getting out of it. Nothing I can say or do to stop my future from plowing into me like a freight train.

Maybe I wouldn't feel the way I do about it if they'd just asked. Just *asked* what I wanted to do. *If* I wanted that. But of course they didn't. Because it was a family business, they assumed I wanted to be a part of it. And I might have, if not for my dad. The firm was something my grandfather built from the ground up, but something my father turned so ugly I didn't even recognize it anymore. It's no longer the small firm with a soft spot for philanthropy my grandfather started. Now it's all about the profits. In the years since my father's taken control, he's laid off good people only a couple years from getting their pension and hired recent grads for half the salary. He's found every possible short-cut he can take so he can pocket more profits. And the thing that cuts the most is when he closed the foundation Grandpa created, building homes for low-income families—the only thing I was able to look forward to. The one thing I'd have so I could get past having to work for my dad. He told me he shut it down because it wasn't good for the bottom line.

In other words, it wasn't satisfactory for him to be bringing in less than a small fortune every year, despite the reason for that being helping others in need. All that matters to him—to both my parents—is the next dollar that comes into the bank, the next brand-new car, the next vacation to Paris or Saint-Tropez or Tahiti. It's always about the quality of what they have, how fancy it is, and to whom they can show it off.

And that includes their one and only child.

It's on nights like this I miss my grandpa the most. My grandma died when I was young, in elementary school, so my memories of her are faded, but he talked about her like she hung the moon. And the stories he shared sounded like fairy tales to me, because the life I lived, the love I saw between my parents wasn't love at all. It was a commitment built on mutual benefits . . . on what they could both gain. When my dad aligned himself with my mother's family—the very epitome of old money—he married into the life he always wanted.

The life my grandpa tried to show me there was so much more than.

My phone buzzes in my pocket, and I take the welcome distraction, fishing it out. Tessa's name flashes across the screen, and I close my eyes, blowing out a deep breath. Guess it won't be much of a distraction at all.

Bringing the phone up to my ear, I answer, "Hey."

"Jason?" Tessa's voice is higher pitched than usual, panic seeping through, and I bolt upright.

"Tess? What's wrong?"

"Oh, um, nothing much. It's just—oh shit. Haley! Bring me another bucket from under the kitchen sink!" Her voice is loud and frantic as she yells to Haley, before she speaks into the phone again. "Yeah, um, do you happen to know anything about pipes?"

"Like . . . water pipes?"

"Yeah . . ."

"Tess, what's going on?"

"I just . . . I forgot to leave a trickle of water running in the bathroom, and it was so cold today, the pipes froze. And . . . burst. There's water *everywhere*. I don't . . . I don't know what to do." Where it was frantic before, her voice has softened, wavering just slightly, and I don't care that I know jack shit about plumbing. I set my beer down, thankful I'd managed to have only a couple swallows, and get up from the couch, grabbing my coat and slipping on my shoes before I'm out the door, phone still at my ear.

"I'll be there in ten," I say, then hang up, rushing out into the cold November night to help a girl I'm trying my hardest not to think about.

Tessa

There is *so much* water. Buckets upon buckets, and with every emptying of them, it's another reminder of how I screwed up.

Again. Of how this never would've happened if Cade had been here. He never would've *let* it happen.

The pipes froze once, when I was nine. Though we'd been in the house for a few years by then, the previous winters had all been mild, so we'd never had to deal with it before. But that particular winter was harsh and brutal, colder than it'd been in a long time. It was after my dad had passed away, so it was just me, my mom, and Cade. And even though he was only eleven, Cade still stepped in and took charge. Like he just *knew* what needed to be done.

Then every year after that, he or my mom were diligent in making sure to always leave the tiniest trickle of water running on days it got well below freezing. Every freaking year, they remembered to do that. And the one year I'm here by myself, I can't even manage to turn on a fucking water faucet.

I'm biting back a fresh wave of frustrated tears—which serve only to piss me off more—when the back door opens, and Haley calls out for Jason. He murmurs something to her, then the floors creak as he makes his way toward me.

"Tess, what—" He stops in his tracks in the doorway, freezing as he takes stock of the situation in front of him. His eyes dart around—to the puddles of water on the floor, the bucket I'm holding under the vanity in front of the pipes, and finally to me and what a hot mess I'm sure I look like. I'm soaked from head to toe, and I don't even want to imagine what my makeup is doing right now.

Clearing his throat, he darts his eyes up to mine before he averts his gaze. "Did you, um, did you shut off the water?"

I stare at him for a minute, and then a hysterical laugh bursts out as a fresh wave of tears spring up. Because, no. No, I did not shut the water off. I hadn't even *thought* of that, and what kind of idiot does that make me?

"Hey. Hey . . ." he says as he squats next to me, his hand rubbing tentative circles on my back through my water-soaked T-shirt. "It's okay. I'll go in the basement and get it shut off, then we can figure out what to do, okay? It's fine."

As he stands to do what he promised, all I can manage is a shake of my head as I close my eyes and sink further into the failure I've been so good at.

jason

The water's been shut off, a plumber called, and Tessa is hiding in her bedroom under the guise of changing. And while it's a damn good thing she is, the part of me who's been having fantasies about her can't help but be disappointed.

When I arrived, stepped into the doorway leading to the bathroom, and saw her sitting on the floor, her legs sprawled out in front of her, her makeup smudged down her face, her hair flattened against her head, and—God help me—her pale pink shirt plastered to her chest, I had to look away. Immediately. Because in those two seconds, I glanced at her body beneath a shirt that did absolutely nothing to hide it, and I got more of an eyeful than I ever imagined I would. Turns out, light pink acts the same exact way as white when soaked through. Which means I got a front-and-center viewing of Tessa's breasts, as clear as if she'd been standing in front of me naked.

I groan and close my eyes, scrubbing a hand over my face.

Haley's in bed, finally, and I'm waiting for the plumber to arrive, all the while trying to get the image of Tessa's perfect tits out of my mind.

"Hey." Her voice is soft, defeated, and when I sit up and twist around to glance at her, she looks just like she sounds. Her hair is just damp now, settling into soft waves, her face clear of all the smudged makeup she was wearing before, and she's changed into a plaid flannel button-up and some sleep pants, and it still doesn't stop her from being sexy. In fact, if it's possible, she's even sexier.

Could be the fact that I know the exact shape and size of her nipples now, and all it takes is a flash of my mind to conjure them up, despite the layer of dark blue and gray she's hiding behind now.

"Hi." I clear my throat and avert my eyes, because I'm afraid I'm going to drop them right to her chest again, like it's a fucking beacon or something. "I called a plumber. He should be here within the hour."

"Okay. Thank you. I probably should've just done that in the first place instead of dragging you into it, but this water was pouring out everywhere and I couldn't even take a second to think." She moves and sits on the opposite end of the couch, tucking her knees against her chest and bringing a throw pillow in front of her. Shaking her head, she stares down at her legs. "What an idiot."

My brow furrows as I look at her. "Hey, you're not an idiot. Why would you think that?"

A humorless laugh escapes her, and she rolls her eyes. "Only everything. It was my fault the pipes burst in the first place. I didn't think—I didn't remember to leave some water running so it wouldn't happen. Do you think that ever happened to Cade?

Not once in the thirteen years since the first time it happened. I'm here for five months by myself and I managed to fuck up the very first winter."

"Tess—"

"And then I didn't even *think* about shutting the water off or calling a freakin' plumber. I just kept filling up buckets and dumping them out, and Jesus, Jason, how did I think I could do this on my own?" Her voice is wobbly, her eyes glassy, but she swallows, not letting any tears fall. She's so strong. Why can't she see it for herself?

"It was stressful. And sometimes in situations like that, we have our heads up our asses. It could've happened to anyone."

"But it didn't happen to anyone. It happened to *me*."

I turn to face her on the couch, my arm stretched over the back toward her. "Look, I know you're stressed. And you feel like you're failing. But you're not."

She rolls her eyes again, and I reach out and yank on a strand of her hair. "Hey!"

Shrugging, I say, "I figured that was better than flicking you in the forehead like I used to in high school." She glares at me, and I keep on. "You weren't listening to me, so I needed to get your attention. *You are not failing.*"

"Sure feels like it," she mumbles, avoiding my eyes.

"Believe me, I get it. But you're *not*. You get your daughter up every day, get her ready, take her to school, go to work, come home, feed her, and get her ready for bed, and at the end of the day, you're both alive and happy and healthy. That's not failure, Tess. So you've had a few bumps along the way. So fucking what."

She snorts. "A few? Try a fuck-ton."

"Fine, so you've had a fuck-ton of bumps along the way.

You're still figuring all this shit out. You need to give yourself a break. You're not going to step in and automatically know what to do all the time."

"You did. I mean, I didn't even think to turn the damn water off."

"The only reason I did is because I remember the last time this happened. We were in sixth grade, and your mom was rattling off orders to Cade. Adam and I were here, getting in the way. First thing she said was to shut off the water." I shrug. "Makes sense you wouldn't remember. I think you probably locked yourself in your room, playing Barbies or whatever the hell you used to do for hours in there."

Through my explanation, her face has softened slightly until a frown isn't pulling at the corners of her mouth, and her shoulders relax.

"Are you finally back to being Regular Tess instead of Tess the Grouch?"

She laughs her first real laugh of the night and tosses the pillow at my head. "You're such a jackass."

Smiling, I catch the pillow and set it in my lap. Tessa's legs stretch out from being up against her chest, and she doesn't stop until her toes press into my jean-clad thigh. She gives me a light shove. "Thanks. For coming right away."

I shrug, waving her off. "It's no big deal."

"It is," she insists, her eyes intent on mine. "When it all happened and I was trying to figure out what to do, you were the first person who popped into my head to call. I can always count on you, and that means a lot. Especially now. So thank you."

Despite the part of me that likes knowing I'm the one she called first, that I'm the one who's always here to help, me being here all the time is part of the issue. Part of the problem I have of not being able to get her out of my head. But as I look at her, a little lost, a little scared, a lot thankful, I realize there's nothing I can do about it.

Because even though I have a hundred warnings going off in my head, a thousand reasons to stay away, I can't. I can't help myself, and I'm not sure I want to. I'd be here in a heartbeat if she needed me. And that's not going to change.

FOUR

Tessa

"Mama! It's time to call Uncle Cade!"

"Okay, okay, just give me a second," I say as I hurry to clear the plates from dinner—another meal my brother would be ashamed even got prepared in his kitchen. I try my hardest, but the fact is, some nights I don't have the time—or energy—to do anything other than microwave something.

"It's ringing!" Haley yells from the living room.

"Answer it, then."

She does and then her voice is animated as she chats with Cade, telling him all about story time at school and the project she brought home from Miss Melinda's. They chat for about ten minutes—just long enough for me to get the counters wiped down and the dishes loaded into the dishwasher. I walk into the living room and find Haley leaning so close to the laptop, her face—well, her nose and mouth, anyway—takes up the entire portion of her side of the screen.

"Move back, baby. Uncle Cade can see you better that way."

"I was giving him a kiss, though."

I huff out a laugh. "Okay. Why don't you go ahead and say bye? It's time to get your jammies on."

"Bye, Uncle Cade. Talk to ya later!"

"Love you, short stuff."

"Love you, too!"

"Remember, no messing around, or we won't have time to read a book tonight," I call after her fleeing form. A brief wave of her arm is the only response I get, and I plop on the couch, rolling my eyes. "Already with the sass."

"Gee, wonder where she gets that from."

I look up at the screen, Cade's smiling face filling it. He looks good. Ever since Winter got back a couple months ago, he's been better, happier. And he loves his job, which helps things. I'm so happy for him, that he got this amazing opportunity right out of school. But, God, I miss him.

"Even though this is Skype, I can still hang up on you, you know," I say.

"So we're in a bad mood tonight, then."

"I'm not . . ."

"What's up?"

Shaking my head, I answer, "Nothing."

"Tessa, this isn't like talking on the phone. I can actually see your face. You've never been able to lie to me. Now, what's going on?"

"It's really nothing. I'm just . . . feeling a little overwhelmed."

"With work?"

"And Haley and home stuff and . . ." I sigh and slump back on the couch. "Life."

He frowns, his brow furrowed, and I know without his saying anything that he's feeling guilty for leaving me. And that makes me feel even worse.

I sit up and lean forward again, pointing a finger at him. "Don't. Don't even start that. This is *my* fault, not yours. I just haven't found my groove yet." I shake my head, closing my eyes as I rub them with my fingers. "It's been a bad week. Tuesday, I was late getting Haley again, and then I fell asleep on the couch. Haley got into my makeup—which I didn't even know about until the next morning when I saw the pile it was in under the sink."

"If she got into your shit, how could you not know? That girl loves painting her face like a clown."

"Jason must've cleaned her up before putting her to bed."

Cade's eyebrows lift to nearly his hairline. "Jase?"

"Yeah, he stopped by that night. And then . . ." I take a deep breath and close my eyes briefly. I know I have to tell Cade about the pipe—he'd want to know—but voicing my failure *sucks*. "He was here again night before last because, um, the pipe in the bathroom froze and burst."

He opens his mouth to say something, then closes it, probably realizing I'm already beating myself up over it and I don't need his help. Before he can say anything, I continue, "Anyway, I called Jason and he came over. Helped me get the water shut off and called a plumber. It's all fixed now, but . . . it's just been an exhausting, taxing week."

He's quiet for a minute, just staring at me, then says, "I'm glad you got everything fixed." Clearing his throat, he looks off to the side, then back at me. "So, has Jase been stopping by a lot?"

I shrug. "Yeah, ever since you left."

"Hmm . . ."

Narrowing my eyes at his tone, I ask, "What's the 'hmm . . .' for?"

He shakes his head, and just like that, his face is wiped free of the suspicion I saw a moment ago. "Nothing. So the pipe burst—it happened to Mom, too, remember?"

"Yeah, I remember. Which is why I should've remembered what to do to prevent it."

"Cut yourself some slack. You're still beating yourself up over what happened Tuesday with Haley, too, aren't you?"

I avoid his eyes, and that's all the answer he needs.

"Tess. So you were a little late and you fell asleep. Remember when I fell asleep watching her and she used markers to draw all over the couch cushions? It happens."

I don't say it, but all I can think is that it shouldn't happen to *me*. And maybe that's me putting too much pressure on myself, but I'm her mother. Not her uncle or a babysitter or a family friend. What if she got into the kitchen? If she grabbed a chair and climbed on the counter and pulled out a knife? Or got into the cupboard where the matches are kept? What if she drank Lysol or fell down the basement stairs and I didn't even hear her cry because I was so fucking exhausted?

"Don't." Cade's sharp tone snaps me out of my thoughts, and I look at him on the screen. "I know exactly what you're doing. Every worst-case scenario just went through your head. You're only going to drive yourself crazy. You're a great mom, Tess. And she's a great kid, because of *you*. Don't ever doubt that."

I take a deep breath and nod, knowing he won't drop it unless I do. "It's fine. I'll be fine." I shake my head a little and wave my hand in front of the screen, sitting up again and moving closer to the computer. "Enough about me. What's up with you, Mr. Super Important Chef?"

He snorts, the smile I know and love lighting up his face. "Still feeling like I should pinch myself."

"It's going good, then?"

"Better than. John's been giving me more responsibility in the kitchen, especially when Oscar, the head chef, is off. I think . . . I think he's testing me. He's been traveling a lot, looking at different sites for new restaurants."

My heart speeds, hope and excitement bubbling up. "Yeah?"

"Yeah. Don't know where yet, or even when. He'll build from scratch, more than likely, so it's looking like several months, at the earliest."

"How do you like Chicago?"

"It's . . . different. I mean, it's great. I love being in the city, and Winter enjoys it, but . . . it's not home."

I nod, realizing how much he misses it here. It wasn't just me it affected when he moved. Yeah, I lost my brother, my help, and my companion, but he left *everything*. I'm not sure I'd have the courage to do that. Just another reason he's the one person I've ever looked up to.

I hear a feminine voice in the background, and Cade turns his head, nodding with a smile on his face. When he turns back to me, he says, "Hey, I gotta run."

"All right. Tell Winter I said hi."

"I will. I'll talk to you later."

"Bye."

I close my laptop, then fall back against the couch. Even though nothing got settled, I feel better for having talked with Cade about what's been going on. I've tried so hard to put on a front for him since he left, keeping all my worries buried, because the last thing I want is for him to feel guilty. He had enough doubts about leaving in the first place. He doesn't need my problems heaped on him as well.

I just need to get into a routine, figure out how to do this on my own, and then everything will fall into place.

I'm sitting for only a minute before Haley comes rushing out of her room, her princess nightgown hanging to just below her knees. I look over at her, my reason for everything, and smile. "Ready, baby?"

"Yep!"

I let her grab my hand and pull me up, following behind her down the hall. At least it seems no matter how much of a clusterfuck I think life is, she remains unaware. And that's exactly how I want to keep it.

jason

The professor dismisses class, and I pack up my shit, shoving it into my backpack as I shoulder it and head toward the door, the three people I was assigned to work with on a group project left behind at the table. I don't get far before one of the girls tugs on the sleeve of my hoodie.

"So, you'll call me, right?"

I glance at her, walking a little too close to be the friend she's been pretending to be. When I don't answer, she continues, "You know, to talk about the project?"

I don't mention the fact that she didn't ask either of the other two in our group to do the same. It's easier to placate her. "Yeah, sure. I'll see you later, Kristi."

"Bye," she says with a wave, her smile too bright, her eyes hidden behind layers of whatever shit it is girls put on their eyelashes. She doesn't look all that different from how I found Haley the other night.

I take the stairs two at a time until I'm outside. A quick glance at my phone shows I have about half an hour before my next class, so I detour to the coffee shop to grab a caramel macchiato. The line's not too long, fortunately, and it takes me only a couple minutes to get to the front.

"Hey, Jason," the barista says.

"Hey"—a quick glance at her name tag fills in the blank for me—"Stacy. How's it goin'?"

"Good." She smiles and leans forward a little, giving me a glimpse down her shirt. "You want the usual?"

I look—of course I look—and then glance back up at her face. I don't recognize her, so I don't think she's in any of my classes. And I don't come in here that often, so the fact that she knows my usual order is a little disconcerting. "Uh, yeah, thanks."

"Sure thing."

She moves away from the register and makes my drink, even though there are others still in line behind me. When it's finished, she hands it over with another smile. "See you later, Jason."

"Yeah, later," I say as I head out the door. I don't need to take the sleeve off the coffee to know she's written her number underneath it on the cup. I don't even know that girl, but it's obvious she's heard of me.

I'm about halfway across campus when my phone rings. Caller ID shows it's Cade. "Hey, man."

"Hey, you busy?"

"Nah, just walking to class. What's up?"

"Not much. Talked to Tessa last night."

"Yeah? She tell you about her week from hell?" He doesn't say anything, and I pull the phone away to make sure I didn't lose the connection. "Still there?"

"Yeah." He clears his throat. "She, ah, she said you've been coming by a lot since I left."

"Yeah, I guess," I answer with a shrug.

"Why didn't you ever say anything?"

"Why didn't I ever say anything about what?"

"That you were seeing her so often."

"I . . . don't know?" Except I do know. It's because the thoughts I've been having about Tessa aren't exactly the kind of thing you share with her big brother. Playing it off as nothing more than the favor he asked of me before he left, I say, "You told me to watch after her. Sorta figured you'd take it as a given that in order to watch after her, I'd have to, you know, physically see her."

He grunts, but doesn't say anything more.

"What's that shit for?"

"Nothing."

"Don't bullshit me."

"Don't fuck with her, okay?"

I stop dead in my tracks. "What the fuck is that supposed to mean?" The tone in his voice suggests what I already know—that if he knew . . . if he had any idea the kinds of thoughts I've had about his precious baby sister, he'd beat my ass so hard, I'd be lucky if I landed in the hospital instead of a graveyard. And I know the reason for his trepidation about me and her is because he knows *exactly* what kind of history I have. He knows the name of every single girl I've ever been with—not to mention detailed descriptions of what I've done with most of them—from tenth grade on, and the list is extensive.

Proving me right, he says, "Look, man, I know how you are. And that's fine. That's cool. But it's *not* cool with my baby sister."

"Fuck you, Cade." I laugh it off, though his words sink into my chest. Despite figuring that's what he'd think, hearing him confirm it . . . knowing he thinks so little of me fucking sucks.

"I'm serious."

I clench my jaw. Voice hardened, I answer, "So am I."

Instead of hearing the steel in my voice and backing off, he presses. "You get an itch, go to one of your fuck buddies. Don't scratch it with Tess. Am I making myself clear?"

"Crystal," I mumble. "I gotta run. I'll talk to you later."

I hang up before he can say anything more, pissed off that he thought he even needed to have that conversation with me. I'd never use Tess like that. Despite the incessant thoughts about her that I can't seem to get rid of, I'm well aware she's not one of the dime-a-dozen girls who throw themselves at me every day. And it pisses me the fuck off that he thinks that's how I see her.

That's never been how I've seen her.

She's always been someone more . . . someone different, even if there wasn't anything between us. And this conversation just once again proves exactly what I've known all along.

That she deserves a hell of a lot better than an asshole like me.

FIVE

jason

Even after an afternoon full of classes, I'm not any calmer after my phone call with Cade this morning. I've done nothing all day but stew over what he said, and little by little, I've just gotten more pissed off. I know I don't have the best reputation with girls, and I own that. I've never had a problem with the way people view me.

Or I didn't until today.

I've always thought of Cade like family—he and Adam both kept me sane when my parents threatened to drive me off the edge. They kept me sane after my grandpa passed away a few years ago. They're the brothers I never had. And it's always been a joke between us—the revolving door in my bedroom—but something about the way he said it, or maybe whom he was referencing, pissed me the fuck off, whereas normally it'd just roll off my back.

Just as I walk through the door to my apartment, my phone buzzes in my pocket, and I pull it out to see Adam's name on the screen. I wouldn't put it past Cade to call him and get him to bitch me out about this as well. Blowing out a breath, I answer, "Don't tell me you've called to warn me to stay away from her, too."

There's a beat of silence on the other end before he says, "Stay away from who? And who told you that?"

I groan, dropping my head back on my shoulders. I totally fucked myself over with that one. "Whatever, it's not a big deal. What's up?"

"Nothing, just sitting in traffic. So who are you supposed to stay away from?"

After a brief pause, I say, "Tess."

"Tess? As in . . . Tessa? *Our* Tessa?"

"Well, *Cade's* Tessa, if he has any say in it."

"Wait a minute. What am I missing here? Since when is there anything at all with Tessa?"

"I don't know, man. All I know is I'm here, looking after her and Haley, doing exactly what Cade asked me to, and then I get a phone call today because I've been spending time at their place."

"O . . . kay," he replies, clearly confused.

"Basically told me to dip my dick somewhere else."

"Shit."

"What the fuck, right?"

"Did Tessa say something to him?"

"I don't know, she probably told him I was there helping out a lot last week. And then he flips out."

"You know how he is with her. I'm surprised he doesn't have surveillance on her."

"Yeah, I know how he is with her, but I don't give a fuck. That shit's not cool."

"I'm not saying it is." He's silent for a minute, then he clears his throat, and I've known him long enough to realize he's about to ask something that's going to make me uncomfortable. "So . . . *is* there anything going on with Tessa?"

"Oh Jesus. Not you, too."

"Hey, I don't care one way or another, so long as she isn't just another chick in your bed."

"You know she'd never go for that, even if that's what I wanted."

"Well, do you?"

"No," I say immediately. When only a weighted silence greets me, I groan. "Fuck, I don't know. I mean . . . did you realize how hot she is? When the fuck did she get hot?"

He barks out a laugh. "Uh, yeah, I knew. You saying this is new information to you?"

"I'm saying I never saw her as . . . *that*. Or I didn't let myself see her as that, whatever. But lately"—I scrub my hand over my face—"fuck, I don't know."

"You already said that."

"Yeah, well, the sentiment is still accurate."

"You better know before you start anything with her."

"I'm not going to start anything with her."

"Why not? I know Cade would be a pain in your ass—"

"That's putting it lightly."

"—but who cares? He'd get over it. Eventually."

I'm shaking my head even before he can finish. "It's not gonna happen. And it has nothing to do with Cade and everything to do with me. C'mon, man, you know Tess wants the real deal.

That's why she's been doing that online match bullshit. That's not me." Before he can say anything more, I change the subject. "Besides, I have other shit to worry about. My parents have finally added a deadline to my ongoing undergrad career."

"No shit? That mean you're gonna graduate this year?"

"Looks like."

"And then what?"

"Then I go to whatever school Dad deems appropriate to get my master's and learn the ropes at the firm while I'm at it so I—and I'm quoting—don't fuck everything up."

"So your dad's still an asshole, then?"

"Yep."

"On the bright side, think of all the secretaries you'll be able to go through. That'll really piss him off."

For the first time all day, I laugh. "You have a point."

"All right, I gotta run. Keep me posted on the Tess thing."

"There's no Tess thing."

"Like I said . . . Later."

I shake my head as I end the call, knowing he's wrong. He has to be. There can't be anything between me and Tess . . . period. She is the very definition of off-limits.

And a night out is exactly the thing I need to remind me of that.

tessa

I slip out of Haley's room, having just tucked her in, and head into the living room. I have time to do only a quick pickup of the shit lying all over the floor before the back door swings open. I glance up to see my best friend, Paige, standing there with a pint of Ben & Jerry's. "Hey," I say as I go over and give her a hug. "What's with the ice cream?"

"I broke up with Tom."

"Who's Tom?" I follow behind her as she heads straight for the kitchen.

She pulls out two spoons, offering me one, then uncaps the container and digs in. Despite partaking in my ice cream obsession with me, she never manages to gain an ounce. Or if she does, it goes straight to the right places—the places that give her the perfect hourglass shape. The first time I met her, I had her pegged as a snooty, real-life Barbie doll with her long, wavy blond hair, her bright blue eyes, and a figure that makes girls hate her. And then she opened her mouth and swore like a sailor, and we've been best friends ever since. Around a mouthful of ice cream, she says, "I met him last weekend when I was out."

"And you were seeing each other seriously enough that you had to have a breakup conversation? I didn't even know about him."

"Well, I stayed at his place the whole weekend . . . and a couple times this week."

I roll my eyes and scoop out some ice cream. "When are you going to realize you're not going to meet a good guy in a freakin' bar?"

"Hey, Winter and Cade met in a bar," she says, pointing her spoon at me.

"That's different. She worked there, and Cade's not a sleazy asshole."

"I'm just saying . . . you never know what kind of guys are going to be there."

"But you *do* know! They're the same assholes you've been spending nearly every weekend with for the last six months!"

She waves me off before digging in for another bite. "Whatever."

"So what was wrong with this one?"

Scrunching up her nose, she shudders a little. "He left his used floss on the sink. If that's how he is after only a weekend with each other, can you imagine how he'd be after a year? *No thank you*." She scoops another bite and around the mouthful asks, "How about you? Any keepers in the sea of online dating?"

I groan, slumping in my seat. My thoughts about wanting someone around to share the burden, someone around to make the nights less lonely come back to me, and I'm even more defeated. Because I haven't gone out with anyone I can see a future with. "I don't know. They're all . . . *fine*. I mean, on paper they're perfect. And then I meet them, and I . . ."

"Want to punch yourself in the face?"

Laughing, I say, "Something like that. I just haven't clicked with anyone. I want to *click* with someone, you know? Where when that first kiss happens, it's like all that cheesy stuff you see in the movies." I sigh. "It's stupid, but I want to be swept off my feet."

Paige just stares at me, blinking a couple times. She shakes her head and sighs. "Sweetie, it's time to put the romance novels down, m'kay? Shit like that doesn't happen in real life. Hell, I'm just thrilled if the guy gets me off before he passes out on top of me, to hell with sweeping me off my feet. I don't think that's too much to ask."

I cough, nearly choking on the bite of ice cream I just inhaled. "God, Paige."

"What? It's the truth. Haven't these guys ever heard the saying 'ladies first'?"

"Yeah, well, at least you're having sex. I'd just be happy to be getting *any*."

"And, see? That right there is exactly why my ass is going to be at the bar again this weekend, searching for the elusive Mr. Right Now. I get grumpy without sex."

"I don't even remember sex."

"Who was the last guy?"

"David."

"*David?* Jesus, Tess, that was over a year ago. You got any cobwebs up there?" she asks, twirling her spoon in my direction.

I snort. "Oh, you're hilarious."

She shrugs and gives me a self-satisfied smirk. "I think so. But seriously, we need to work on that."

"What do you think I'm doing? I have date number two with someone on Friday. He didn't do anything for me the first time, but maybe . . ." I shrug.

"And who is this someone?"

"He's the one I went out with a couple weeks ago. Greg, the orthodontist."

She scrunches up her nose. "Oh, honey. An orthodontist is never going to fuck all those cobwebs out of you."

Laughing, I turn away and put my spoon in the sink. "You keep going to the bars and finding your losers and leave me and my nice guys out of it."

"Whatever you say. Let me know when you're ready for someone a little more dangerous."

Without my permission, my mind immediately conjures up an image of Jason. From his carelessly mussed dark hair to his mischievous eyes to his ever-present smirk, he's got the looks and the charisma, not to mention the reputation . . . He's *exactly* the kind of dangerous she's talking about.

And that's exactly the reason I'll never go for a guy like him. I've done the dangerous thing before. Tried the whole taming-a-bad-boy thing—and it got me pregnant and alone at seventeen.

Regardless of how boring these nice guys are, it doesn't matter. Because I've already been down the road of heartbreak and loneliness, and I have absolutely no interest in traveling it again.

SIX

tessa

After spending a shit-ton of money on an after-hours call to the plumber, plus the repairs needed, my budget this month is shot. The last thing I need to do is shell out money on a completely unnecessary slice of white chocolate raspberry cheesecake. But that's exactly why I'm going to do, because it's been one thing after another for too long, and now to top it all off, I had a giant block of cancellations at the salon this morning. I totally deserve this plate of deliciousness and all the calories that go with it, and I'm not going to feel guilty about it. I'm also not going to feel guilty about eating it before I even delve into the salad currently sitting off to the side.

Despite being midday, the café isn't as busy as I would've thought it'd be. There are a handful of students inside, every one of them with a laptop open in front of them. I generally hate getting lunch by myself, though it's rare I ever actually have the option to do so. I hardly ever get a minute to myself to just *breathe*, either too busy with work or Haley or life, and I want to bask in the feeling of having absolutely nothing to do.

Although I might do better if I weren't sitting idle, because whenever I do, I automatically think about everything that's happened in the last couple weeks—in the last several months—and then I'm right back at square one, feeling overwhelmed.

Even after my talk with Cade earlier this week, after his reassurances that everything is fine, that I'm doing fine, I still don't feel it. I feel lost and in over my head, and I don't know what to do to make it change. I wish I had a pause button for life—that I could just freeze everything for a little bit to try and get caught up. To try and feel like I actually have my shit together.

The bell on the front door jingles as I take another giant bite of my cheesecake, staring out the window at the people walking around campus. I hardly ever get over here anymore, not since Cade graduated, but while he was still in school here, he got me hooked on the desserts in this place. And even though there are half a dozen little salad-and-sandwich shops that have acceptable desserts within two miles of the salon, it's totally worth the ten-minute drive to come to this one.

"Tess?"

With a giant bite brought to my lips, my mouth open wide to eat it, I startle and freeze, like the food police have come to haul me off for eating my dessert first. Instead of the food police, Jason is standing in front of me, an amused smirk on his face and his eyes nearly dancing right out of his head when he pointedly glances at the dessert on my fork, then to my clearly untouched salad.

"Oh, shut up. I've had a bad day. I'm an adult. I'm allowed to eat dessert first, you know."

He chuckles, holding his hands up. "I didn't say anything."

"You didn't have to *say* anything. Those eyes and that smirk spoke volumes."

He grabs the chair across from me and pulls it out before sitting down, dropping his bag next to him on the floor and shrugging out of his coat. "Bad day, huh? What's going on? Haley give you a rough time this morning?"

I drop my fork full of sugar back to the plate, sighing. "No, she was great. It's just everything—all of last week and then I had a huge chunk of cancellations at the salon this morning." I pick up my fork again and wave it in front of his face. "I totally need this. That's why I drove all the way over here."

"Again, I didn't say anything. Eat your dessert first. In fact, I'll do the same. Be right back."

He pushes off from the table and goes up to order something. He rubs a hand through his hair as he looks up at the menu on the wall above him, then braces his arms on either side of him at the counter. His back flexes as he leans forward, the muscles clearly visible through the thin cotton shirt he's wearing, and without my permission, my eyes drop to take in his ass. It's a great ass—especially in those jeans. He shifts, and that subtle movement jolts me out of whatever ass-induced trance I was just in, because seriously? Was I seriously checking out *Jason's* ass? I haven't done that since I was a starry-eyed fourteen-year-old girl.

I snap my head away from looking in his direction and stare blankly at the empty seat across from me. The conversation I had with Paige last night is still fresh in my mind, about me needing someone dangerous.

Someone like Jason.

He's the epitome of the kind of guy I've stayed far away from, ever since Nick. I don't touch guys like that with a ten-foot pole. Guys who are irresponsible and carefree and who've had more sexual partners than there were students in my graduating class. For some people, that's fine. For *Paige*, that's fine. That's exactly the kind of guy she wants, and I don't begrudge her for it. I'm glad she's happy. But I couldn't be happy with someone like that—with an arrangement like that. I never could have no-strings-attached sex. My heart always gets involved.

The last thing I need right now is a complication like Jason. And that's exactly what he'd be: a complication of the greatest proportion.

I have enough of those to last me a lifetime.

jason

Tess is deep in thought when I set my tray on the table across from her. Her eyes snap up to mine, and I have to remind myself that this isn't a big deal. We're friends. Friends get lunch together all the time. They hang out and talk and eat together, and it's no big deal. I'd do it with Cade or Adam without a second thought.

Except if I grabbed lunch with either of those two, I definitely wouldn't feel a twitch in my jeans when they pursed their lips around a straw and sucked . . .

Clearing my throat, I avert my eyes and take a seat, occupying myself with sorting out my lunch. Dessert isn't really my thing—unless it's whipped cream licked off the smooth stomach of a willing partner—so I had no idea what to get. I just ordered something different than what Tess had that I thought she might like.

"Ohhh, you got the crème brûlée. That's another good one, but I don't ever get it because I love this too much." She holds up a bite before she puts it in her mouth, and then her lips wrap around the fork, her eyes flutter closed, and she lets out the softest hum in her throat, and *Jesus fucking Christ*, I'm hard as a rock in two-point-three seconds.

"So good." She opens her eyes and looks at me, her eyebrows rising when she notices me staring. "Did I get it all over my face?" Grabbing a napkin, she brings it up and wipes the corners of her mouth, and I almost laugh at what she'd do if I fessed up to what I was actually so focused on. She'd be mortified and maybe a little offended. Ever since that crush she used to have on me when she was fourteen faded away, she hasn't looked at me with any sort of interest.

Waving her off, I pick up the sandwich I ordered and say, "No, I was just zoning out, thinking about classes and shit."

She hums, taking another bite. "How's that going, anyway? Did you decide what you're going to do about your parents?"

And maybe I should have told her I was picturing my dick in her mouth instead of that fork because then we wouldn't be talking about the rock and hard place I'm stuck between, and the inevitable future I don't want any part of.

I take a huge bite so I don't have to say much and offer a shrug and a mumbled, "What's there to do? No changing their minds."

She stares at me, her eyes narrowing. "You know, for someone who's so stubborn, you sure are bending over for them without much of a fight."

"What kind of fight should I give, Tess? The kind that gets me permanently kicked out of my family?"

She shakes her head and says softly, "They wouldn't do that."

"They would, and we both know it. The only reason they bent on me going to art school in the first place was because my grandpa paid the first year against their wishes. After he died, they didn't think it'd look good to have me transfer schools. Again. They only placated me because in the end, they were getting their way—having me at the head of the company. And *that's* something they won't bend on. Having no son is better than having a disappointment of one who can't get a good job—at least in their eyes—to save his life." I grab a couple chips and shrug, affecting nonchalance, though I feel anything but. I put on a good front, but the truth is, I'm still hoping some sort of promise will shine through from my parents, giving me a glimpse of what it was like before my grandpa died. I'm not sure I'm ready to just throw that away, even if they are.

We're both quiet as we eat, and I never noticed before how comfortable it's always been between the two of us. Even before this attraction on my end started, we'd always been able to just hang out—talking or not talking. I've gone out with more girls than I can count, and while they've always scratched an itch, it's never been as *easy* as it is with Tessa.

When she's nearly done with her salad, she says, "If you don't want to be the CEO or president or whatever your dad wants you to be, just tell them. Talk to them. They might surprise you."

"They're not going to surprise me, Tess. You know how I know that? Because it's going to be sophomore year in high school all over again, when I wanted to get involved in the web design club and they wouldn't sign off on the papers. They made me run for student council instead."

Her eyes grow wide and she stops picking at her salad as she looks up at me. "I thought that was your idea. You made it seem like you loved it."

"Yeah, like sixteen-year-old me is going to fess up to my parents pulling all the strings behind the curtain? Of course I acted like I loved it."

"Well, that was a long time ago. Maybe their reaction would be different now."

But based on my father's words during his ultimatum, on how he feels about the "arts and crafts" school I go to, I know that's a futile hope. My future's already been mapped out for me, whether I like it or not. And no amount of negotiating will get me a different outcome.

SEVEN

jason

Even though I know how the conversation will go before I show up, I still try. Tessa's words have stayed with me since our lunch yesterday, and I can't get them out of my head.

Which is how I find myself at my dad's ostentatious building, walking down the halls to stares and stiff smiles as I make my way toward his corner office.

"Hi, Jason," the receptionist says with a smile. She's blond, late twenties, if I had to guess, and probably one of the reasons my father spends a lot of his evenings here instead of at home. "Your dad doesn't have anything on his schedule right now. Let me just buzz him and make sure he's free."

"Thanks."

As she picks up the phone and calls him, I stand with my hand in the front pocket of my jeans, looking around the space at all the trimmings that are unnecessary. Just like in my parents' house. God forbid there's no outward show of their wealth. Can't have people thinking they're not raking in buckets of money.

Pulling me out of my thoughts, she says, "You can go ahead and go in," and gestures me down the hall toward the closed door of my dad's office.

I don't bother to knock before I go inside. He's sitting behind his desk, the floor-to-ceiling windows providing the backdrop to his stiff shoulders set in his gray suit.

"Jason," he says, glancing up only long enough to give me an appraising look before he returns his eyes to the paperwork in front of him. "Next time you come here, I'll expect you to be in something more presentable than jeans and a T-shirt. This isn't the gym."

"Nice to see you, too, Dad," I say as I shut the door behind me, then sprawl out in the chair in front of his desk.

"What can I do for you?" he asks. "I have a meeting in ten minutes."

"Well, then, I'll cut right to it. We both know working here isn't my first choice, but you've given me little other options."

He bristles, his spine straightening as he looks at me with hard eyes. "I think we've done a hell of a lot more than give you little other options. We let you go to that damn arts college, despite all the trouble we knew it would cause down the line— down the line being now, when I had to persuade the admissions department to let you into the master of architecture program without so much as a single piece in a portfolio."

I blow out a humorless laugh at how he's rewritten history. "You didn't *let* me go. Grandpa paid for it, and after he died, you only went with it so you could save face in front of your friends. What kind of student transfers schools three times, right? Certainly not a Montgomery." I close my eyes and take a deep breath, trying to get my temper under control. I can't ever have a normal conversation with him. "That's not why I came to see you. I'm here about what I want to do once I start working here."

"You'll be doing what I'm doing. I've already laid the ground-work. If you keep on, you won't have anything to worry about."

"That's not what I mean."

"Well get to the point already. Seven minutes," he says as he taps the face of his Rolex.

I swallow, stare right at him, though his attention is focused on the papers in front of him rather than me. "I want to start up the Elise Montgomery Foundation again."

His pen freezes above the paper he was jotting notes down on, the only outward appearance he gives that he heard me.

Continuing, I say, "I'll still take my place in your shoes, I'll do what you want me to do here, run it however, but I want the foundation up and running again. And I want to head it."

Carefully, calmly, he sets his pen down, then he leans back in his chair, both arms braced on the armrests as he smooths his tie down the front of his shirt while he's appraising me. "You want to resuscitate a nonprofit company I shut down no more than three years ago."

"Yes."

He laughs then, a sound I can't remember hearing in a long while, and shakes his head. "No."

Just like that. No. He doesn't ask me why I want to start it back up, doesn't let me tell him that doing so would give me a purpose, allow me to swallow all the shit he's done to this com-pany because it would mean that I'm able to give back in some way. It'd mean that I'd be able to give life to the legacy my grand-father left. The legacy my father shit all over.

He leans forward and rests his forearms on his desk, clasping his hands together as he stares at me. "I know you and your grandfather had grand plans for that. Ever since he started it, that's all you two would talk about, all you'd spend your time on, even when you were younger. Used to go with him to those build sites and get your hands dirty, doing work we hire people for. You both were weak when it came to doing what needed to be done to get ahead." Which, to him, means never spending time, much less money, helping those less fortunate than he is. "Unfortunately, you're the only one bearing the Montgomery name who can step up to lead this firm once I retire. I'm not going to let you come in here and take this company your grandfather built but all but pissed away because of that fucking foundation sucking all the profits, and run it into the ground after I've finally made something of it. After it's finally started to see generous revenue. And the group of partners will see to that. They'd never approve it." He says it with such a smug satisfaction that I have to clench my hands around the arms of the chair so I don't do something I'm not sure I'd regret. Like wipe that smug satisfaction off his face. With my fists.

He glances at his watch. "Time's up. If that's all . . . ?" He doesn't wait for me to say anything before he stands and walks over to the door, twisting the handle and pulling it open for me. Body language relaxed, cool smile in place. Showing everyone beyond the closed door just how perfect everything is in our little family of three.

"Thanks for stopping by. See you for dinner next week," he says loudly enough for the few other employees in the hall to hear. They offer me the same stiff smiles they did before as I make my exit. I give the receptionist a tight smile and nod when she waves and says good-bye, then I'm down the hall and jamming my finger in the button for the elevator, anxious to get the hell out of here.

I don't know why I put myself through this. Why I don't just tell them to fuck off and do what I want to do. Yeah, I'd be out the money they're shelling out every month for me to live comfortably. I'd have to move somewhere else, figure out a job really damn quick, but I could. If I had to, I could. I've interned every summer for the same graphic and web design company, and I have little doubt they'd hire me on. Probably as something lowly, but at least I'd be able to use my web design and interactive media degree. At least I'd be in the field I want to be in. At least I wouldn't be working for a shady asshole who cares more about money than anything else in the world.

I glance over at the wall next to the elevator, an outdated picture of my grandfather hanging there, his kind eyes seeming to stare right at me. And I know why I don't just tell them to fuck off and go on with my life. Because despite all the shit they've put me through, all the hoops I have to jump through to get even an ounce of approval from them, they're my family—the only one I've got, unfortunately. Grandpa's words—the ones he'd say frequently—ring in my ears as I step into the elevator and push the button for the lobby. *Family is everything. Don't ever turn your back on it.*

It's those words that follow me out to my car, those words that have stayed with me as long as I can remember. And it's those words that have me deciding to give it another shot. Maybe I can talk my father into resurrecting the foundation. Maybe he'll come around and see it from my side. Maybe.

EIGHT

jason

This girl's laugh is too loud, her voice too high-pitched, her entire demeanor just . . . off. Not long after my friends and I got here, she pushed her way through the crowd and somehow infiltrated herself into the middle of the group I'm here with, casual as all shit. Except she can't exactly pass as one of the guys, just hanging out to watch the game. Not with her skintight dress and boots that go up to her knees with heels that look dangerous as hell. Not with her bright red lips or dark, overdone eyes. She nods along with the trash-talking about who's going to beat whom in the game on Sunday, but she has no input, and her eyes keep coming back to me, lingering along my chest or lower. She's certainly not shy about what she's after.

I should be eating it up. I should be trying to figure out how I'm going to get her back to my place, especially after the talk I had with my father earlier today that put me in a shit mood. Especially after the talk with Cade about Tessa. But all I can think about is the couple sitting at one of the low tables on the outskirts of the place. I glance over at them, and this odd feeling creeps into my gut, twisting and making me uncomfortable. It takes me a minute to realize it's jealousy—something I can honestly say I've never felt regarding a girl before. The feeling is unwanted and completely unwelcome. And I don't know what the fuck to do about it.

I noticed Tessa right away—how could I not? Unlike the blonde next to me, Tessa's put together and sexy as hell without looking like she's trying too hard. She's got a fake smile plastered on her face as she sits across from a guy who looks too old for her. Something bright red and groan-inducing is covering all the good parts of her body—the parts I got an unintentional front-row viewing of the night the pipe burst—and I sort of want to punch her date for getting to stare at her all night . . . for getting to feel it on her later.

And then I sort of want to punch *myself* for thinking that. Tessa isn't mine—not by any stretch of the imagination. She's never been and is never going to be—especially if her brother has anything to say about it—so what do I care that she's out on a date with a nice—albeit seemingly boring-as-hell—guy?

Even knowing this, I can't stop my gaze from returning to them, over and over again. She looks bored out of her mind, her eyes continually darting around or staring longingly at the dance floor. She loves to dance—always has—and she'd obviously like to get out there tonight, but this dipshit doesn't even notice. He's got this hot-as-hell woman across from him—a woman so far out of his league, he shouldn't even be able to breathe the same air as her—and he can't even pay attention to the signals she's giving off.

When the waitress places a third glass of wine in front of Tessa, I can't stay hidden any longer. I need to make sure she's okay, that he'll get her home safe, if for no other reason than I promised Cade I'd watch out for her. It has absolutely nothing to do with the unwanted feeling spreading through me like cancer.

I slap Justin on the back, telling him I see someone I know and that I'll be right back, and head toward the not-so-happy couple. I don't miss the way the blonde pouts a little as I leave, but it still doesn't stop me.

Tessa's eyes widen when she notices me approaching, and she glances at her date before shifting in her seat.

"Hey," I say when I get to the table.

"Hi." Her eyes flit to her date again, but mine stay glued to hers. "Um, Jason, this is Greg."

Finally, I look over at her date, sizing him up and wondering if that's really the kind of guy Tessa's attracted to. If he is, I'm totally fucked. He's scrawny, his arms lost somewhere in the sleeves of his dress shirt. Wire-rimmed glasses sit perched on a perfectly straight nose—no fights for this guy. His hair is combed neatly, and I notice he's drinking a glass of wine. Fucking *wine*.

He stands halfway and extends his hand to me. "Ah, the infamous Jason." The fact that Tessa's talked about me to him comes as a surprise. I look over at her and raise an eyebrow. She glances back at me, and if I hadn't known her for so long, I would miss the way she bites on her nail and can't maintain eye contact. But I notice both, and I know she's uncomfortable. Unaware, or just uncaring, of our exchange, Greg continues, "Nice to meet you." He sounds genuine, his smile sincere, and it hits me that he doesn't see me as a threat. Not even a little.

Just for that, I grip his hand harder than necessary and offer a tight smile. I sort of want to give him a reason to see me as a threat. "Yeah, you, too."

Once Greg sits back down, Tessa asks, "Did you come out with the guys?"

"Yeah." I look over my shoulder to where they are, and see the blonde hanging all over Justin in my absence. Rolling my eyes, I turn back to find Tessa's gaze focused where mine just was. "Looks like your date for the night has moved on."

Raising both eyebrows, I stare at her. "Been watchin' me, Tess?" I get a smug satisfaction at that, that even if she is here with another guy, she's obviously been keeping her eye on me. And it sends a thrill through me that she was aware I was here even before I came over.

My question makes her nervous, and she shifts in her seat, taking a sip of her wine as she shakes her head. She doesn't say anything more, and her date keeps clearing his throat, like he wants me to get the hell out of here, but he's too polite to ask.

Well, if he wants me gone, he needs to grow some fucking balls and ask. Instead of being a gentleman about it and leaving, I ask, "Why don't you go out and dance?"

Her head snaps to mine, her cheeks flushed. "What? Oh no . . . I don't—"

"Did you want to?" Greg asks, glancing between her and the people out on the dance floor. People who are nearly a decade younger than him, I'd imagine. "We can . . ." He doesn't finish his thought, and it's clear the very idea of it turns him off.

She shakes her head, waving her hand at him even as she tosses me a glare. "No. Thank you, though. I don't know how much dancing I could do in these shoes, anyway."

I look down, over the curves of her shapely calves, down to

her feet, and see the shoes she's talking about. The kind of shoes a girl wears if she's hoping to be wearing *only* them by the end of the night. Clenching my jaw at the thought, I decide maybe it's time to give this guy a reason to see me as a threat. "One dance won't kill you. Come on." I glance at her date. "You don't mind, do you?" Except I don't wait for an answer before I set my beer bottle on the table and grab Tessa's hand, tugging her to stand.

"No, really, I don't want—"

"In fifteen years, I've never once seen you pass up the chance to dance." And, yeah, I threw that in just to remind Greg what kind of history we have, because I'm a dick. "Now come on. He doesn't mind." I tip my head in her date's direction, not taking my eyes off her.

"No, no, of course not. Go have fun." His words sound sincere, and I realize I have some work to do because he's still not at all bothered by this.

I keep hold of Tessa's hand as I pull her out to where the mass of bodies is moving to the beat of the music shaking the speakers. It's packed tonight, like it usually is on a Friday, and I use it to my advantage. She squeaks as I pull her closer to me, wrapping an arm around her back and holding her to me. I shouldn't be doing this. I should be the best friend I am and listen to Cade's warning. I should respect the fact that Tessa's here, out on a date—no matter how mind-numbingly boring that guy seems to be. But I can't help myself. And definitely not when I get a feel of her body pressed against mine from legs to chest and every inch in between.

"Jason . . ." The music is louder out here, and I don't hear what she says as much as the way my name forms on her lips. Her hands are braced on my chest, and though I'm moving to the rhythm of the song, Tessa is still standing still.

I lean down, my lips next to her ear so she can hear me over the din. "Come on, Tess. I've never known you not to dance. Just one song. No big deal."

She stands still for another moment, and then, finally, she moves. Her hips start swaying under my hands, and I have to physically stop myself from gripping her tighter, from pulling her closer to me, from grinding her into my aching cock. It's bad enough that I'm dancing with her like this at all, never mind the fact that her date is watching from fifty feet away.

It doesn't take long before she allows herself the freedom of getting lost in the music, her eyes closing and her movements more fluid. She rolls her hips, her body pressing into mine over and over and over again until I'm certain I'm going to go out of my fucking mind. And then she turns around, her back to my chest, and lifts her arms over her head, finally not caring about anything or anyone but the music playing around her.

Tentatively, I settle my hands on her hips again, diligent in keeping space between us, because the last thing I need is her ass rubbing against my very obvious hard-on. But I can't stop myself from picturing what she'd look like, doing this for me. For *only* me. Dancing in the privacy of her room, maybe doing a striptease or giving me a lap dance, and I curse myself and the path my mind always seems to take when she's around.

The more we dance, the longer she stays out here with me—one song turning into two, then three—the more irritated I become that she's on a date with someone like that in the first place. She needs someone who'll do this with her. Who's not too buttoned up to get on the dance floor—because they can see the longing in her eyes, just because they know it'll make her happy. Someone who'll take her to places she likes, make her laugh with stupid jokes, who'll order a dessert they don't even want just so she can have some.

That thought stops me cold, because I realize with a start that I just described myself. And while she most certainly doesn't belong with someone like Greg, she also deserves someone a thousand times better than me.

And the sooner I get that through my thick fucking skull, the easier it's going to be.

tessa

Guilt, heavy and solid, sits in my stomach. And I have no idea why it's even there, why I'm feeling it at all. I shouldn't be. I absolutely shouldn't be, yet ever since those five uncomfortable minutes when Jason showed up at the table and the subsequent fifteen we spent on the dance floor, it's been there, steady and unbreakable.

And then on top of guilt, jealousy crept in as I watched him go back to his buddies, the blonde who'd been hanging all over his friend switching her sights back to Jason. Even though he didn't seem to be welcoming her advances, never touched her, the fact that he could if he wanted to, that he *should*, sent a wave of unease through me.

And it rocked my whole goddamn foundation.

Jason is very nearly the exact opposite of the kind of man I'm looking for—the kind of man I want to have a future with. The kind of man who will fit perfectly into my and Haley's lives. He's irresponsible and wild and unsteady. He's a bad boy, and I have no illusions of turning a bad boy good.

I force my thoughts back to my date, to the perfect-on-paper man in front of me. It's the second time we've gone out, and now I remember why it took me three weeks to get back to him about another date. He's very nice, and he's handsome—if you go for that classic, Ralph Lauren kind of look—but just like I told Paige, he doesn't do anything for me. No butterflies. No breathless anticipation wondering if he's going to kiss me. No flutters when his fingers brush the backs of my arms. Nothing.

Nothing like what I had in spades during those few minutes I was on the dance floor with Jason.

But Greg, unlike Jason, *is* the kind of man I'm looking for. He just turned thirty, is looking to settle down, and he seems to be smitten over the idea of Haley, though he hasn't yet met her. He has a great job—an orthodontist. Except instead of thinking about how dedicated he must be, how intelligent, all I've thought about is what my teeth look like to him. Are they white enough? Are they straight enough? Can he tell I didn't wear my retainer every night like I was supposed to after I got my braces off? Will this guy expect me to floss every night? And then I think about what Paige told me about her last guy, and I start picturing used floss on my bathroom counter, and I'm *done*.

"I'm sorry to cut this short, but it's been a long week at work and I'm a little tired. Would you mind if we headed out?"

"Oh sure. Of course." He moves to stand, then reaches for my coat. "Here, let me help you with this."

He's always the gentleman, helping me out of the car, opening doors for me, pulling out chairs. And it's something I should want, right? That kind of man is exactly what I'm looking for.

But if he's what I want, why can't I even muster up a shiver of excitement when I'm around him?

And why do I feel so much when I look across the room, my gaze automatically seeking out Jason, and find him staring back at me? The butterflies I've been desperately searching for, the same ones who've been absent in Greg's presence, suddenly make themselves known and flutter rampantly in my stomach.

From a single glance.

From a single glance from the wrong man.

NINE

Tessa

"Come on, come on," I say, turning the key in the ignition once more. When only a soft clicking greets me, I slam my hand on the wheel. "Goddammit!"

Haley gasps from the backseat. "That's a bad word, Mama."

Closing my eyes, I rest my forehead on the steering wheel, counting backward from ten. It feels like one thing after another is happening, and I just keep getting buried under it all. I need for something to go right. I just need a goddamn break. When I finish counting down and reach zero and it hasn't helped a bit, I take a deep breath and say in as calm a voice as I can, "I know. Sorry, baby." I unbuckle my seat belt, then get out and open her door. "Let's go inside. Mama's gonna have to call someone and get the car looked at."

"What about school?"

"Looks like we're skipping school today. I'll call them when we get inside."

"Can we skip Miss Melinda's, too, and have a jammie day?" Her big brown eyes peer up at me, her expression so hopeful. I quickly go over my schedule in my head, trying to figure out if I can swing it or not. It's not a packed day, so I know Brenda, the receptionist, will be able to reschedule my clients easily.

Instead of committing to it until I know for sure, I say, "We'll see."

Once we're inside, I get her set up with a coloring book and crayons while I grab my phone and figure out what the hell I'm going to do. Normally, I'd call Jason. But after last Friday night, things are different. Strange. Tense. We haven't talked since we parted ways on the dance floor and he went back to his friends while I rejoined my date—something highly unusual for us. I don't want to think about how much I've come to count on his company, how much I've come to enjoy it.

And I definitely don't want to think about the way my body positively came alive when he was pressed against me on the dance floor.

Unfortunately, the only other person here whom I could count on—Paige—knows even less about cars than I do, so with a sigh, I dial Jason's number, waiting only a moment before his deep voice answers.

"Hey."

"Hi . . ."

The hesitancy in my voice must be obvious because he immediately asks, "What's wrong?"

I blow out a deep breath. "I'm not sure. My car won't start. It just clicks whenever I try, so I don't think it's the battery, but I don't know. Do you know anything about cars?"

"I can take a look at it. I'll be right over."

I glance at the clock, seeing it's just after eight. I remember him telling me he had early classes nearly every day this semester. "You don't have class?"

Instead of answering, he says, "See you soon."

While I'm waiting for him to arrive, I call Haley's preschool, letting them know she won't be in today. I wait to make any other arrangements, hoping Jason can get my car started once he gets here. If that's the case, I can make it to work on time and drop Haley at Melinda's on the way.

Not even ten minutes later, I hear a car pull up outside. "Haley, Mama's gonna go out and see if Jason can figure out anything with the car. I'll be right back in."

"'Kay," she says, her eyes not moving from her coloring book.

Grabbing my coat, I open the front door and head outside, slipping my arms in the sleeves as I walk down the path. When I get to where Jason is, he's already got my hood up and is looking under it, fiddling with different things.

"Hey, thanks for coming."

He glances at me over his shoulder, his eyes taking a slow perusal of my body, and just like last Friday night, my entire body lights up from it. "No problem. So it just clicks, you said?"

"Yeah, doesn't turn over at all."

He hums, his eyes focused once again in front of him. After a few minutes of him reaching out to mess with different parts of the car, I look back and forth between his expression to where his hand is, and a smile tugs at my lips. "You have no idea what you're doing, do you?"

Glancing over at me, his lips curve at the corner. "Am I that transparent?"

Laughing, I say, "Probably not to most people, but I've known you a long time."

"Yeah." His eyes hold mine for a minute until I look away. He clears his throat, then closes the hood. "I'm not sure what the problem is, but I can call my mechanic and find out what he thinks."

"You have a mechanic?"

He rolls his eyes. "My parents."

"Your parents have a mechanic?"

"They have an everything."

In all the years Jason's been a part of my life, I've met his parents only a couple times. When the guys were still in middle and high school, Jason spent a lot of time at our house when he wasn't with his grandpa. I rarely remember Cade going over there. The lasting impression I have of them is that they're the epitome of elitist parents, and Jason's surety that they won't budge about his future, despite how little he wants it, only proves that fact. How they ended up with a son like him, someone so laid-back and genuine, I'll never know. And the really sad thing is that they're probably disappointed in the man he's become.

Realizing I don't know anything more about his situation, since we haven't talked in a few days, I ask, "Did you decide to do anything? Talk to your parents?"

"About what?"

"The whole school thing . . ."

He laughs, though it's harsh and humorless. "Yeah, actually. I went and talked to my dad. Told him I could swallow going to work there if we could resurrect the Elise Montgomery Foundation."

"The one your grandpa started? Building homes for low-income families?"

"Yep," he says. "His answer . . . well, it was a much more colorful version of *no*."

"Just like that? He won't even entertain the idea?"

"Nope. And the partners will make sure of it. Not good for the bottom line, giving away your profits like that. So, not only do I not get to do the one thing that was ever worthwhile for that company, but I'm still stuck there thanks to being the only Montgomery left after my dad."

The stiffness of his shoulders and the harshness of his words prove what I already know—that he doesn't want this. "Why do you let them do that to you? Why don't you just say the hell with it and do what you want?"

"They have a very specific idea of who I should be, whether or not it's something I want."

"But you're not the kind of guy to go along with something if you're not into it. You never have been."

"Except where they're concerned."

"But why?" I ask, genuinely perplexed. If Jason doesn't want to do something, he doesn't. That's how it's always been. "That's what I don't get."

"My grandpa always told me you don't turn your back on family. I just keep thinking maybe they'll change." He shrugs, acting like this doesn't bother him, but I know it does. "And if I pushed back on this, they'd consider me out of their lives for good. Out of the family. And even though they're shitty parents, they're my shitty parents and they're all I've got."

Frowning, I reach out, tugging the sleeve of his jacket. "They're not all you've got, Jason. We might not be blood, but you've got me, Haley, and Cade. Adam, too. We're family."

He stares at me for a moment, his eyes searching mine, and I wonder if he's looking for reassurance or simply the truth in my words. He offers me only a short nod, and then he pulls his phone out of his pocket and turns around. With his hand on the small of my back, he guides me into the house as he dials his mechanic. "Hey, Dan, this is Jason. I've got a problem—"

I tune out his conversation, trying to keep Haley entertained so she doesn't interrupt the phone call. My powers go only so far, though, and as soon as Jason hangs up, Haley runs at him full force. He lifts her easily into his arms, and she starts talking a mile a minute.

"Guess what, Jay? The car didn't start and then Mama punched it and said a bad word and now it's a jammie day!"

He looks at me with a full grin on his lips. "Is that right? Hit the car *and* said a bad word? What does Mom have to do when that happens?"

I glare at him, definitely not in the mood to deal with his teasing.

"She hasta make me cookies. Any kind I want!" she yells right in his face with a smile. Haley turns toward me, her finger on her lips as she looks to the ceiling, deep in thought. "Chocolate peanut butter, I think."

"Thanks a lot," I say to Jason.

"Hey, you're the one with the potty mouth."

"I was frustrated. And like you wouldn't have said something a million times worse. Now what'd your guy say?"

"That it's probably the starter and he can get it fixed today. He's sending a tow truck over now."

Groaning, I drop my head back and close my eyes. The last thing I want to do is wait at the shop for them to fix my car while a rambunctious four-year-old runs circles around me. Never mind how much it's going to cost me with the tow truck and then the repair. After the burst pipe, my savings isn't as padded as I'd like it to be, and this is just going to drain it further.

"It shouldn't take too long, so I'll ride over in the tow truck and leave my car here in case you need it."

I snap my head up to look at him. "Wait, what?"

Shrugging, he says, "It'll be a lot easier for me to wait for them than for you and this one." He tips his head to Haley while he tickles her stomach. She falls into a fit of giggles, leaning backward over his arm until he eventually drops her on her back onto the couch.

"I—"

He holds up his hand to stop me. "It's not a big deal."

"Don't you have class?"

"Missing one day isn't going to kill me . . . or my GPA."

"Well . . . okay. If you're sure."

He shrugs again, then turns his smile on me. "Better make a double batch of those cookies, though."

Knowing I can't afford to miss an entire day of work, I sneak off to call Brenda and have her reschedule today's appointments for my next scheduled day off, and take today off instead. Once that's taken care of, I make my way back into the living room, finding Jason and Haley lying on their stomachs on the floor, each coloring a page in her coloring book, and I freeze, a flush sparking right in the center of my chest and working its way all over my body.

A little while later, the loud beeping of the tow truck echoes from outside, and Jason says good-bye to Haley, then tosses me his keys as he walks out the door.

I watch out the front window as he speaks to the guy hooking up my car. After Jason opens the door to the truck, he turns around and gives me a quick wave before disappearing inside the cab. As they drive away, I'm left wondering when Jason became the guy I call when I'm in need of help.

And when he started always showing up.

jason

It takes only a couple hours for Tessa's car to get towed to the shop and repaired—one of the benefits of having someone on call to drop everything for your needs. It's not quite noon, and I should probably hurry and drop off the car, then head to my afternoon classes. Except I know once I go inside and see her and Haley, I'm going to want to do anything but.

We haven't talked since I saw her and her date out on Friday, and part of that is because I needed the space to get my head on straight. Whatever I feel—whatever this draw to her is—needs to go the fuck away. Having made up my mind that night, I flirted with the blonde after Tessa and Greg left, let her put her hands on my chest and brush against me. I was ready to take her home, just to wash away the thought of Tess . . . to forcefully push it away. And I would have, too, if the girl hadn't stumbled around in a drunken haze. Apparently trying to keep up with the guys left her a little inebriated. And no matter how much I needed to fuck the thought of Tessa out of my system, I have some sense of integrity. I wasn't about to screw a drunk girl, especially not while I was thinking of another the entire time. Instead, I made sure she got home okay, then went to my apartment. Alone.

And today, seeing Tessa again, I realize I'm no better off than I was three days ago.

I pull her car into the garage and enter the house through the side door. Singing is coming from the TV in the living room, so I head in that direction. I come around to the front of the couch and nearly laugh at the sight in front of me. A very happy Haley looks up, chocolate crumbs all over her face, while at the same time a very guilty-looking Tessa meets my eyes, cookie halfway to her mouth.

"Jay! Guess what? Mama made cookies and that's what we're having for lunch!"

"Shh! You're not supposed to *tell* him," Tessa hisses at Haley.

I grin. "Is that right? Cookies for lunch . . . Must be a special occasion."

Haley nods her head. "And I got to pick out the movie. See? *Tangled*!"

"You're a pretty lucky girl." Haley's attention is already back on the TV, so I focus again on Tessa. "Did you save any cookies for me?"

She rolls her eyes. "We didn't eat four dozen cookies for lunch."

"*Four* dozen?"

"I told you I'd make extra."

"No you didn't, I just asked."

"Yeah, well . . ." She shrugs.

"Shhh!" Haley interrupts, her eyes still glued to the movie.

I stare at Tess for a minute, her eyes meeting mine quickly before looking away. When she glances up again, I tip my head toward the kitchen and head that way, Tess pushing off the couch to follow behind me.

Before I can say anything, ask how her date went even though I really don't want to know, she asks, "So what's the damage?"

I lean back against the counter, legs crossed at my ankles. "It was the starter, like he thought. Got it fixed, though," I say as I grab a cookie from the cooling rack. Now that I can get a good look at her, I see Haley wasn't joking with the whole pajama-day thing. I raise an eyebrow and gesture to her clothes. She's in some wide-legged cotton pants with sea horses all over them, and she's wearing a tank top that has to be from high school—maybe even middle school. The hem is tattered, the material thin and clinging and doing absolutely nothing to hide an ounce of her figure from me. A blink is all it takes for me to recall her in the pale pink shirt when the pipe burst—the *translucent* pale pink shirt—and I have to turn away. Clearing my throat, I tease her about her pants, though it sounds strained even to my ears. "Sea horses. Nice."

She slaps the back of her hand against my stomach as she walks past me to the fridge. "Shut up." She pours a glass of milk before setting it in front of me and putting the jug away. "How much is it gonna set me back?"

I wave her off, shaking my head. "Don't worry about it."

"Jason."

"Tessa."

She huffs, rolling her eyes. "Don't do that. Tell me how much it is."

"It's roughly four dozen cookies."

I hold her gaze as she stares at me, her jaw set. She crosses her arms, the act pushing her tits up, and—Jesus—that's all it takes for me to remember the exact shape of her nipples I saw through her shirt. Immediately, I lift my gaze to meet hers again, and she lifts her eyebrow. Caught. Fuck.

Rather than calling me out on it, she says, "Well, I'm going to be short on payment. This is our lunch, after all."

"Okay, how about three dozen and a pajama day?"

She sputters, her eyes growing large as she gawks at me. "A what?"

I gesture toward her sea horse pajamas, then tip my head to the living room. "Pajamas. Movie. Cookies."

"Oh, right. Yeah, of course." She looks visibly flustered, and I wonder briefly what she thought I was referring to. "You're not going back to school?"

I know I should. I should leave, if not to stay on top of my classes then to get some much-needed space between me and Tessa. Because I just keep digging myself further into this hole I've somehow found myself in where she's concerned.

But instead of walking away, I shake my head. "Nah. I could use a little *Tangled* today. That Flynn Rider, he's so dreamy."

She laughs and turns around, leading the way into the living room. "You would go for someone tall, dark, and handsome."

I watch her walk away, noticing the sway of her hips, and there is something seriously wrong with me if I'm actually thinking her ass looks good with fucking sea horses all over it.

"Don't forget cocky, too," I say.

"So you're attracted to a mirror image of yourself? Nice."

"Aw, Tess, you think I'm handsome."

"Oh please, everyone in the state of Michigan thinks you're handsome. It's not a newsflash."

Except it is coming from my best friend's kid sister . . .

someone I never saw as anything more than that until recently. Someone I *still* shouldn't see as anything more than that.

Tessa curls up on the couch, pulling the blanket over her, and Haley looks over at me. "Sit next to me, Jay!"

I snap out of my thoughts and do as I'm told, taking a seat to her right. She gives me some of the blanket, then frowns. "Your jeans are scratchy. You should be in jammies."

"Sorry, shorty, I didn't bring any jammies with me. Are you gonna kick me out of your pajama party now?"

She thinks about it for a minute, her brow furrowed as she seriously considers it, then she shakes her head. "You can stay. But you gotta be quiet."

"Got it."

I glance over Haley's head and find Tessa's eyes on me. I drop my gaze to her lips, and for some inexplicable reason, I want to lean over and find out what that full bottom lip feels like between mine, find out what her tongue tastes like. Shaking my head, I break my gaze and turn back to the TV, trying to get my thoughts under control.

As much as I hated the phone call Cade made to me, I can't really blame him for it now. Not with the thoughts I'm having about his baby sister. And I could probably use another reaming, because it seems I didn't get the message the first time.

TEN

tessa

"Mama, Auntie Paige is here!"

I poke my head around the corner from the kitchen and see my best friend's car pull into the driveway. I also see a hyper four-year-old jumping on the couch cushions, her hair flying around her. "Haley Grace, you know better than to jump on the couch. Down. Right now."

She pouts, her bottom lip sticking out almost comically, before she drops to her butt on the cushions. I can't see her anymore, but I don't have to to know she's got her arms crossed against her chest, a petulant look on her face. I roll my eyes and go back into the kitchen to finish preparing dinner for our weekly girls' night, knowing Paige will let herself in.

Not even a minute later, the front door creaks open, then Paige says, "Hey, Haley girl. Did someone give you a fat lip?" And try as she might—and I know how hard she tries, stubborn little thing—Haley starts cracking up, soft snorts turning into full-blown giggles, and just like that she's good as new.

While Paige entertains Haley, I finish up. The spaghetti—yes, boxed noodles and jarred sauce—I'm serving is a far cry from when Cade used to spoil us on these nights with test recipes he was trying out, and that makes me miss him—for far more than just his stellar cooking. We've Skyped a couple times since the burst-pipe fiasco, and every time, he's been a little off. Still asking questions about Jason and when the last time I saw him was. I don't know if I'm giving off a different vibe or not, and the thought is disconcerting. I'm terrified that this sudden interest in Jason is seeping out to talks with my *brother*, of all people.

"Hey." Paige snaps me out of my musings, and I smile at her.

"Hey yourself. How were classes today?"

"Awful, as always." She pokes her head over my shoulder, peering down at the saucepan. "Smells good, whatever it is."

"Spaghetti. And it only smells good because your standards have finally become lowered since Cade left."

She snorts. "Well, you're no professional chef, I'll give ya that."

Before I can flip her off, Haley calls for her from the other room, and with a grin in my direction, she's off to play with dolls. In all honesty, I'm glad I've got a while to get my thoughts together before I tell Paige about what's going on. We never really get into the meat of our discussions until after Haley's in bed, and tonight, I'm thankful for it.

Mostly because I don't know what the hell I should tell her. Mostly because I don't know what the hell I'm feeling. I'm confused and overwhelmed, wishing for something with someone who I'm not even sure exists, all the while wanting something with the one person I have no business wanting it with.

ONCE HALEY'S IN bed, Paige pats the cushion next to her on the couch, and I plop there, my head resting against the back.

"You look exhausted," she says.

"I *am* exhausted."

"More than usual? What's going on?"

I give a rueful laugh. "What isn't going on?" I rub the heels of my hands against my eyes, groaning. "I'm just . . . so completely over my head, and I never realized it. How did I never realize it?"

"You mean since Cade left?"

"Yeah. I was so stupid, pushing him away, blowing off his concerns about how I was going to do it on my own. I was such a cocky shit."

"Well, from where I'm sitting, I think you're doing a damn good job."

"You also didn't see when I let Haley eat four cookies for lunch the other day."

"Still not seeing the problem."

Expelling a deep breath, I say, "I feel like I'm trying so hard to catch up, and I'm never going to."

"You will. You just need to give yourself a little time."

"Yeah, that's what Jason said."

She raises her eyebrows as she studies me, but instead of pressing me on it like I know she wants to, she says, "Well, he's right. You'll get there soon enough."

"I hope so. I just feel like I'm letting Haley down left and right."

"Oh please. That girl would be happy if she could play dolls all day and eat cookies for lunch, and it seems like you're doing a stellar job of that."

"But that's the problem. I don't know . . . Some days I feel like I'm trying so hard to prove that I'm the *mom*, you know? That I'm capable of doing this. And I feel like I'm failing."

"Tess . . ." Paige shakes her head and reaches out to give me a quick hug. I accept it without fight, relaxing into it until we pull away. "You love that little girl more than anything. You pursued the best avenue to get yourself a good, steady job for her stability. You gave up the years where you were supposed to be wild and crazy and not worry about anyone but yourself. And you did that for *her*, so don't tell me about you failing at being a good mom. You are the most amazing mom I know, and I know damn well you're better than any other twenty-two-year-old with a four-year-old kid. You need to cut yourself some slack."

I smile at her after she finishes her tirade. That, right there, is why she's been my best friend for the last five years, ever since she transferred to a brand-new school as a junior, walking in like she owned the whole damn place. "Do you plan this stuff before you come over or just go off the cuff?"

She shrugs. "Off the cuff, mostly. You know how damn witty and quick I am."

We both laugh and I relax farther into the couch as we munch on the bag of chips she brought out. Once we settle on a movie and get about ten minutes into it, she says, "You never told me about your date."

Flashes of that night come to mind, except none of them are

actually of my date, but rather the fifteen short minutes I spent with Jason on the dance floor. I groan, resting my head against the back of the couch, and turn to face her. "It was fine."

Laughing, she says, "For the record, that is not an appropriate response to something that is *fine*. That response is reserved for fucking awful and/or incredibly awkward and uncomfortable. So which is it?"

I force myself to think only about my time with Greg, not yet ready to divulge everything else that happened. "God, I don't know. All of the above? I mean . . . I tried. I really did. And he is so sweet. He came to pick me up, brought me flowers." I point to the dozen roses filling a vase on the dining room table. I *hate* roses. Paige knows this, and she scrunches her nose up as she looks back at me. Taking a deep breath, I say, "He helped me into my coat and held open all the doors for me and asked about Haley . . ."

"He sounds like a regular Prince Charming."

"I know, right? But when I get around him? I don't *feel* anything. No excitement. No butterflies. Nada."

"Hmm, seems like a chemistry thing to me. And you know how mediocre sex can be when you don't have it." I nod in agreement, and she continues, "And you know how freaking awesome sex can be when you have amazing chemistry."

Except I don't. The small handful of partners I've had haven't ever done much for me, save for Haley's dad—my first everything, and I think that was probably just the excitement of everything being so new, not necessarily *him*. I just always assumed the problems I had with partners since then was me—body issues from pregnancy or something. It never occurred to me that it might be because we simply weren't sexually compatible.

And then I think about what it felt like on the dance floor with Jason, how his body felt behind mine, all solid and strong, and how it sent tingles from my head straight to my toes and all the little places in between—places no one had been able to coax a reaction out of in a long time. And he was able to do it with a simple dance.

"What's got you thinking so hard over there?"

Trying to hide the heat in my cheeks, I cover for the path my thoughts took and say, "I've never had that."

"What?"

"That—I don't know—that all-consuming *need* to be with someone. I've never had the urge to rip my boyfriend's clothes off and screw him on the floor because I couldn't wait to get to the bedroom." *Until Jason*, I leave unsaid.

"Oh God, the floor fuck is my *favorite*."

And for a minute, for one tiny minute, I'm jealous of my best friend. She's everything I thought I'd be back when I was sixteen and dreaming about my future—college and sororities and boy-friends. Going to clubs on Friday nights and having hangovers the next morning and just being *young*. She has complete freedom over her life. No one to answer to. No one to be responsible for except herself. And she enjoys every minute of it.

And then I feel guilty for that jealousy because if I were able to experience all those things, I wouldn't have Haley.

"So you've really never had that? What about the butterflies?"

"When I was younger, yeah. With Nick. But I think it's because I was so young and he was so experienced. It was prob-ably nervous butterflies instead of excited butterflies."

"Not since? None of the guys you've met recently have given you even a little flutter?"

No, definitely not any I've met recently. That seems to be reserved completely for the man I've known the majority of my life.

Noticing the look on my face and the way I avoid the question, she presses. "Ohhh . . . what? Who? One of the online guys?"

I snort. "I wish."

"Well, *who*? Jesus, the suspense is killing me." She tugs a pillow into her lap and bounces on the couch.

"It's nothing. It really isn't. I just . . . I'm confused, I think, and trying too hard with these guys, hoping something fits, so I'm naturally gravitating to something completely different. And because of that, all this shit starts happening with Jason. It's like my own mind is conspiring against me."

"Whoa, whoa, whoa . . . What shit with Jason?" She sits up abruptly, leaning toward me. "Girl, what's going on? Did you sleep with him?" Her voice gets high-pitched, and she reaches out and grips my arm, shaking it back and forth. "Goddamn, if anyone could fuck the cobwebs out of your lady business, it's that boy. Whew." She fans herself and lies back against the couch cushions.

"God, Paige!" I stare at her, mouth hanging open. "Why the hell would you automatically assume I slept with him? You've got dick on the brain, apparently."

"I can't help it when it comes to him. He is *fine*, with a capital F. With his smile—Jesus, those dimples—and all his laid-back charm, but you just *know* he would throw you down and fuck the shit out of you."

"Oh my God."

"Oh please, like you haven't noticed how extraordinarily attractive he is. Or how he's been looking at you lately."

Reluctantly, I get ready to agree with her about how hot I've found him lately when the second part of what she says finally registers. "Wait . . . what? What do you mean? How's he looking at me?"

She stares at me for a moment, studying me. Then she gapes, her eyes going wide. "Holy shit, you actually didn't notice."

I definitely didn't notice anything on his end, though, admittedly, that could be because I've been so preoccupied with everything going on in my own damn head. "No, I didn't notice anything."

"Well, I'm telling you . . . he looks at you different now. Not pervy or anything, but there's a definite hunger there."

"How long's this been going on for?"

She shrugs. "I don't know . . . couple months? I honestly thought you knew and were just ignoring it, that's why I never said anything. You do like to put your head in the sand."

Shaking my head, I look at my hands, having no idea what to do with this information.

"Okay, so if you didn't sleep with him, what do you mean by shit happening with him? What's going on?"

"I've . . . I don't know. Lately, I've been thinking about him differently. Ever since Cade left, Jason's been here a lot. A couple times a week, checking in and helping with whatever he can."

"That's sweet."

I nod. "It is. You know about the burst-pipe stuff. And then he helped me get my car fixed the other day when it wouldn't start. Then skipped classes to stay and have a PJ day with Haley and me."

With each piece I tell, her eyebrows inch higher on her forehead until they're lost under her bangs. "Okay, so . . ."

I blow out a deep breath. "So, I don't know. I've just been thinking about him as something more than my brother's best friend. And I don't think it's a very good idea."

"Well, that could be the cobwebs talking, too. The thinking-about-him bit, not the bad-idea bit."

"God, will you stop with the cobwebs already?"

"I'm just sayin'. He wouldn't be a bad one to get your groove back with. And what about the butterflies? Are there any when he's around?" She asks the question, waiting for an answer, but from the look on her face it's clear she already knows what it is.

And even though I don't have to, I reply honestly, "So many it's overwhelming."

"Well, there ya go, girl. Go get you some of that."

"Just like that?"

"What do you mean, 'just like that'? It doesn't have to be a whole production, Tess. Sometimes sex can just be sex."

"Okay, first of all, you know that's not true. Not for me. Not anymore. Not ever, really. And second, 'just sex' with my brother's best friend? Do you honestly think that'd be a good idea?"

"Look, I know Cade would probably lose his shit, but who cares? He needs to finally cut the damn cord. You're a grown woman with a *kid*, for fuck's sake. I think you're old enough to make your own decisions, including decisions about who you'd like keeping you company in your bed."

She's right. Of course she is. If I wanted to, I could call Jason up right now, invite him over, and get on with it. Except where would that leave me in the end? The last time I did that, threw caution to the wind and got involved with a bad boy simply because he made my stomach flutter, it led to a road I have no plans of traveling in the near future.

"He's not what I need, Paige."

"And what do you need?"

"Someone responsible. Steady. Someone who's older and knows what he wants, which happens to include a relationship with a woman who comes with a built-in family."

"So someone like your boring-ass match dude."

"I just . . . I feel like I need to give it another chance. Maybe I had an off night?"

"Or maybe you're completely delusional and talking yourself into it because you're scared as hell of actually *feeling* something for someone who doesn't fit into your perfect little mold. It doesn't have to be a giant production, Tess. You're allowed to have a little fun, even if it doesn't lead to a white picket fence." At my scowl, she raises her hands. "You do what you gotta do. Go on another date where you talk about the stock market and the price of gas. But when you come to your senses, let me know."

ELEVEN

jason

If I thought I was fucked before, spending the day with Haley and Tessa, everyone piled on the couch all day watching movies, only made it ten times worse. And now I've turned into some sort of pansy-ass fucker who can't get a girl out of his head. I'm thinking about the way she *smelled*, for Christ's sake. I feel like Cade after he got all googly-eyed at Winter. No, worse. I feel like Adam. Bastard always was a sap when it came to women.

And the worst thing is that I can't talk to either of them about it. Adam will shove me in Tessa's direction, telling me all the reasons it's a good idea, and Cade will . . . Jesus. I don't even want to think about what Cade will do.

Which is exactly why I need to get her out of my mind. School isn't working. Stressing about my impending doom with my father's company only goes so far, and unfortunately has absolutely no bearing on what or whom my dick is interested in.

What I should be doing right now is calling one of the two dozen girls whose numbers I've got stored in my phone. I should be going out, hitting a bar, and finding someone to distract me. Someone to distance me from everything I'm suddenly desperate to have.

Instead, I'm going right back into the lion's den.

I pull up outside Tessa's house and just stare at the large picture window out front. Behind the drawn curtains, I can see shadows moving around inside, and for a minute, I consider just leaving without talking to her. Without doing what I need to and telling her what's been constantly on my mind.

But I've never been a coward, so I take the keys out of the ignition, get out of the car, and walk up the front path while thinking of a hundred different ways to have this conversation with her.

What's the best way to tell a girl you've known more than half your life that you can't get her out of your head? That, suddenly, I see her as so much more than the pesky younger sister of my best friend?

Taking a deep breath, I knock twice on the door and wait for her to answer. And even though I have a few moments to compose myself, no amount of time would prepare me for what I see when she opens the door. She's wearing a dress—black this time—that's formed to her body and leaves her shoulders and arms completely bare and doesn't cover nearly enough of her legs, unless she's planning to wear this only for me. She's changed her hair again since the last time I saw her a few days ago—purple streaks here and there amidst dark brown. And I love when she wears it like this, kind of wavy and tousled. Sexy. Like she just rolled out of bed. And that only makes me think of Tessa in a bed, her hair spread out on the pillow and only a thin sheet covering her body, which isn't helping anything.

Her lips—painted in a deep red—form an O when she sees me, her eyes widening in surprise. "Jason! What are you doing here?"

I shrug. "Thought I'd stop by. You going somewhere?" I ask, gesturing to her dress.

"I . . . um. Yeah. I am. Or I was." Her phone rings from somewhere inside, and she opens the door wider before running off to grab it. "Amanda! Hi! No, thanks for getting back to me so quick." She pauses for a minute, listening, then her mouth draws down at the corners, her eyes flicking to mine briefly before looking away again, her shoulders sagging. "Oh sure. No, I totally understand. It was really short notice. Okay, have a good night." She hangs up the phone and tosses it on the couch behind her, muttering nearly every swear word in the book as she does so.

With raised eyebrows, I ask, "What's up?"

She heaves a sigh and turns around to face me. "My babysitter got food poisoning this afternoon and called to cancel on me about fifteen minutes ago."

Suddenly, the thought of postponing what I came here to talk about seems like the best idea in the world. What's another couple hours when I've already waited weeks? Months, if I'm being honest. "I can watch Haley if you need to go somewhere."

"I—" She looks at me, then toward the hallway leading to Haley's room, where I can hear her playing. "I don't know if that'd be a good idea."

I frown. "You don't trust me with her?"

"No! No, that's not it at all. Of course I trust you with her, Jason." She expels a deep breath and avoids my eyes. "I'm just not sure everyone would be . . . comfortable."

"Who wouldn't be comfortable?"

"Um, you."

"Why the hell wouldn't I be comfortable? I hang out with Haley all the time." When she doesn't answer and brings her thumbnail to her mouth, chewing on it relentlessly as she avoids my eyes, I say, "Tess, I have no idea what the hell you're talking about. Just spit it out already."

She drops her arm and meets my gaze, her shoulders back as if she's bracing for my reaction. "I'm going on a date with Greg. That's why I called a babysitter."

And she was right to brace herself, because I feel like I just got punched in the goddamn stomach. For days, I've done nothing but think about her, about that night on the dance floor and the time spent with her and Haley when we all skipped our obligations, and try to figure out how I could possibly make this work. I came over here tonight with the intention of telling her, asking if she might be interested in trying, despite the warnings from her brother. Despite knowing it's a bad idea.

And while I was doing all that, she was making plans to date the boring-as-fuck dude I know is better suited to her than I am.

I stare at her, my jaw flexing as I try to get myself under control. When I think I can talk and not give anything away, I affect nonchalance as I shrug and say, "So go on your date."

Her head snaps to mine, her eyes wide. "You . . . you don't mind?"

"Why should I mind, Tess?" My voice is low, controlled as much as I can manage.

"Just . . . the other night . . . and . . ." She shakes her head, snapping her mouth shut. "Nothing. Of course. Well, if you're sure . . ."

I pull off my coat and toss it on the couch, shrugging as I cross my arms against my chest. "I'm sure."

Her gaze is pulled away by lights shining into the living room, and she goes over to look out the window. "That's him. I'm just going to go say good night to Haley."

Not a minute later, the doorbell rings, and I answer it, coming face-to-face with an obnoxiously large bouquet of flowers—roses—and I'm smug in the fact that I know Tessa thinks roses are a cop-out. She hates them. "Aw, Greg, you shouldn't have."

His face betrays his surprise before he's composed again, the smile he wore the whole time I intruded on their date last week once again present. "Jason. Hi. Sorry about that. I assumed Tessa would answer."

Moving away and falling to sit on the couch, my arm stretched out along the back, I say, "She went to say good night to Haley."

"Oh. So you're . . ." His eyebrows are raised as he trails off.

"Staying with Haley. Her babysitter canceled."

He frowns, his attention focused on the hallway where I can hear Tessa going over the rules with her daughter. "She didn't need to call you. She could've canceled. Or we can just stay in. I'm sure you have other things to do."

"Nah. I'm here for them. Whenever they need it." I maintain eye contact with him, and it's physically obvious the moment he registers my words as something that may threaten what he has with Tess. Before, even when I dragged Tessa away to dance, he didn't see me as anything more than her brother's friend. Someone so much younger than him, less established than him, someone who was no competition at all.

That was before he knew I was in the game.

tessa

I have no idea what I was thinking when I agreed to have Jason watch Haley. The very person I'm trying to forget about, trying to push out of my mind, here while I go out on a date with the man I'm trying to fill the void with.

After saying good-bye to Haley and reminding her to be good, I slip out of her room and head back to the living room. Jason's lounging on the couch, the picture of ease, his arm spread across the back, his legs wide, taking up as much space as possible. Greg is stiff by the door, and he offers me a tight smile.

"Hi, sorry about that," I say as I walk toward him. "Babysitter canceled at the last minute."

"Yeah, that's what Jason here was just saying." He clears his throat, his eyes briefly taking in my outfit. And even with his gaze raking over me, there's not even a whisper of excitement in my body. In every other circumstance, I'd ignore it or push it to the back of my mind, but having Jason arrive a mere five minutes ago, his eyes doing the exact same thing and my body responding with full-blown goose bumps, the differences between these two men and how they affect me are obvious. And staggering.

"Did you want to grab your coat? Our reservations are at seven."

"Oh sure. Yes." I turn around, glancing at Jason as I pass. His body language still exudes calmness and disinterest, but his eyes are sharp, boring into me as I walk across the room and grab my coat from the hook by the back door. Once I slip it on and grab my purse, I stop next to Greg and turn to face Jason. "So, I shouldn't be gone too long. You've got my cell if anything happens."

He nods. "Take your time." And even though he says the next words to me, his eyes are focused directly on my date. "I'll be here when you get home."

The tone of his voice, the way it was almost a warning to Greg has me frowning as I look between the two of them, wondering what I missed while I was in with Haley.

"Ready?" Greg asks.

"Ah, yeah."

Greg's hand goes to the small of my back, and he guides me to the front door, opening it for me. Before it closes behind me, I glance once more at Jason, and the intensity of his stare stays with me long after we leave.

TWELVE

jason

I don't realize how hard I'm clenching my jaw until the door shuts, and I drop my head back on the couch cushions. I want to take those goddamn flowers he left on the table by the door and shove them down his throat. With a groan, I scrub my hand over my face. I should've called Katie or Jess or Laura. I should've gone out with the guys and gotten shit-faced. I should've done a million things other than seeking Tess out in the first place.

Because now I'm stuck here for who knows how long while the girl I've done nothing but fixate on for the last several months goes out on a date with some too-old jackass. The image of them leaving comes to mind, the look he threw over his shoulder as I watched them walk out the door. I wanted to break his fucking fingers when he put them on Tess's body, pulled her close, and guided her out of the house. Away from me. And that's exactly what he was doing. Though when we met, he didn't see me as anything but some friend, it's obvious he finally gets it. He finally realizes I'm someone he needs to be wary of.

And worse than seeing him with his hands on her is imagining them on her later. I know this is their third date, and combined with the dress and the shoes she wore out of here, it's perfectly clear what she plans on doing tonight. The thought makes me want to stab my eyes out with a spoon just to get the image of them out of my head.

Before I can think too much on it, a high-pitched voice says, "Jay!" and Haley runs out of her bedroom full speed—that girl doesn't do anything slow. I barely have time to protect my junk before she collides with me, launching her body at me on the couch. When she's in my lap, she puts her hands on my shoulders, her face too close to mine and her voice too loud, her excitement obvious. "I'm so excited you're gonna watch me tonight while Mama goes on her date! Come on, come *on*! Let's play tea party."

She climbs off my lap and reaches for my hand, yanking with all her four-year-old might to get me off the couch. I play along and let her pull me up, then lead me down the hall to her bedroom, where she already has everything all set out.

"When'd you get all this set up?"

"Just now when Mama told me you were stayin'." She has two places set at her midget table, and she goes over to pull out a chair for me.

Raising an eyebrow, I say, "Isn't that my job?"

She giggles and goes to her pretend stove while I fold my too-tall frame in these step stools she calls chairs. I just know before the night is through, I'm going to break this thing and end up sprawled out on my ass.

"Don't forget your hat."

"My what?"

"Your hat," she says like it's the most obvious thing in the world. "You have to wear a hat for the tea party. It's the rules."

I look over to where she's pointing. There's a whole pile of pink and purple and bright yellow hats in a heap in front of her bed. I'm sure my face must show the horror I'm feeling when I look back at her. "Can't I wear a baseball hat? I have one in my car. I can go grab it. It'll only take me a minute."

Her smile turns to a scowl in the time it takes me to blink. "Baseball hats aren't allowed at tea parties. You have to wear one of *those*." She crosses her arms, her little toes tapping out her impatience. "Uncle Cade wore them."

I snort, shaking my head. "And don't think I won't remind him of it the next time we talk. All right, hand me the yellow. I think that's my color."

She nods seriously and goes to grab it, then brings it back and places it on my head, adjusting it a little before it's apparently just right.

"All done?" I ask.

"Yep. It's dinnertime now."

I grab the play bowl in front of me and bring it to my lips.

"No! Not like that! Tea first. And don't forget to drink with your pinky out."

"My pinky."

"Yes."

"Why?"

She shrugs. "Dunno. That's just what Mama told Cade, so you have to do it, too."

I laugh, shaking my head, and do as she told me, watching

her bounce from thing to thing, thankful I'm here with her tonight, because if anyone can keep my mind off Tess and what she's doing right now, it's this little girl.

tessa

I'm not sure I've ever been to as fancy a restaurant as the one Greg brings me to, and I'm not sure I've ever felt more out of place. It's intimate, the small dining room holding only a dozen or so tables. Candlelight flickers everywhere I look, the overhead lights of the chandeliers set low. The waitstaff is dressed in tuxedos, and there are way too many utensils spread out in front of me to know which ones are appropriate to use.

I was uncomfortable from the minute we walked in, and that feeling hasn't abated at all. Not through the fresh bread with some kind of fancy, homemade butter they brought out, or our soup course, or when they served the salad. And now that our main dishes are sitting in front of us, I'm wondering if this pit in my stomach is going to ever go away.

While my mind should be focused on the handsome man across from me, who's spent the last fifteen minutes talking about world events, it's actually across town with two people who are probably talking about what dress to put on which doll.

"Tessa?"

"Hmm?"

"I asked if your dinner was all right."

"Oh yeah. Yes, it's delicious." I glance around, taking in what would most definitely be considered a romantic restaurant by anyone with half a brain. Apparently I don't have even half a brain. "This place is really something."

He studies me for a minute as he cuts into the piece of steak on his plate that's arranged more like a piece of art than a meal. "It's too much."

Immediately, I shake my head as I hold up a hand. "No, no, it's really nice."

He sighs. "It *is*," he agrees, then adds, "but it's just not you."

I cringe a little and offer him a sad smile. "It's really not. But it's great. And the food is delicious."

"I'm sorry."

"No, don't be. Please. This is all on me."

After a few minutes of silence, he says, "Can I ask you something?"

"Sure, of course."

"Where do you see this going?"

I sputter a little, having just taken a sip of my wine, and dab at my lips with the cloth napkin. "I'm sorry?"

"I'm sure I don't need to remind you that this is our third date. Usually by that time, you have a pretty good feel for the other person. I like you, Tessa. A lot. And I'd like to see where this can go, but I can't be the only one willing to go on the trip. I don't want to put you on the spot, and I apologize because that's exactly what I'm doing. It's obvious that you've been through a lot—a lot more than I have in my life, despite our age difference. And I get that. I've been aware of it and understanding. And I'm willing to wait. But not if there's nothing here to wait for."

It's not an unreasonable request. He's been up-front about the fact that he's actively looking for someone with whom to get serious. And that's what I've been looking for, too. Someone in it for the long haul. I think about what he said, and he's absolutely right. By this time, I should know whether or not I want to move forward with this guy. And the thing is, I *do* know. I've known since before we went on our second date; I was just too stubborn to accept it.

Because the truth is so much scarier than this safe, secure man sitting across from me.

"You're a great guy, Greg."

He must hear my apology in my tone, because he expels a deep breath and offers a nod. "Yeah, that's what I thought."

"I'm sorry," I say for what feels like the hundredth time tonight.

"No, don't be." Repeating my words from earlier, he says, "This is all on me. I tried to make this work, even though I was pretty sure it wasn't going to."

"I *have* enjoyed spending time with you."

He offers me a genuine smile, and not for the first time, I'm frustrated with myself that I'm not attracted to him. "Same here."

The rest of our dinner is filled with stilted conversation and uncomfortable pauses, and when he drops me off at home, saying he hopes we can stay in touch, I lie and say I'd like the same thing.

The windows are dark as I walk up to the front door, and I slip into the house, listening for signs of life. When I hear none, I take my shoes off and hook them on my fingers as I walk down the hall toward Haley's room. Carefully, I push open the door, and what I see inside stops my heart and makes the butterflies lying dormant in my stomach burst to life.

Jason and Haley are both asleep on her bed, my little girl

curled under his arm, her body fitting perfectly into the nook of his side. She's in full-on princess gear, the tulle of her play-dress bunched up by her knees, her pretend high heels discarded below her small feet. The tiara I'm sure was once perched on her head now sits on Jason's shoulder. And while seeing that would warm any mother's heart, that's not the part that's making mine skip a beat. No, that achievement is because of the too-tall man whose legs are falling off the sides of Haley's twin bed. He's wearing one of Haley's tea party hats with a bright pink feather boa wrapped around his neck, and I almost can't breathe.

Seeing something like this isn't anything new. I used to come home from working a late shift or a date or a night out with Paige to find Haley and Cade curled up the same way. And I remember thinking then what I wouldn't give to find a guy who would do that with my daughter. Who would forget about being a manly man for an hour and play dress-up with a little girl who thinks he hangs the moon.

And all this time while I've been searching for him, I've been looking in all the wrong places. Trying to fit a square peg into a round hole. Because while Greg was safe and steady, someone who looked great on paper, I could never see him doing something like this. The realization that this has been in front of me the whole time—that *he* has been in front of me the entire time—is jarring, and I stumble over some toys lying on the floor as I make my way out of the room, quietly shutting the door behind me.

I press my back against the wall outside Haley's room, my eyes closing at my epiphany. I don't have enough time to process it, though, before her bedroom door opens and Jason comes out, now free of all dress-up gear. He shuts the door again, then leans against the wall opposite from me, arms folded across his chest and ankles crossed.

His pose is casual, just like how he was when I left him earlier, but his eyes are appraising, searching for something. They travel the entire length of me from my head all the way to my bare feet, darting up to see the shoes hanging between my fingers. And just like earlier, his eyes, the way they seem to almost caress me as his gaze travels over my body, light something inside me.

"How was your date?" His voice is low and raspy from sleep, and I don't want to admit what the sound does to me, that it sparks something deep when touches from other men haven't evoked even a quarter of the response.

I could lie. I could tell him it was wonderful, that Greg took me to a beautiful restaurant and I had a good time, but I don't feel like pretending. Not tonight. "Not great."

"Why not?"

I shrug. "We just didn't click."

He stares at me for a long moment before he says, "Why do you keep going out with guys like him, Tess?"

After a pause, the truth tumbles out of me. "Because he's what I thought I needed."

"And what about now?"

I look at him, take him in, from his carelessly mussed hair to his dark butterscotch eyes to the jaw sharp enough to cut glass, only marred with a slight shadow of stubble, and my knees go weak. "Now I'm not sure."

He pushes off the wall and moves to stand right in front of me, so close I can feel his breath ghosting over my exposed collarbone. "Were you ever sure about him?"

His nearness has stolen my voice, and all I can do is shake my head.

With his voice dropping even lower he asks, "Did he ever make you feel good?"

And he could mean a dozen different things. He could mean intellectually or emotionally or physically, but it doesn't matter which one he's talking about because the answer is the same regardless.

"No." It comes out raspy and breathless, and when did I become *that* girl? The one who loses all composure at the nearness of a guy. A hot guy, sure, but a guy nonetheless. Apparently allowing the tension to build up so much that it has no choice but to explode wasn't my brightest idea.

He reaches out, his fingers tracing along my shoulders, and I shiver, a wave of goose bumps erupting all over my skin, my nipples tightening into hard points against the satin material of my dress. "I could," he says, his voice so quiet I barely hear him. But I do. I do, and I want exactly what he's suggesting. "I could make you feel so good, Tess."

Of that I have no doubt. Jason's competence in that area has never been in question, not since we were in high school.

"Do you want me to? Just say the word, and I will."

He leans forward, his lips brushing against my neck, and my head hits the wall, my shoes forgotten and thudding on the carpet by my feet. I can't seem to make my arms go around him, to press my fingers into his hair and pull him to me, so instead I flatten them against the wall behind me.

"Tell me, Tess." His voice is low, gritty, and the desperation in his tone is what finally breaks me.

"Yes," I whisper, finding my voice.

jason

The word isn't out of her mouth before I lean down, her face cupped in my hands as I press my lips to hers. And her lips—Jesus, her fucking lips. They're soft and warm, and she doesn't hesitate to move them along with mine. With a groan, I press into her farther, trapping her body between mine and the wall, and Christ, she feels good. Her hands finally come away from the wall and press into my sides, her fists bunching up the material of my shirt, and I want more. I want to feel them against my skin, all over my body. I want her gripping and grappling and scratching. I want her teeth marks on my shoulder and scratches from her nails down my back. I want her moaning and writhing and panting and crying out my name. I want to sink into her, to feel her pussy pulsing around me, to see what she looks like under me as I fuck her.

I pull my mouth away from hers and kiss my way across her cheek to her ear. I trace the shell with my tongue, loving her moans of encouragement. "How much, Tess? How much will you give me?"

"What?" And I can't deny how much I love the raspy timbre of her voice, the breathless and almost confused way she answers. Like her mind is focused only on the responses from her body. Like I got her so worked up, she can't comprehend a simple question.

I pull back to look at her face. "How far do you want this to go? Can I take you to your bedroom?"

Her eyes go wide and panicked for a minute, and I rub my thumb along her jaw, soothing her.

"All right, no bedroom. It's okay. I won't push." I press a quick kiss to her lips. "I can do a lot in a hallway." With a smile,

I duck down, sucking on the skin of her neck, and her head falls back against the wall again, her hands pulling me to her.

"No sex," she says, and I don't know if it's my ego imagining it or not, but it seems like she has to force the words out, as much to warn me off as to remind herself of it.

"No sex," I repeat, nodding, already leaning in for another kiss.

She mirrors my efforts, her tongue searching for mine even before I can coax her mouth open. The sounds she makes, the way she moves her body against mine, gets me harder than I can remember being in a long time. And I don't know if it's the taboo of this—if it's because I've finally got someone who's been off-limits for so long in my hands—or if it's simply Tess.

Our height difference makes it awkward to kiss her and grind up on her in the way that makes her moan, so I reach down and grip the back of her thighs, lifting her up and against the wall as I guide her legs around my hips. With one hand gripping her ass to hold her up, the other trails up her leg, not stopping when I get to the material of her too-short dress now bunched around her hips. Knowing the only thing keeping me from her pussy is the thin scrap of lace I feel against my fingers makes me groan and press against her harder, my hips swiveling and trying to find the right rhythm that gets her exactly where she needs to be.

This is what I'm good at, what I've always been good at. Finding what makes a girl moan, scream, melt into a boneless heap under my hands. What gets her off. And while I want to do all that with Tessa, too, before it always felt like a duty. Like the least I could do for these women who agreed to spend nothing more than a night in my bed was to make sure they had a good time while they were there.

But with Tess . . . with her it's so different. For one thing, I want so much more than a single night. I think I could spend days studying her body and not grow tired of it . . . not grow tired of her. And for another, I *want* to get her off. I want to give her pleasure, to see her come apart in my arms, to know *I'm* the only one making her feel like this.

I want to feel her soft and warm and wet, slip my hand under the material of her panties and make her come around my fingers. I want to pull the top of her dress down, put my mouth on her tits, suck her nipples until she screams, but I don't want to push her too far. Instead, I grip her ass in both hands and press my cock against her, moving until she gasps against my mouth, her eyes heavy and sleepy-drunk as she stares into mine. She's restless against me, her rhythm long since lost, her body seeking the release it desperately wants.

Against her mouth, I say, "Come on, baby. Let go. Just let go. Let me make you come."

And even though I had it in my mind that I wasn't going to, that I didn't want to push, I move my hand up to the top of her thigh and slide my thumb over until it slips just under the material of her panties. She's wet and smooth and Jesus Christ, I'm going to come in my goddamn jeans like I'm an inexperienced teenager again.

She tenses, gasps, then moans, and it doesn't take more than a brush of my thumb against her clit before she comes, her head thrown back, her neck exposed, her chest heaving.

The complete and utter satisfaction I feel at being the one who was able to do that for her should embarrass me, but I can't seem to muster up any shame. I love the fact that I got her off with little more than a swipe of my thumb against her and a few kisses.

The thought of what she'll be like when I've got a bed to work with, when I'm able to use my fingers and my tongue and my cock, sets my head spinning.

This is usually when I start thinking about my next conquest, already bored with the girl I'd just made come, but the thought of not doing this with Tess again makes my chest twist. And I realize with panic that I'm not bored. Quite the opposite.

I could see myself doing this for her every day for a month and not tiring of it. And that's scary as hell.

THIRTEEN

tessa

When I was younger, I had a crush on Jason. How could I not? He was everything my gangly, preteen self wanted in a boyfriend. He was older and more experienced. He was funny and ridiculously hot and knew how to have a good time. Unfortunately, he saw me as nothing more than his best friend's younger, annoying sister.

But still, I was a tenacious little thing, even then, and I harbored the completely unrealistic fantasy that one day soon he'd come around. He'd realize we were meant to be and he'd come to my room one night when he was hanging out with Cade and he'd kiss me. And then we'd live happily ever after.

It's hard to believe I was ever that girl . . . the one who was so innocent and naive. The one who pined for nothing but a kiss.

That all changed my freshman year of high school when we were all in the same school again. I was forced to watch Jason day in and day out show off a different girl on his arm. I'd see him in the halls, pressing some faceless blonde or brunette or redhead—he never was discriminatory—against the lockers, hands and lips everywhere they could get away with, and I was devastated. Absolutely heartbroken—or as heartbroken as a fourteen-year-old could be when finding out her crush was unrequited.

And then I moved on.

I set my sights on other guys, cultivated crushes, and then, eventually, found my first boyfriend and got my first kiss. I forgot about Jason and his girl of the day and never looked back.

But even if I forgot about it on the surface, it's never really gone away, because here I am, lying in my bed completely sated from none other than the man himself, and all I can think about is the fact that he's probably done that with a hundred other girls. Hell, he probably did that with one yesterday. And the thought sends my stomach twisting, my heart racing, my mouth going dry.

I don't want to be just one girl in a long line of too many to count.

Somehow he went from the guy I didn't want to the guy I wanted above all others, and that thought scares the shit out of me, especially having been a front-row observer of Jason's past indiscretions.

When he left, he seemed fine. He was all smiles and soft words, telling me he'd call me tomorrow, but for all I know he tells that to all his conquests.

My phone buzzes on my nightstand, yanking me out of my thoughts, and I'm equal parts relieved and disappointed to see Paige's name instead of the guy I was thinking about.

"Hey."

"Damn, I was hoping you weren't going to answer."

I huff out a laugh. "Why?"

"Because I would hope you wouldn't answer the phone if you were being fucked good and proper."

"God, Paige."

"What? That was the goal of tonight, wasn't it? Date three? God knows you didn't get your vag waxed for *me*."

And though I didn't have sex tonight, someone else at least got to feel the benefit of it. Just the thought of Jason running his thumb over me has me tingling all over again.

"Holy shit. You *did* have sex!"

"I didn't say anything!"

"Please, you not saying anything said more than if you'd said anything at all."

"What does that even mean?"

Ignoring my question, she barrels on, "But, hell, it's only ten and you're already home, so that means he was a two-pump chump, huh?"

"I swear to God, I don't understand how your brain works."

"But you love me anyway."

"Most of the time."

"So fill me in. Give me the details. Did he at least have a horse cock to make up for his other shortcomings?"

"Oh my God. What's wrong with you?"

"I don't think there's anything wrong with hoping my best friend gets some solid action."

"I'm not sure I'd want to screw someone who has a horse cock, to be perfectly honest. *Ouch.* And stop talking about sex! I didn't have any."

"Well you had some something. I can tell."

"Oh, get off it. You can't tell anything over the phone."

"I absolutely can. You're all . . . jittery-sounding. Nervous. And that's exactly how you'd be after sex, because for some unknown reason, you don't think you should be having it."

I exhale an exhausted breath. She is going to go round and round in circles until I spill. "I didn't have sex, okay? I just . . . did something else."

"Ohhhh, I can work with something else. Did this something else involve a tongue by any chance?"

"No, no tongues."

"Fingers, then."

"Mmm . . . not exactly."

"Jesus, Tess, do we need to play twenty fucking questions or are you just going to tell me what the hell happened?"

I could avoid her question, refuse to answer, but the truth is, I need to talk this out with someone. I stare at the ceiling and blow out a breath before the words rush out of me. "Jason dry humped me against the wall."

"Say what now?"

"Oh God. It's bad, right? It's so bad. I can't believe I did that. I can't believe I *did* that. God, I can't believe I let *him* do that to me. And right after I got home from a date *with another man.* What kind of person does this make me? I mean, at least it wasn't sex, though, right? I told him that right away—no sex. But that doesn't really make it any better, does it? He's still the same kind of guy he's always been, the same one I've always known him to be. And even knowing that, I let him hold me up against the wall and grind all up on me until I came. Oh *God.*"

Paige is quiet for a moment, and when I don't say anything more, she asks, "You done with your word vomit now?"

"I think so."

"Okay, first things first. Was it good?"

I think about how it felt being in his arms. The length of his torso against mine, the bunch of his muscles under my fingers. How I wanted to reach under his shirt and feel his skin against my fingertips. I think about his breath on my neck and my chest and against my lips and in my mouth. How it felt when he pressed against me, how hard he was, how easily I came when he just slipped his thumb under my panties and applied the faintest pressure.

"It was amazing."

"Well, at least you can admit that. This might not be as hard as I thought."

"What might not be?"

"Me convincing you to give this a go with him."

"Give *what* a go with him? This is Jason we're talking about. Jason, who was banned from that coffee shop on Center Avenue because he got caught screwing some girl in the bathroom. This isn't Greg, who was actively seeking someone to get serious with. Jason actively seeks ways *not* to get serious with someone."

"Yeah, but it's *you*."

And I want *so badly* to believe the words she's saying. But I just can't. "That's not going to matter, Paige."

"What did he say before he left?"

I blow out a breath, remembering his words, the expression on his face, and for one minute, a tiny part of me harbors the hope that maybe Paige isn't completely full of shit. "That he'd call me tomorrow."

"Well, then, I'll guess we'll see what happens tomorrow."

jason

I'm not even home before the guilt kicks in, settling like a lead weight in my stomach. Guilt is the last thing I want to feel right now, especially considering I left a blissed-out Tess at home. And though there probably should've been awkward conversation or uncomfortable silence following our make-out session, there was neither. She was breathless and all smiles, and I left her with a kiss and a promise to talk tomorrow.

So then if everything was fine when I left, why is this feeling creeping in my gut? I know I didn't take advantage of her. I gave her plenty of times to say no, to stop it, and I know she wanted it as bad as I did, but still, that nagging sense that I did something wrong is eating me alive.

It doesn't take a genius to figure out what it is, though. That unwavering sense of loyalty to my best friend is the reason. Just a couple weeks ago, he told me to stay away from her, and instead of listening to him, instead of backing off like I know I should've, I pushed her up against a wall and made her come. Something her brother would have my balls for.

The drive home is quick, and I pull into my parking space before heading into my apartment building. Once inside, I toss my keys on the kitchen counter and throw my coat over a chair. Knowing I need to unwind before I'll ever be able to sleep, I grab a beer from the fridge and relax on the couch.

My phone rings just after I've turned on the TV, and for one second, I think it might be Tess, calling to say what a mistake it was. I don't want to admit what the thought of her saying that does to my chest.

The display on my phone shows the last person I want to talk to now—the very person I feel like I betrayed. Groaning, I drop my head to the back of the couch and close my eyes. I don't need Cade's warnings or his overprotective bullshit right now, but I know if I don't answer, he'll probably call Tess, and I don't want her to have to field his calls now. I don't want her second-guessing what happened between us any more than she already may be.

Knowing I have little choice, I answer, "Hello."

"Hey, man, what's going on?"

"Not much. Just got home."

"What is it, ten there? Early night for you."

"Yeah, I guess."

"Slim pickings at the bar?"

Though his tone isn't accusatory or mean, I still bristle at his comment but clench my jaw to keep myself composed. It's not his fault he still thinks of me as the guy who'd go home with one girl Friday night and a different one Saturday. It's not his fault he hasn't been around to see how different Tess is for me.

When I think I can speak without betraying how much his comment got to me, I say, "Actually, I didn't go out tonight. I was at Tessa's."

He's quiet for a moment, and I want to bang my head on the nearest hard surface for telling him that in the first place. I should've kept my fucking mouth shut.

"Tessa's, huh?" He clears his throat, and though I know he's aiming for nonchalance, his voice is strained when he asks, "What were you doing there?"

It's probably not the best idea to tell him that I made his sister come against a wall, so instead I give him a tiny piece of the truth. "I was watching Haley for her. She had a date."

Those four little words bring back images of that guy with

his hand on the small of her back, guiding her out of the house . . . away from me . . . and it's like a punch in the gut. While I feel like an ass about what we did, I sure as fuck don't want to see her out with other guys.

He blows out a breath, and I can practically hear his relief over the phone. "Oh yeah? This the dentist still?"

"Orthodontist."

"That's right. You meet him yet?"

"Yeah."

"And?"

"And . . ." I sigh heavily, taking another drink of my beer. "I don't know, man. He's boring as fuck. And he's too old for her."

"How old's too old?"

"I'd guess at least thirty."

"Jesus Christ," he mutters, and even though I know I shouldn't lead Cade to believe Tessa's still seeing that guy, I can't pass up this chance to get him off my ass about her. "You're keeping an eye on her, though, right?"

I huff out a laugh. "Fuck, Cade, make up your damn mind. Last time you called, you told me to stay the fuck away from her. Now you want to make sure I'm watching her. Which is it?"

"I want you to look after her—I just want you to keep your dick in your pants while you do it."

"Look, man, she's a grown woman. She can make her own decisions. And if that's dating a thirty-year-old dude, or getting mixed up with someone you might not approve of, that's her choice. And I'm not going to let you monitor her through me. I'll make sure things are going okay for her, help her when her car breaks down, watch Haley when she's in a pinch, but if you want to find out what she's doing in her love life, ask her. Stop running interference through me."

He doesn't say anything for a minute. When he finally does, he surprises me. "You're right. I know I shouldn't do that, but it's hard as hell being so far away when she's going on these dates with these assholes she meets online. Who the fuck knows who they are? They could be creeps or psychos, and there's nothing I can do about it. I'm not used to not being able to keep an eye on the guys she gets mixed up with."

"Give your sister a little credit. She's not an idiot. It's not like she gets a message online and the very next day meets them in the woods somewhere. You just have to trust her to know what she's doing." While it fits for what we're talking about, I want to have it encompass so much more—I want to have it pertain to *us*, too . . . to me and Tessa.

"Yeah. I do. I trust her." Someone says something to Cade— the voice low and feminine—and then Cade laughs. "Winter says I need to leave Tess alone and start talking about something else."

"I always knew she was smart."

He chuckles. "Yeah, she is. So what's new with you? How're classes going? You gonna finally graduate this year?"

The last time we talked, I was so pissed at him for telling me to stay away from Tess I never filled him in on the ultimatum my parents gave me. "Yeah, looks like."

"No shit? Finally declared a major, huh? What brought that on?"

"Well, when your parents tell you you're going to be cut off if you don't get your shit together, that sort of lights a fire under your ass."

"They said that?"

"Yep. They hit me with it a couple weeks ago at dinner. I start going for my master's in January while I'm shadowing my dad at the firm, or I'm booted from the family."

"Jesus, those were their terms?"

"Well, I added the booted-from-the-family part, but they didn't have to say that to make it true. You know how they are. Only the best or get the fuck out. Can you imagine how it would look at the club to have a son doing something other than wearing a suit five days a week and golfing every chance he gets?"

He's quiet, and then he blows out a breath. "I'm sorry, man."

"For what?"

"I feel like an ass."

"Well, you are an ass, but I'm used to it by now."

"I'm serious. You've been dealing with all this shit, and I've been an asshole best friend, doing nothing but badgering you about Tess."

"Don't worry about it."

"For what it's worth, I think you should tell them to go fuck themselves."

"Yeah, you and everyone else." And I'd love to. I'd love nothing more than to give them the finger and turn around, walk away, and never look back.

But the thing is, I didn't grow up in the house Tessa and Cade did. I didn't grow up with a set of parents who loved me unconditionally, who pushed me toward my interests, who supported me in my choices. I grew up with two people who cared more about what my decisions would look like to their friends at the country club than what was best for me, what would make me happy. And even though I've spent the last however many years doing everything I could to push the limits—taking as long as I

possibly could toward my undergrad degree, racking up a reputation that I knew would reflect poorly on them—I've always
known just how far I can go, just how much they'll bend. In the
end, after everything they've piled on me, all the unreasonable
expectations they've set, I'm still seeking their approval. Especially now that my grandpa is gone—the one and only person in
my family who ever assured me I was worth more than just what
I could do for someone.

That I'm still seeking their approval is a pretty fucked-up
thing, considering I'll never get it. I'll never fit into the image they
have in their minds of the perfect son.

I've never been that guy, and I never will be.

FOURTEEN

Tessa

Paige was so sure last night on the phone, her voice unwavering as she told me exactly what I needed to do. I wish I had her confidence for only five minutes. To be so *certain* about something must be refreshing. For as long as I can remember, that's been missing. I feel like I've done nothing but second-guess every decision I've ever made since that morning in the bathroom five years ago, staring at a stick that linked me to a future I never knew I wanted—at least not at seventeen.

Everything I do now is done with Haley in the back of my mind. How it'll affect her, *if* it will . . . if it makes me the kind of person I'd want my daughter to look up to. And as for last night, letting some guy get me off against a wall? No, I can't say I'm very proud of that person, not as a role model for her.

While it felt good in the moment—it felt *amazing* in the

moment—I can't help but wonder if it was a mistake. Not the *what* but the *how*. We could've waited longer. Gone out on a date or two, gotten to know each other as something other than the friends we've been for the last fifteen years. Hell, we could've walked down the hall to the living room so we weren't right up against the wall outside Haley's bedroom.

I exhale a deep breath and close my eyes, letting it go. There's nothing I can do about what happened last night, and though a part of me knows it was irresponsible . . . the other part is still tingling with memories of every moment of our time together and wondering when it can happen again.

I glance down at Haley, snuggled against me in my bed, her cheek puffed out against my chest as she smiles at the cartoon on TV. This has been our Saturday morning ritual for as long as I can remember. At first, it was started for purely selfish reasons— so I could sneak in a few more minutes of that ever-elusive sleep when I was an exhausted, new mother working my ass off while going to school. And, admittedly, catching another half hour of sleep still happens sometimes, but it's grown into something more. She's always more open in the mornings, and definitely more so when she's preoccupied with animated characters. It's my secret mom-weapon for getting her to talk about stuff she otherwise might not. I only hope it continues when she gets older.

A commercial comes on, the TV losing her attention, and she twists around to lie on her stomach, propped up on her elbows as she stares at me.

"What're we doin' today, Mama?"

I reach up, brushing her hair away from her face. "I'm not sure. What do you want to do?"

"Get ice cream!"

"Baby, it's, like, twenty degrees outside and you want ice cream?"

"I *always* want ice cream."

I laugh. "Me, too. I think it's supposed to storm today, though, so maybe we can have a campout in the living room with ice cream instead of going out. I have double fudge brownie in the freezer . . ." I say with a grin.

Her eyes get wide, a smile stretching her face, and I love her so much it hurts. She's perfect—the best parts of me mixed with an amazing array of traits that are all hers. When I get down on myself, frustrated with everything I'm not doing right, I just need to look at her. Stop and really look, because she reminds me of exactly everything I'm doing right.

"Can we do a slumber party in the living room? And do makeup? I'll try not to get blipstick all over your face again."

My smile grows until it nearly splits my face in half. I'm going to miss these days when she eventually says all her words right and doesn't want to spend undivided time with me.

"Yeah, we can. Maybe we'll paint our toenails, too."

"*Yes!*" she hisses, flopping on her back and wriggling around in her excitement. She freezes and flips back over, her head popping up, her hair a mess on her head, partially covering her face. "Can Jay come, too?"

I freeze from pushing her hair back again, all the nerves that faded into the background leaping to the front once again. "I don't think he'd like to have his toenails painted very much."

"We don't have to do *that*, but he can watch movies with us and have ice cream and popcorn and maybe read to me in those funny voices and this time he can bring his jammies so there's no scratchy jeans."

While I always knew that whatever I did in my social life would affect Haley, this is like a slap in the face and exactly the kind of reminder I need. Haley is already invested in this thing with Jason. Regardless of whether or not anything romantic happens between us, he's situated himself so far into my little girl's life that she can't see it without him. She asks for him when he's not around, she clings to him when he is, and she loves him every minute in between.

I only hope Paige is right about the outcome from last night. Because if there's fallout from my actions, if something happens thanks to my choices, I'm not the only one who's going to be affected.

IT CAN'T BE more than a half hour later with me dozing in and out of a light sleep when Haley gets restless, notifying me there's another commercial on. She's squirming and bouncing on the bed, trying to tickle me while she giggles hysterically, when I think I hear something. Immediately, I'm wide awake.

"Shh, baby, be quiet a minute."

Her giggles die off, and then just the soft cadence of the commercial meets my ears, the rest of the house silent. When I relax back against the bed, she starts up again, giggling and bouncing, and this time I *know* I hear something. For a second, I panic, my entire body going taut as I prepare to reach for the baseball bat Cade made sure I had by my bed. And then I hear Jason's voice booming through the house, and I panic for another reason entirely.

"Hello?"

"Jay!" Haley's eyes are as wide as her smile when she bounces off the bed and tears out of my room and down the hall.

I glance down, seeing the ratty tank top and flannel pajama pants I slept in last night, knowing without a doubt my hair is a crazy mess on my head. I'm wearing no makeup, and I haven't even brushed my teeth yet. I throw the covers back and fly out of bed, slipping into the bathroom before Haley can drag Jason down the hallway.

One look in the mirror proves my fears, and I finger comb through my hair to get it in some sort of order, then proceed to scrub the remnants of last night's mascara from under my eyes. A quick swig of mouthwash, a swipe of my toothbrush, and a couple slaps on my cheeks later, I slip out again and follow the sound of laughter. Instead of my bedroom, where I thought Haley would take him to show him her favorite cartoon, I find them in the kitchen, Haley perched on a stool, her butt bouncing as she kneels, animatedly telling Jason a story.

In the middle of Haley's explanation of what words start with their letter of the week, Jason glances over her head and our eyes meet. His are deep and dark and bottomless, and they're focused completely, intently on me.

When I was alone with my thoughts, stuck in an empty bed last night, it was easy to brush all my feelings aside, assure myself I was mistaken. That I didn't feel this overwhelming want around him. That it wasn't as all-consuming as I imagined.

But here . . . now . . . when he's standing ten feet away, his gaze spreading over me like fire? I realize I'm a liar and I'm very good at pretending.

Except he doesn't look like he has any interest at all in pretending.

jason

Before I could second-guess myself, I got up and showered this morning, stopped off to grab some donuts because Haley loves them, and headed over to Tessa's. I needed to see her, despite any lingering apprehension I had. And that need made me feel like a pussy, but I didn't even care.

With my parents taking every ounce of independence I have left, taking any choice I had in my future away, taking away the hope I had of doing the one thing I always enjoyed, I want this. Selfishly and foolishly, but neither are going to stop me.

I knock a couple times with no answer, so I use my key to let myself in, figuring Tess is preoccupied or just can't hear me. After calling out a hello, I hear Haley's voice echoing down the hallway, and then her tiny feet are pounding the floors. She crashes into the back of my legs as I'm walking into the kitchen to drop off the donuts.

"Hey, shorty. What's shakin'?"

"Nothin'. Did ya bring me a donut?"

I lean down and slowly open the box for her to peek in. Whispering, I say, "I brought you *two*."

Her eyes crinkle as her mouth splits in her wide smile. She climbs up on the stool to sit and digs into her chocolate-covered with rainbow sprinkles, all the while telling me about her week at preschool and day care, even though she already told me some version of it last night. Haley doesn't even pay attention when her mom comes into the room behind her, but I can't help but glance up. Tessa's hair is messy and sexy as hell, her face flushed, and before I can stop myself, I glance down, taking a quick sweep of the rest of her. And for one minute, I almost wish I hadn't, because she is abso-fucking-lutely not wearing a bra, and the sight of her nipples pressing against the not-nearly-thin-enough material of her tank top makes me want to groan. And then press her up against a wall and have a repeat of last night, this time without the blue balls that accompanied it.

It isn't until Haley pokes at my hand repeatedly that I remember there's someone else here besides the two of us, and thinking about anything at all having to do with Tessa's tits is wholly inappropriate right now, despite what my dick thinks.

"Well, do ya?"

Shaking my head to clear it, I glance down at Haley's face, her mouth covered in smears of chocolate. "Um, yeah, sure." I don't even know what I'm saying yes to, but it's pretty obvious I don't say no to much where this one is concerned.

"*Yesss!* Last one has to be middle!"

Without another glance, she climbs down from the stool and runs out of the kitchen.

"Do not climb into my bed before you wash your face and hands, Haley Grace!" Tessa yells down the hall toward the retreating form of her daughter before she turns back to me. Once her gaze meets mine, she lifts her eyebrows in question. Her look of surprise makes me panic for a minute about what I actually accepted from Haley.

"What'd I just agree to?"

Her shock gives way to suspicion and then amusement as a

small smile sweeps across her face. She crosses her arms, and no, I'm absolutely not going to look down at what that does for her tits. "You didn't hear a word of what she said."

"Say what now?"

She huffs out a laugh and shakes her head. "Yes, exactly. You could've agreed to allow her to try out her new makeup on you or curl your hair."

"Oh Jesus, please tell me it's neither of those things."

"Well, she was talking about painting toenails earlier, but I said you probably wouldn't be up for that. You just agreed to do our Saturday-morning ritual with us."

I put the lid back on the donuts and walk to stand in front of her. I want to reach out and touch her, to lean down and kiss her breathless, but I'm not sure where we stand—if last night was a fluke or the start of something. The worst part is, I don't know which is scarier. I pop the rest of my donut in my mouth, not wanting to think about that at this moment. "And what's that? You guys drinking pig's blood later?"

"Worse. Watching Disney Junior while confined in a bedroom."

"In your bedroom or in hers?"

"You'd better hope mine. That'd be a lot of people on her twin mattress."

The thought of me and Tessa in her bed . . . alone . . . is enough to squash any uncertainty I had as to whether I wanted last night to be a fluke, because there's nearly nothing I want more than to see her under me, breathless for *me*. I lean forward, my lips nearly brushing hers. "Oh, Tess, I do hope yours. But at another time and for another reason entirely."

I watch her eyes widen slightly, her lips part, and I know she's remembering exactly what we did in the hallway mere hours ago.

I hope she's remembering how it felt to come apart in my arms, because I like knowing she's thinking about me like that . . . thinking about us like that.

"Mama! Jay! Hurry up! It's already starting!"

"You heard her. Last one gets middle." And with that, I slap Tessa on the ass and jog past her down the hallway and into her bedroom. Haley's tiny frame is taking up entirely too much of the mattress as she pats the spot next to her.

"Got any jammies?"

"Still no jammies here, shorty."

She heaves out a dramatic sigh, rolling her eyes as best as a four-year-old can. "Fine. But no shoes. Mama gets real mad if you do that."

Just as I slip my shoes off, Tessa sneaks into the room and leaps onto the bed, giggling as Haley goes up on her knees, clapping and then pointing to me. "You have middle, Jay!"

Not that long ago, I would've been doing something far different on a Saturday morning while sandwiched between two girls. But now? I can't find it in me to care that this is exactly how I'm going to be spending this particular Saturday morning.

Haley scoots down on the bed and pats the spot in the middle, encouraging me to climb in. With a raised eyebrow in Tessa's direction, I silently ask for permission. Her not refuting Haley's invitation in the kitchen and then flying into bed seemed like she was okay with it, but I want to be sure.

When she gives me a smile and a slight nod, I climb in and take over the majority of the bed, sprawling out on top of both Tessa and Haley. "You're right, this *is* comfortable. This pillow is so soft," I say as I bounce a little on a giggling Haley.

"Jay! That's me, not a pillow!"

"Oh, so sorry, miss. Pardon me," I say in an exaggerated British accent.

Her giggles grow louder as I mumble gibberish in the accent while still lying partially on top of her. When she's able, she tugs my arm off her, and I'm barely relaxed back against the headboard before she's burrowed her way under my arm and is snuggled into my side. I've always had a soft spot for this girl—since the day she was born, though I fought it a lot. Because, really, what kind of nineteen-year-old guy was enamored with a baby?

But now, feeling her laugh against my chest . . . seeing her look up at me with those dark eyes so much like mine, this warm ache spreads through my chest, and I think for a second what it'd be like if she *were* mine. If both of them were mine. And I wonder if *this* is what my grandfather always talked about—the kind of family that's worth something. The kind of family that's worth *everything*.

I've fought a connection like this since I was old enough to get involved with women, struggled against what it might mean to get involved with someone because of how my parents' relationship turned out. But I can't fight it anymore, not with Tessa and Haley.

And I realize I don't want to.

FIFTEEN

tessa

"Do you guys seriously spend all day in bed like this?" Jason's voice is low, mumbled softly against the top of my head, and I fight back a shiver.

It's been an hour or so since he arrived. An hour filled with full-body touches and the feel of his rumbled voice under a layer of cotton as I rest my head against his chest. As soon as Haley burrowed her way into his side, he tugged me closer, too, smashing the both of us to him and not letting go. Not that I put up much of a fight.

"No, we usually find our way to the kitchen at some point for sustenance."

"Yeah, ice cream!" Haley yells with a raised fist, though we're all no more than two feet apart.

"You've already got her addicted to ice cream, do you realize that?" Jason's breath tickles my forehead, and I have to remind myself to slow down. To pull back. Paige thinks I can have sex just for the sake of having sex, but I can't. I never could, as much as I wanted to, sometimes just needing that physical connection, that release. But whether I want it to or not, sex causes emotional turbulence for me, and with our history . . . with how close Jason and I are, I have no idea what the outcome from a shared night would be.

And the constant churning in my stomach is proof enough that I'm scared as hell about that.

Needing some space, I use this as an excuse to get up. Jason recoils as I jab a finger in his side and say, "Better ice cream than wine." I slip out of bed, walking out of the room and toward the kitchen. A glance at the clock on the microwave shows it's nearly noon, and I grab everything I need to throw together some sandwiches for everyone. Can't have ice cream or cookies for lunch every day . . .

It isn't long before Jason walks into the kitchen, no Haley shadow behind him.

"How'd you manage to slip out of there?" I ask.

"Some Princess Sophie show or whatever came on."

"Princess Sofia. She loves that one."

I slather a layer of mayo on three slices of bread, then proceed to top them with ham and cheese. Jason doesn't say anything more, but it's mere seconds before my entire body ignites. Though I can't feel him, I know without a doubt that he's stepped closer to me. The hairs on the back of my neck stand on end, goose bumps erupt on my skin, and it's not until my nipples tighten into points against the cotton of my tank top that I remember I'm not wearing a bra.

He leans forward, his breath warm on the back of my neck, my short hair baring that part of my body to him, and I close my eyes in anticipation. Of what, I don't know. His lips? His tongue? His words?

And I want all of them. Any of the above, or all three at once.

When none of them come, I can't take it anymore. I stop what I'm doing and rest my hands against the counter, using the support to hold myself up as I drop my head forward and close my eyes.

"What are we doing, Jason?" My voice is barely above a whisper, my words said to the floor, but he still hears me. Where before I could only sense him behind me, now I *feel* him. He takes a small step forward, bringing the line of his front against my back, and I can't deny how amazing it feels. How amazing *he* feels. He smells like soap and laundry detergent and just a hint of cologne—nothing overpowering. It's light and fresh and everything Jason is wrapped up in a mouthwatering scent.

"I'll do whatever you want me to, Tess."

"That's not fair. Don't put this all on me."

"It *has* to be all on you. I know how I am; we both do. If I put my mind to it, do you think I couldn't get you in your bed? Even if you thought it was a bad idea? I need you to be sure. I want you, Tess. Don't doubt that. I've wanted you for months, and I'm finally owning up to that. But you have to want it as bad as I do."

Before I can say anything, before I can even *think* about his words, his warmth is gone and the voice of my daughter fills the room.

"Yes, ham and cheese! Can we have chips, too?"

It takes me a moment before my parched mouth can form words. "If you eat your carrots."

She nods enthusiastically, taking her place at the breakfast bar next to Jason, but I can't look at him. My face has erupted in flames, a wave of heat engulfing me at his words—at the honesty in them and the truth in what he wants.

Me.

I busy myself with everything I can just to avoid eye contact, because I know I'll get lost if I look into those dark whiskey-colored eyes—eyes so similar to my daughter's it's jolting sometimes. And he's right. This does have to be on me.

I'm just not sure I'm ready for the leap.

THE SNOW IS falling in sheets, those perfect flakes that come only once or twice a season covering the ground. Despite the accumulation, it's a nice day, even though winter descended exceptionally early, the temperature hovering right around thirty degrees, perfect for snowman building and snow angel making and snowball fights.

I don't know if Jason could sense I needed time to myself, or if he really is that much of a kid despite his twenty-four years, but regardless of the reason, he offered to take Haley outside and work off some of her endless energy. He got her ready, covered head to toe in winter gear, then took her outside only to arrive back five minutes later because Haley forgot to use the bathroom. He was patient, never getting frustrated for the extra ten minutes of work as he unbundled and rebundled her, and then they were out the door again.

It's been nearly an hour, and I'm still standing frozen in my place in front of the kitchen sink as I look out into our backyard, hearing the pealing giggles of my little girl followed by the deeper baritone of Jason's chuckle. And just like last night with him curled up on Haley's bed with her, the sight of them in the backyard isn't anything new. Cade used to take Haley out in the snow all the time. It's her favorite season, and she never tired of playing outside, even in the frigid temperatures. But there is something new about the scene in front of me now. It fills my chest with a warmth I wasn't expecting, a warmth I hadn't banked on when Jason started spending more time with us after Cade left.

I think back to how he's been in the last five months, checking it against what I've known of him the last fifteen years. He's been a constant—his support unwavering and unquestionable. It's no secret he's smitten with Haley. That girl has him wrapped so far around her pinky, it wouldn't take much more than a bat of her thick eyelashes to get him to agree to anything.

Paige's words come to me, a reminder that I'm not a new infatuation for Jason. That, according to her, he's been looking at me differently for months. And his words from this morning prove that.

Somewhere along the way, I started looking at him differently, too.

But still, I'm holding back.

A few months of new behavior doesn't discount the years before. The years full of girls, of one-night stands—neither of which I'm judging him for. He was never committed to any of the women he slept with, never misled anyone, and if that worked for him, great. It *doesn't* work for me, though, and I'm worried this is just a phase. Something that won't stick, and then where will that leave me? Where will that leave *us*? Because as much as I'd like to make the decision based solely on what my body is begging me to do, there's another person I have to take into account. Another person who'll get stuck in the fallout if this all blows up in my face.

But as I look out at the two of them playing in the snow, Jason running away from Haley but not so fast that she can't catch him, I don't think he'd even be here if he hadn't thought it through a hundred times. He wouldn't hurt Haley like that, and after being in our lives so frequently for the past few months, he has to know just exactly how much it will affect her.

Haley tosses a snowball at him, a weak excuse for a throw, but Jason goes down, crumpling to the ground as sure as if it were a major-league pitch hitting him. She's on him in a second, her head tossed back in the absolutely unrestrained laughter that can come only from a child. She is so happy, so full of love. For Jason. It's clear in the way his laughter meets and melts with hers, in the way he tosses her in the air, and in the way he smiles just for her that he feels the same.

It's then, in that very moment as I stare out at a blanket of white, that I know I'm in trouble.

"HOW IS SHE not tired yet?" Jason's sprawled out on the couch, his head resting against the cushion. After an hour and a half outside, they came in to warm up the same way that's been a tradition since *I* was a child—with hot chocolate. Once they were toasty again, Haley talked him into a tea party followed by a rousing game—or seven—of *Mario Kart*, and now despite all the activity outside and the nonstop goings-on in the house, Haley is still practically bouncing off the walls.

"It's cabin fever. It's like she knows we can't get out even if we wanted to." I glance outside at the snow still falling, the once-perfect flakes transforming into a blur of white, the wind gusting and blowing and the ground piled high with more than a foot of snow.

"Well, I'm ready for a nap," Jason mumbles, his eyes closing.

"No naps!" Haley yells as she spins in circles.

"It's the donuts from this morning," I say to Jason. "You only have yourself to blame."

"Oh, so that hot chocolate with twenty-seven marshmallows and a candy cane stir stick didn't do anything, right?"

I smile. "It's tradition. It's what my mom used to give us whenever we played outside."

With his head resting back against the couch cushion, he turns to face me. "I remember."

His voice is soft—not tentative, but wistful. And even though he's not a Maxwell, even though he didn't live in this house, he'd come to count on my parents, my mom especially, as sure as if they were his own, because God knew his parents weren't worth shit. There's comfort in that, in shared memories and not having to recount the little details, of not having to try and tell someone how amazing my parents were. He already knows. He already knows so much.

"Let's play a game!"

With a sigh, I glance over at Haley. "It's almost bedtime, baby."

She slumps, her lip going out in a pout. "Come *on*. Just one game?"

"Yeah, just one game?" Jason mimics, his lip popping out just like Haley's.

I narrow my eyes at him. "I thought you were ready for a nap?"

"The faster we play the game, the faster I'm going to get one."

"Yes!" Haley takes that for an answer and pumps her fist in

the air before running down the hall to her closet where all the games are stored.

When she comes skipping back in, a giant smile on her face and a white box with bold letters over the front and huge circles in red, green, blue, and yellow in her hands, Jason looks at me with a question I can't misinterpret, his eyebrow raised. He knows just as well as I do that this is going to do nothing to extinguish the bubbling chemistry between us. And me agreeing to play the game is akin to stepping right into the wolf's den.

jason

"Left foot green," Tessa says, blowing the hair out of her face as she looks at Haley.

This is what my Saturday night looks like. Not body shots, not beer pong or strip poker.

Twister. And not even naked Twister with a group of coeds.

We've been at this for fifteen minutes. Fifteen agonizing minutes where too much and not nearly enough of Tessa has come in contact with me. When Haley came running out of her room with this game of all that she could have chosen, I knew exactly what would happen if we played it. Tessa and I have combustible chemistry when standing on opposite ends of a room, but throw us together, contorting and bending over a small mat, and all bets were off. I've had to restrain myself more times than I can count from leaning forward and biting the ass that somehow keeps ending up in my face. The only thing that's stopped me is the four-year-old cock-blocker currently having the time of her life.

Listening to her mom's order, Haley stretches, attempting to reach a green dot, but the closest open one isn't close at all, and with a grunt, then a giggle, she collapses on the mat, taking her loss surprisingly well. "I'll be the spinner! Mama, you gotta beat Jay, 'kay?" She sits on her knees off to the side, bouncing up and down as she sends the arrow spinning. Tessa watches, waiting for it to stop. When it does, she smiles smugly, then easily moves her left hand to the blue space.

I'm not so lucky—or luckier, depending on how you look at it. Haley's spin for me lands on right hand red, which is on the other side of the mat. Carefully, I move, diligently keeping myself held up over the mat, and bring my hand down on the other side of Tessa, her back brushing against my chest. She took a shower while Haley and I were out playing in the snow, and the citrusy-fresh scent of her shampoo—the same scent she uses on me when I go to her for a haircut, the same scent that taunts me for days after—assaults me. I'm lost in thoughts of what that hair will look like spread over my pillow, when Haley calls out the next move, having already memorized which section on the spinner is for what body part.

With a twist of her body, Tessa moves her foot to the nearest yellow, her hip brushing up against my cock, and just like that, the semi I was sporting goes to full wood, and I groan under my breath. Tessa looks over at me, her green eyes darkening, her lips parted, and if there was any question about whether she feels this thing between us, I have my answer right here.

She holds the pose for a moment, then she drops one elbow to the floor, maintaining eye contact with me the entire time. Haley groans in the background, but it's drowned out as I focus on Tessa's eyes. I read everything I need to in that gaze. The want, the desire, the acceptance . . . the fear.

She's scared she's going to be just like any other girl for me, that this won't be different. I'm scared of it, too. But then I remember I could have a dozen different girls if I wanted to. Ones I could call up and they'd be on me in the blink of an eye. Instead, I've spent my time dressing up in hats and feather boas just to see a little girl smile. I've spent a Saturday curled up in bed, then freezing my balls off for the sole purpose of hearing Haley laugh. I've spent all my time lately getting closer to the two girls who've come to mean the world to me, and because of that, I'm certain this is different.

She is different. And I'm ready to prove just how much.

SIXTEEN

tessa

I threw the game. Despite my daughter wanting me to win—*for girls everywhere*, she said—I couldn't. I feigned exhaustion, letting my body slump to the ground. Because my blood was boiling, my body on fire as I pressed against Jason's body during a stupid game of Twister, and I couldn't take it anymore. If Haley hadn't been in the room, I would've pulled Jason down on top of me and let him strip me down right there on that stupid plastic mat.

In reality, I had a four-year-old to attend to instead of doing everything I wanted to. In the thirty minutes since putting Haley to bed, my urgency has faded, leaving behind only a subtle hum under my skin, but it's there. This vibration of need when Jason is around that I never bothered to notice before. Or that I willingly ignored, which is probably more the case.

Despite that, despite wanting him, I'm in the bathroom under the guise of freshening up, even though I showered just a couple hours ago. I'm stalling, and I don't know why. Haley's asleep, Jason's in the living room, presumably waiting for me, and I'm hiding in the bathroom.

Several minutes go by before a soft knock sounds at the door, sending me jumping nearly a foot in the air.

"Yeah . . ." I try to say, except my voice comes out all scratchy and breathless, so I clear my throat and try again. "Yeah?"

"Do you want me to just go home, Tess?"

"What?" I whip the door open, eyes wide and frantic, because that is absolutely *not* what I want. Not even a little bit. Leaning his shoulder against the doorjamb, Jason's eyes snap to mine as soon as the layer of wood isn't separating us anymore, and in that split second when our eyes meet, the heat between us cracks and sizzles just like it did while we were playing the game. Just like it's been doing anytime we're within twenty feet of each other. Shaking my head, I say, "No. I don't want you to go home."

His eyebrows lift up on his forehead, his expression one that clearly says he thinks I'm full of it. "You sure? Because you've been hiding in here for ten minutes."

I open my mouth to argue with him about the hiding bit, but there's no use. Instead, I simply nod and swallow, not sure I can find the words to tell him exactly what's going on with me.

Mostly because I don't even know myself.

It's not like I'm a virgin, and even though it has been a while, I've never gotten like this with any of my previous partners. Never had this overwhelming nervousness, and I don't know where it's coming from. No idea why there's this swarm of bees buzzing around in my stomach. Why I'm all breathless with anticipation and anxiety.

But then Jason steps forward, right into my space, one hand coming up and cupping the back of my neck while the other goes to my hip, his thumb slipping under the material of my shirt to graze the skin above my waistband, and I know *exactly* why there's a tornado in my belly.

"Last chance," he murmurs, his breath washing over my lips, and I don't think I could tell him to stop even if I wanted to.

But I don't. I don't want to, so I shake my head, and finally—*finally*—he closes the distance between us and puts his lips to mine. The kiss is tentative at first, a question, and even though he gave me an out just a moment ago, I love that he's not pushing it. When I don't pull away, don't do anything but grip the front of his shirt in my fists and pull him closer to me, he takes that as an answer and swipes his tongue across my lips. On a moan, I open to him, desperate to taste him again in a way I didn't allow myself to think about before now.

Jason's grip on me tightens, his thumb rubbing in circles against the pulse point at my neck, and I know he can feel my heart flying. It's nearly pounding right out of my rib cage. His other hand curls around my hip, pulling me closer to him, flush with him, and I can't stop from gasping into his mouth. He's against me, all of him, strong and solid and *hard*, and I didn't realize how much I wanted this until this very moment.

He's already good at reading my cues, because no more have I thought it than we're walking, fumbling down the hallway and into my bedroom. The door isn't even closed before I start tugging up his shirt, desperate to feel his skin against mine. With a grunt and a curse, he reaches back and yanks his shirt over his head before his lips are back on mine, his tongue sliding against my own, and I can hardly breathe I want this so badly.

In the dozen-plus years of his being in my life, I've seen him without a shirt on too many times to count, but I've never *felt* his bare skin. Not like this. He's sinewy and muscular, the body of a runner, all tall and lanky, the muscles in his abdomen defined but not obscene, his biceps cut but not bulky. I run my hands over every part of him I can reach, sliding from his chest to his stomach, following the trail of hair down then hooking into the waistband of his jeans, and I want those off, too.

"Jesus, Tess," he groans into my mouth, and the roughness of it washes over me like a warm rain, comforting me in a way I didn't realize I needed. He wants this. *Me.* Desperately. It's reassuring to know I'm not in this on my own.

His lips brush across my cheek, his teeth nipping at my chin, his tongue licking a line up the column of my neck, and I think I might die right here. I might actually die, because my heart feels like the pounding hooves of a thousand horses, and I can't seem to get my clothes off fast enough.

Jason huffs out a laugh at my growl of frustration when I can't get my shirt over my head without forcing his mouth away from my body.

"It doesn't bode well for you to laugh now," I say, abandoning my mission to get my shirt off as I reach out and cup him through his jeans. He's just as hard as he was last night when I felt him pressing against me, and I revel in the fact that I'm the one doing that to him. "Just help me get out of my clothes."

Groaning, he drops his forehead to my shoulder. "You're killing me. You're actually going to kill me." With urgent movements, he brushes my hands to the side and takes over on the task of getting me naked. I don't want to think about how many times he's done this before that in less than thirty seconds he can unhook my bra with one hand and have me on my back on the bed, wearing only my panties.

I don't even have time to worry about the wisps of silvery stretch marks on my hips or the slight curve of my lower stomach before he's stretched out on top of me. The only things that separate us are my underwear and his, two thin pieces of cotton, and I can feel every inch of him against where I'm aching.

He sinks his teeth into the juncture where my shoulder meets my neck, and I bow off the bed, my hands latching on to his hair. "Oh God . . ."

Jason lifts himself off me only enough to cup one of my breasts, bringing it closer to his mouth. "Haven't been able to stop thinking about these perfect tits," he mumbles, then flicks his tongue out, tracing my nipple before he engulfs the entire thing in his mouth. He's thrusting against me, his hips rocking into mine, his movements just as frantic as I feel. Our frenzied breathing fills the space around us, and I want him in me, *now*. I slide my hands down his back into the waistband of his boxer briefs, then reach around to try and pull his cock free.

But before I can come in contact with him, he stops, freezing with his hand still on my breast. His eyes find mine, and he says, "Wait. Tess, wait . . ."

And my whole world stops.

jason

Tessa's eyes are wide, and her entire body deflates against the bed when I stop her. I don't want to. I nearly came undone at the thought of her hand on my cock, but I don't want this to be a rush job, either. I don't want this to be a five-minute fuck where we both get off, but that's it. I don't want it to be like every other sexual encounter I've ever had.

Not with her. This is *Tessa*.

I lean down to kiss her, because I can. Because, at least for right now, she's mine. "Slower, baby. I still want you. Christ, I want you," I say as I let my hips press once again in the cradle of her thighs so there's no question just how much I do. "I just want it slower. I didn't get to see you last night, and I don't want to rush it. I need to have you slower. Can we do that?"

She exhales, her eyes fluttering closed before she opens them again and gives me a subtle nod. That's all the encouragement I need before I lean down to kiss her. I was never much for kissing before. It was always the thing I had to do to get to the thing I *wanted* to do. But it's different with Tessa. She's so responsive, her body arching into mine with the slightest brush of my tongue against hers. She hums into my mouth when I scrape her lower lip with my teeth, then moans when I suck it into my mouth.

I drop my head to her neck, brushing my lips and tongue against her, scraping my teeth along the way, spending time getting to know the spots that make her squirm in anticipation, the ones that make her shiver, the ones that make her gasp in pleasure. Her hands are restless against me, her fingers slipped into the front of my boxers, running back and forth, brushing against the head of my cock at each pass, and she's driving me fucking crazy. I lift up and sit back on my knees, pulling her hands out of my waistband and gathering her wrists together before I pin them over her head.

And then she's spread out for me just like in a thousand different fantasies I've had of her over the last almost-year, her tits pushed up and heaving with every breath, perfect pink nipples that have haunted my dreams hard and pointed right at me, and I want to memorize how they feel under my hands. Under my mouth and my tongue. I want to know what they'll look like, bouncing in time to my rhythm when she's under me. What they'll look like when she's on top, riding me . . .

I reach for her, my fingers brushing up the curve of her waist, up up up until I capture one of her breasts in my hand. I lean down and let my lips sweep across her chest, lick up the line between her breasts. Rubbing my thumb back and forth over her nipple, I watch as it tightens even further before I lick against it with the flat of my tongue. That earns me a sigh. Tracing around it with the tip of my tongue pulls a gasp from her, but it's not until I suck it into my mouth and flick my tongue against the peak that she finally lets out a long, low moan, and I smile against her.

I file that tidbit of information away for future reference.

Her head shifts from side to side on the pillow, her eyes clenched tight, and fucking *Christ*, she's gorgeous. And she's mine. For now, at least, she's mine.

I press her hands into the mattress before I let go of them, a silent command to keep them there. We'll see how long she lasts. Leaning over her, I caress both her breasts, moving my mouth from one to the other and back again. Her body is writhing on the bed, her hips rolling restlessly against nothing, and it's taking everything in me not to rip her fucking panties off and bury myself into her in one thrust, give her what she's seeking.

Instead I concentrate on the taste of her skin below her breasts, how soft the curve of her stomach is against my lips, and then my hands are gripping at the sides of her underwear and I'm pulling them down her legs and tossing them over my shoulder. Tessa's head is turned to the side, her face pressed against one of the arms that's still over her head, prone against the bed. She opens her eyes and peeks at me when I don't move to touch her again, too busy letting my eyes feast on the sight before me. It fucking killed me that I didn't get to see any of her last night, and I'm soaking up every inch of her now. She's all delicate features and soft curves, and I can't believe this is actually happening. After months of fantasies I tried to will away, after trying to deny myself this with her, she's here, under me and naked for me, waiting and writhing for my fingers, my tongue, my cock.

And I'm going to enjoy every fucking second of it.

Sliding backward down the bed, I start at her legs, lifting her foot to rest against my shoulder as I kiss her ankle, her calf. Then the inside of her knee and the inside of her thigh, and I can *see* exactly how much this is affecting her, exactly how much she wants me. Her pussy is wet, glistening, and it takes everything in me not to go straight for that, bury my tongue inside her, and instead brush right past it with no more than a breath and repeat my path on her other leg.

She makes an impatient noise in the back of her throat, and her hips lift off the bed, subtly rolling, and I smile as my lips trace up the length of her thigh.

"Not funny," she grumbles, shifting in vain to try and bring me closer to where she wants me.

As much as I'd like to continue dragging it out, it's torture for both of us, so when I get to the place where her thigh meets her pussy, I don't deny either of us any longer, licking a long line up the crease. And then I place a kiss above her clit, spreading her open with my fingers before taking a swipe with my tongue up the length of her slit. She nearly shoots off the bed, her hands flying to my hair, gripping hard.

"Jason!"

I groan against her, the sound of my name on her lips while she's already teetering on the edge sending a wave of possession through me, desire coursing through my body and pooling in my cock.

"Oh shit. Shit, shit, shit," she breathes, her hands tightening in my hair, clamping me to her.

Like I'd go anywhere else.

I trace circles around her clit before I flutter my tongue against it and slip a finger inside her. Her mumbling has advanced to something completely unintelligible, and I double my efforts, sliding another finger inside as I increase my pace.

Her legs tighten around my head, her fingers pulling at my hair, and then she's frozen, pulled taut until she groans and squeezes my fingers, pulsing around me and coming against my mouth. As much as I want to deny it, there's a smug satisfaction at how quickly I made her come, how much she wants this. I lick her slowly, gently, slipping my fingers out of her before I kiss her thigh and then move up her body to hover over her.

A soft smile plays on her lips, and her eyes are closed, and I fucking love that I was the one who got to put this blissed-out look on her face. She blindly reaches out for me, her brow furrowing when she comes in contact with the material of my boxers.

"Why are you still wearing these?" she asks as she snaps the waistband.

"Hey!" I lean down and nip at her jaw while she giggles. Pulling back, I look down at her, all teasing gone. "I just want to be sure you're sure."

"Jason . . ." She shakes her head and reaches up, her fingers along my jaw. "Stop asking. I'm sure. I promise. Now take those boxers off and get inside me."

SEVENTEEN

Tessa

My words ignite something inside him, because he doesn't even pause as he strips off the rest of his clothes, and then I hear the tearing of a condom package. I shouldn't be staring so intently as he rolls it down his hard length, but the sight of it—how he strokes himself a couple times after he's sheathed—is completely mesmerizing.

"You like to watch, huh?" His words are low, just soft murmurs in the otherwise quiet room, but with how my face heats up, he might as well have screamed over a loudspeaker. He grins at my reaction, then leans down to kiss me. Against my mouth, he says, "I'll remember that for next time."

Next time.

A part of me I didn't even realize was coiled tight, waiting for the other shoe to drop, relaxes infinitesimally. From what I've heard over the years—from what I've *witnessed* over the years—Jason always has one foot out the door before mutual orgasms are even achieved. That he's already planning to be here for a next time speaks volumes, and though before I even decided I would give this a go with Jason, I hoped this was different, that *I* was different, this is reassuring nonetheless.

A tiny part of me wonders if we should've talked about that . . . if we should've discussed what it'll mean now that we're taking this step. Because as sure as I am that he'll be able to make me scream his name again tonight, I'm also sure sex for him has always meant something totally different than it has to me.

Before I can worry too much on it, he kisses me again, his lips no longer the question they were at the start of all this. He kisses just like he does everything else—with a confidence and sureness I would usually find a turnoff. But not with him. He coaxes my mouth open with his tongue, sliding it against mine, tipping my head the way he wants it so he can kiss me harder, deeper. Then he releases my mouth, pulling back and dropping sporadic kisses along my cheeks and my jaw, and all I can do is pant. He brings his mouth to my ear, his tongue tracing the shell, before he whispers, "Tell me how you like it, Tess." He lowers his body to mine, relaxing into the cradle of my thighs, and I moan at the hard ridge of him pressing against the hottest part of me.

Clutching at his shoulders, my head tipped back, my neck extended in offering, I groan louder when he pushes harder against me.

"Tell me . . ." he says again. "I want to know what you like. I want to make this so good for you."

His words and the quiet, lilting cadence of his voice combined with the soft, shallow rocking he's doing only spirals me closer to the peak, making me teeter on the edge.

"God, I'm gonna come again if you keep this up." My finger-nails dig into his shoulders, and I'm certain I'm leaving marks, but I can't force myself to care. I'm not even going to examine the part of me that secretly likes that I'm marking him.

He smiles against my neck at my admission. "Good," he says, then kisses the space just below my ear. "Then you'll come again when I'm inside you. You'll come all over me, won't you, baby?"

Those words and a punctuated thrust of his hips is all it takes, and I'm flying.

Jason's mouth claims mine, and before I've even caught my breath, before the last pulses have washed over me, he slides inside, and I lose my breath all over again.

"Oh *fuuuuck*," he groans against my lips, his hips resting flush against mine as he clenches his eyes. "Jesus Christ, you feel good."

And then he starts to move. His thrusts are slow and steady but sure, each pump punctuated with a swivel of his hips. And with each swivel, he presses into my clit, keeping me so worked up I have no doubt in my mind he'll make good on his promise to make me come again.

Reaching up, he curls his fingers around the back of my head, tangling them in my hair as his thumb brushes against the expanse of my cheek, and I almost can't look at him. The heat in his eyes, the want and desperate need I see reflecting back at me—the same emotions I know are written all over my face—are overwhelming. Scary as hell, while at the same time it loosens something inside my chest.

His forehead rests on mine, and I can't help but want to pull him closer. We share breath, never kissing, but our lips never part, either. I grip him around his neck, my other hand digging into the flesh of his ass, encouraging his thrusts, getting lost in the feel of us together.

In all the times I've thought about this with Jason—hell, in all the times I've had sex before—I never thought it could be like this.

He finally kisses me, his tongue slipping into my mouth, and I don't think about anything but the feel of him connecting us completely. He breaks away and presses his lips down my chest to my breasts, sucking a nipple into his mouth. I arch into him, gripping him by his hair to hold him close to me, the movement pressing my clit against him even more.

"*God*," I breathe, my eyes fluttering closed.

After he's shown the same attention to my other breast, he pulls away and sits back on his knees, his hands gripping my hips as he stays motionless, seated fully inside me. I'm laid out in front of him, spread wide open and more exposed than I'm comfortable with. But then he looks at me—really *looks* at me—and the hunger in his eyes is unmistakable. His hands are open, his fingers spread out against the expanse of my stomach, his thumbs brushing just above where I need his touch. My head shifts back and forth on the pillow, my hips arching to bring his touch closer to where I want it, and all he does is chuckle.

"Need something?"

I groan, squeezing my eyes shut as I fist the pillow on either side of my head.

"All you have to do is say the words, baby, and I'll give you whatever you want. Whatever you want . . ." He punctuates that with a thrust of his hips, pulling me onto him.

"Shit, oh God, please," I say, my words jumbled and probably incoherent.

"You want more of that?" he asks, but he doesn't expect an

answer, because he gives another thrust, his attention now focused on the place where he's slipping in and out of me. "Fuck, you look so pretty wrapped around me, taking me all the way in."

His words only stoke the fire inside, building me up without ever actually giving me the push I need to find completion. He still hasn't touched me where I need him to, and the urge is too much. Finally I slide my hand down my body and find myself wet with want.

He groans, tipping his head back before he looks at me again. "Christ, you're trying to kill me."

The smile doesn't get far across my face before my mouth opens in a moan as he thrusts harder and faster, bringing me onto him with a renewed urgency. I rub my clit in tighter circles, my face turned into my arm as I concentrate on the feelings he's wringing from my body.

Keeping up with his thrusts, he leans down, taking a nipple into his mouth, his tongue laving it before he scrapes his teeth against it and then gives a gentle tug.

That's all it takes and my mouth opens in a gasp, my entire body going taut, and then Jason's curses are lost among the thrumming heartbeat overwhelming my senses as I fall over, waves rocking through my body.

"Jesus, Tess . . ." And then he's groaning, gripping me harder as he loses himself, his body bent toward mine, his forehead resting against my neck.

He breathes me in, and I let him, my hands tangled in his hair, trying to regulate my heartbeat again. Trying to make my mind work after he jumbled it all up.

I thought I'd be filled with uncertainty after having sex with Jason. I thought there'd be this giant question mark hanging over my head as to what came next. Instead, everything about it felt right. Perfect.

And that scares me even more.

jason

If I'd known sex with Tessa was going to be like that, I would've stopped being such a pussy about it and fucked her a long time ago. Jesus *Christ*.

I'm not even sure if I can move, especially when Tessa's fingers are running through my hair and over my back, but I need to take care of the messy part of what was an amazing time. With a kiss on her chest, I pull away and pull out of her, eliciting a groan from us both, and walk to the bathroom to take care of the condom. When I get back in the room, Tessa's on her side, the sheet pulled up and covering all the good parts of her I intend to study later and in great detail.

I slip in bed behind her, sliding up until her back is pressed to my front, and place a kiss on her shoulder. She hasn't said anything, hasn't given me a clue as to how she's taking this whole thing. I know she had a good time. *Three* good times, so the chemistry between us obviously isn't an issue. And I tried my hardest to show her exactly how much I wanted her while she gave herself to me.

I also know exactly what kind of history I have and that Tessa hasn't been ignorant of it, and I feel this overwhelming need to reassure her.

"Hey," I say against her skin.

"Hmm . . ."

I glance over her shoulder to look down at her face. Her eyes are closed and a small smile curves her lips, and finally I relax into the bed, letting my head drop to the pillow.

"Okay?" I ask as I wrap my arm around her stomach, tugging her back to me though there's already no space between us.

She shrugs. "Yeah, just okay."

I huff out a laugh, reaching my arm around to cup her breast, my thumb swiping over her nipple. My smile only grows when she arches back to me, her ass pressing harder against my cock, which already has grand plans for round two. "If that's 'just okay,' I'm going to have a good fucking time finding out what's amazing."

She twists back and looks at me over her shoulder, her eyes flitting between my own, and she's trying to figure something out, looking for something in my expression; I'm just not sure what.

Not able to take the silence anymore, I lean forward and kiss her, tracing the outline of her lips with my tongue. Soft and sweet and the complete opposite of everything I want to do to her right now . . . everything I want to do to her *again*, but I don't push.

She smiles against my mouth, then pulls away enough to say, "Keep this up and you just might be able to tonight."

I groan and drop my head to her shoulder. There's no way she can't feel how hard I am against her, and I've never had this before. This *want* to please the woman I'm with. To study her, every single inch of her body and find out all her secrets. I want to give Tessa what no one's given her before. I want to give her what *I've* never given anyone before.

Connection without an expiration date.

EIGHTEEN

Tessa

The early-morning light streams through my window, waking me from a night of not nearly enough sleep. I stretch, feeling the pull in muscles that haven't been worked in a very long time, and smile. Jason got his wish to see what I deemed *amazing*. Twice more.

My eyelids flutter open, and Haley stands off to the side of my bed, her face right above mine. "Haley! *God . . .*" I say with a hand to my chest as my heart attempts to recover from the jolt she just gave it. "I told you not to wake me up like that anymore."

"Sorry, Mama," she says, but she's still grinning, the little shit.

She briefly glances over my shoulder before looking at me again, and I freeze, my entire body going still as I remember exactly who she's seeing. I've never had a guy stay the night before. Even when I was seeing David, my last semi-serious boyfriend, I didn't invite him to stay. I wanted to keep that part of my life separate from Haley. I didn't want her feeling uncomfortable in her own home, and I certainly didn't want to introduce someone into her life who may not be there for the long haul.

None of that even entered my mind with Jason.

Unsure of what to say to Haley, I reach back for Jason. Except instead of finding warm, solid man, my hand encounters cool sheets and an empty bed, and my heart plummets.

Unaware of my thoughts, Haley asks, "Can we have pamcakes for breakfast?"

I answer automatically, my mind going a thousand miles an hour on where Jason is and why he left. "Pancakes," I correct. "And yeah."

She hisses out a yes, then takes off out of my room, and I'm left alone with only my thoughts. Which aren't a great place to be right now.

Maybe he had an early class. Except it's Sunday.

Maybe he had an appointment he had to get to. Except Jason doesn't make appointments for anything before noon.

Maybe he had to be at his parents' place. Except he goes only once a week on Tuesdays, and he'd rather cut off his own balls with a rusty knife than subject himself to more than that.

No matter what I come up with, I can't think of a plausible excuse for him to have bailed other than the obvious answer I don't even want to consider. My stomach churns as I get out of bed, throwing on a pair of flannel pajama pants and a tank, zipping a hoodie over it. I'm going to enjoy my day with my daughter, and I'm absolutely not going to think about why Jason would have sex with me three times, hold me in my sleep, and then bail before I wake up.

Haley's in her bedroom playing with her dolls when I walk past. I poke my head through her doorway. "Blueberry or plain?"

"Chocolate chip!"

"Nice try. You do not need any extra sugar, girl. Blueberry or plain?"

She pouts, but says, "Blueberry, please."

I smile and head down the hall and toward the kitchen, stopping short when I get to the end of the hallway where it opens to the living room. Because there on the couch, his arms crossed over his chest, face turned toward the cushions at the back, is a sleeping Jason. My heart stops, then leaps, my stomach doing somersaults, because he's here.

He's *here*.

He didn't leave like I feared he would. He didn't run off and escape. He didn't bail on me and whatever it was we shared last night.

"Jay!" Haley squeals and tears past me, giving him just enough notice to wake up and protect all the important parts as she jumps on him, bouncing against his stomach. "What're you doin' here?" she asks, leaning right in his face. "Mama's makin' pamcakes. Wanna stay for breakfast?"

He looks past her until his eyes connect with mine, and then he smiles. A smile I've never seen on him before. It's not his confident and sure smile he flashes to everyone. Not his cocky smirk that's nearly a permanent fixture on his face, the one he flaunts when he's getting his way.

His soft expression sends a wave of regret through me that I immediately jumped to the wrong conclusion when I didn't find him in bed with me. Because this smile . . . it's for me.

It's mine and mine alone.

jason

It's been only fifteen minutes, but it feels like it's been fifteen hours by the time Haley is finally engrossed enough in coloring that I'm able to sneak out of the living room and into the kitchen. I walk up behind Tess, bracing my arms on the counter on either side of her as she flips the pancakes.

She smells like her fruity shampoo and sex and *me*, and it does nothing to assuage the overwhelming want I have to bend her over the counter and fuck her against it.

I brush my lips over the base of her neck, smiling into her skin when she shudders.

"You were gone when I got up . . ." She doesn't pose it as a question, but I know she wants to know why I wasn't there.

"Yeah, I set the alarm on my phone for the ass-crack of dawn. I wasn't sure you wanted . . . Well, I didn't know if you'd ever had someone . . ." Christ, why is this so hard to say? Probably because I'd rather slice off my own balls than think of Tessa's previous circumstances . . . circumstances where men might've stayed the night. I clear my throat and try again, "I didn't know what you wanted Haley to know."

She freezes, the spatula in her hand poised and ready to flip a pancake, and then she looks at me over her shoulder. "I thought you left. I thought you bailed."

And even though I figured it would take more than a night full of amazing sex to convince her this was different for me, her words still cut deep. I grip her hips, lower my face until I can press a kiss on the side of her neck. Quietly, I say, "I wouldn't do that. Not with you."

She nods, her face turned toward mine, so I drop a kiss on her lips, too.

"Believe me, I'd much rather have stayed in bed with all your sweet parts pressed up against me." She drops her head back to rest on my shoulder, and I brush my lips down her neck. "Would've been a lot better than lying on a couch by myself at five in the morning."

She laughs, but it dies off, and by the way she's scraping her teeth against her bottom lip, I know she's got something to say. I grab the spatula from her and finish the job of flipping the rest of the pancakes, then I spin her around to face me. Raising an eyebrow, I stare at her and wait.

She tries to outlast me, but eventually she huffs and crosses her arms, rolling her eyes. "I hate when you do that."

"If you'd just tell me what's on your mind from the get-go I wouldn't have to do it."

Her eyes narrow for a moment, then sincerity takes hold of her features. "I wanted to wake up with you, too . . ."

"But?"

She heaves a deep sigh. "But I'm not sure it's such a good idea. Yet."

Despite the disappointment that settles in my gut, I nod. "Okay. Because of Haley?"

She nods in confirmation. "I've never had someone stay the night, Jason. *Never*. And as much as I want to see where this thing between us goes, I have to look out for her. Her comfort is my number one priority."

I get it. I understand completely, even if I wish it were different. But the part I'm focusing on is when she said she'd never had anyone stay the night. And how I can't wait to be the first.

tessa

"Is Cade coming home this week?" Jason asks.

"No, why would he be coming home this week?"

Jason's eyebrows lift as he looks at me over a stack of pancakes drenched in syrup. He's worse than Haley, I swear. "Thanksgiving . . . ?"

"That's *this* Thursday?"

"Yep."

"Crap, I forgot all about it. Um, no, I don't think he is. He was just hoping he'd be able to get back for Christmas. His schedule's pretty crazy right now."

"So what are you guys doing, then?"

I shrug, taking a bite of my breakfast. "I dunno. I'm certainly not cooking a turkey, that much is for sure. Probably just hang out at home, unless Paige drags us to her parents' house."

He's quiet for a minute, the kind of silence that's weighted, and I lift my eyes to meet his. "How about I drag you to mine?"

I stop chewing. I'd probably choke if I attempted to swallow. And then with a mouthful of food, I ask, "Do what now?"

I couldn't have heard him right. Because anything to deal with his parents is a no-go zone. We don't talk about it, unless I bully him into it, and he certainly doesn't bring people to his childhood house unless he's forced to.

"My family dinner was switched to Thursday instead of Tuesday this week, so I have to be there. I want you to come with me."

"To your parents'."

"Yes."

My eyes flit over to Haley, because Jason's parents have never made it a secret that they don't approve of my choice to keep her at my young age. While I've met them only a few times, Cade had that privilege plenty more, and every time he came back, he'd be fuming. Finally I flat out asked him what the problem was, and he managed to evade the question. Then one day both he and Jason came back, and neither knew I was home. Cade ranted to Jason about how narrow-minded his parents were, about how they had their heads so far up their snooty asses, they couldn't see an amazing girl making the right choice for her—a *hard* choice, yeah, but one they should accept and let be. Jason didn't disagree, but neither did he ever extend to me an invitation to his house.

"Haley would be with me," I say.

"I know that."

"And you're still inviting us?"

He stares at me, his eyes locking on mine, locking me in, and there are a thousand things in his glance. This is one way for him to show me I'm different. And that he doesn't give one single shit about what his parents think of us—of me and Haley. That he wants us in his life, and, unfortunately, that life sometimes includes the assholes he came from. The assholes he's nothing like.

He's offering me something he hasn't ever offered anyone before, and yet again, a piece inside me holding tight to fear wriggles loose. I never expected something like this from him, not in my wildest dreams. Never allowed myself to imagine it. But what would it be like if the future I'm so desperate for could be found with the one guy who makes me see stars?

"Okay."

His smile would've knocked me on my ass if I weren't already sitting. Relaxing back into his chair, he gives a satisfied nod, then starts up a conversation with Haley, asking what her favorite foods are at Thanksgiving. And when he bends his head low, his brow creased in concentration as though the fact that she likes green beans over peas is the most interesting piece of knowledge he ever gained, I melt.

Right there at the dining table over a late breakfast with my daughter—the person who's my whole world—and Jason—the person who's beginning to take a place right next to her—I melt. And I'm finally honest with myself.

Despite all my best intentions, all the walls I put up and precautions I made sure I took with him, none of it matters.

I'm falling for him whether I like it or not.

NINETEEN

tessa

I get to the restaurant late, having had to give Haley fifteen good-bye and good-night kisses as she simultaneously talked the ear off Becky, the sitter I use as often as I can because she gets along so well with my daughter. Paige is already seated when I slide into the booth across from her, blowing my hair out of my face.

She looks up at me, a smile on her face. "Hey! I just got here, so I haven't ordered drinks yet."

"I slept with him."

The smile disappears as her mouth drops open. She slams her menu closed and leans toward me across the table. "Girl, you had better give me every gory detail right fucking now."

And so I do. I tell her everything—about Jason coming over Saturday morning, about him spending the day and night with us, about what it was like to see him with Haley and how the chemistry between us was as potent as it was undeniable.

"I knew it. I *knew* it would be good. He totally fucked those cobwebs out, didn't he?"

A throat clears from off to the side, and I look up into the smirking face of our waitress. With my cheeks as bright as a neon sign, I turn to my best friend and shake my head. "Oh my God, Paige. You should not be allowed out in public."

"What?" She shrugs. "I'm just sayin'."

After we order our drinks and dinner, the waitress leaves us and Paige digs for details, completely undeterred by what happened not even three minutes ago. "Well?"

"Well what?"

"*Well*, how was he? God, it's like we've never had the sex talk before. I always tell you *everything*."

"Not because I ask."

"Yeah, well, I'm a good friend that way. I like to share the wealth and all that."

I shake my head at her and thank the waitress when she places a much-needed glass of wine in front of me. "I'm not saying anything."

"For fuck's sake, Tess, I didn't ask you to draw a diagram of his cock. I just wanna know if he was good . . . if he wasn't a two-pump chump and he made sure you got yours before flopping on top of you like a dead fish."

I laugh over the rim of my glass. "Fine, yes, he was good."

"Just good?"

"No, not just good. It was . . ." I sigh and slump back against the booth. "Unparalleled."

Paige stares at me, hanging on every word. "Damn."

"Yeah, and he absolutely wasn't a two-pump chump. And

even if he was the first time, I would've forgiven it because of the sheer quantity of opportunities he had to make it up to me."

"Twice in one night? *Nice.*"

"No, not twice . . ."

Her mouth drops open and her eyes grow wide. "Holy shit, you bitch, I'm jealous. Me, the girl who gets laid every weekend, is actually jealous." She heaves a giant sigh and rests her elbow on the table, palming her chin. "I forget what that insatiable want is like . . ."

"What do you mean, you forget what it's like? You just said yourself you get laid every weekend."

"Yeah, but that's different. These are guys I only know at the most artificial level. It's different when you have a connection beyond just insert peg A into slot B."

"Well, we definitely have that." I take another swallow of wine, then say, "He asked Haley and me to his parents' for Thanksgiving."

Her eyebrows shoot up on her forehead. "No shit? Well, well, well . . . It seems this isn't just insert peg A into slot B for him, either."

"Yeah, I sort of got that when he asked, but, shit, Paige . . . they are going to hate me. They *do* hate me. They think I'm some kind of evil slut woman, what with those three times I had sex— with the same guy—before I got pregnant with Haley. This dinner is going to be awful. *Awful.* And I'm willingly subjecting myself to it."

"It's going to be fine. They're too classy to be openly rude to you. Rich, snooty people always are."

I've been so worried about how they would receive Haley that

I didn't even have time to think about how they'd receive me—the woman I am now. "Oh God. I have purple hair, Paige. *Purple!*" I reach up and grab a stripe of the bright violet as if she can't see it from two feet away. "This is not the kind of hair one has to meet rich, snooty people! There's probably some law against it in their handbook. There has to be."

Paige rolls her eyes and laughs at me. "Since when do you give two shits about what people think?"

"Since they're the parents of my . . . my . . . Jason."

"Your Jason, huh? This might not take as much persuasion as I thought it would."

"What won't?"

"Getting you to see how great you two could be together."

I deflate against the back of the booth, my shoulders slumping, because she's right. It's not going to take much persuasion. Or any at all.

"What's with the slump over there?"

"I . . . I think I'm in trouble."

"Why would you be in trouble? You finally have a man to help you relieve some tension whenever you want."

"I think I'm falling for him."

"With three times in one night, I don't blame you."

"Paige, I'm being serious."

"I know you are, honey, but I don't see the problem."

"This is *Jason*. Jason of the frequent one-night stands. Jason, the aficionado of threesomes."

She shakes her head at me, like I'm an idiot. "Yeah, but this is *you*."

"What's that supposed to mean?"

"It means it's different. I think that boy has been falling for you for a long time, if the secret looks he's been giving you are any indication."

I let her reassurances sink in, hoping she knows what she's talking about, because I absolutely do not want to be the only one falling.

The waitress drops off our food, and before I pierce a bite with my fork, I say, "You know, for someone who's allergic to commitment, you sure are eager to see me fall into the trap."

"I'm not allergic to commitment for *everyone*, just for me."

"Speaking of, when are you gonna move on? It's been almost four years, Paige . . ."

She narrows her eyes at me and swallows the rest of the wine in her glass. "Tell you what, when you *do* draw me that diagram of Jason's cock, we can go there. Until then, let's talk about something more interesting. Like the guy I met on Saturday . . ."

I don't push, letting her change the subject and go right into telling me about Jared and the things he did with his tongue, because if nothing else, it stops me from thinking about the stupid flip my belly did when she said she thinks Jason's falling right along with me.

jason

My last class of the week ends, and I bolt out of there like my ass is on fire. Kristi calls my name, desperate to talk to me about the project she keeps holding over my head, but I offer only a wave over my shoulder before I'm out the door, down the steps, and out into the fucking freezing late-November air. I haven't been able to see Tessa since I left her place on Sunday . . . after I asked her to come to my parents' house for Thanksgiving. And though I want her there—both her and Haley—I sort of want to punch myself in the junk for suggesting it.

My parents have always tried to rule everything in my life, and being able to get my undergrad in a degree I actually wanted, something I *liked*, and then taking my sweet time to graduate were the only ways I could push back, avoid the inevitable for as long as possible. After their ultimatum, I don't even have that. And now they're going to see a part of my life I don't want them to be anywhere near. I don't want them to get their hands on this, too, on the one part of my life I'm not hating at the moment.

My phone buzzes in my pocket, and I open my car door and slide inside before I pull it out. Adam's ugly mug brightens the screen, and I answer. "Yeah."

"Honey, I'm home."

I laugh, despite the mood I'm in. "What the fuck does that even mean?"

"It means I'm inside your apartment. Goddamn, when was the last time you washed a load of laundry?"

"Fuck off," I say through chuckles. "I didn't know you were coming back. When'd that happen?"

"Decided a few days ago. I could use a drink or three. You wanna grab some food or are you busy with your new girlfriend?"

The smile falls off my face, his casual use of the word sending a wave of panic through me. I've never—not once—had a girlfriend. I've had girls, of course, but never anything one could consider serious by any stretch of the imagination. Never more than casual flings or ongoing booty calls.

And now there's Tessa, who totally threw me for a loop,

knocked every idea of relationships I ever had scattering to the ground. And if I'm being honest with myself, the thought of her as just a casual fling or an ongoing booty call sends a wave of a whole different kind of panic through me. Since some point all those months ago when she first caught my eye, it's been building. Slowly, but surely, and now I'm in it. Despite everything I've ever known, despite everything that used to work for me.

"Ah, yeah, I can tonight." I glance at the time on the dashboard, seeing it's just after four. "You wanna meet at Shooters and get in a couple games of pool before?"

"Yep, see you there."

I WALK INTO the bar and order a couple beers from the bartender before claiming one of the free pool tables in the back. I've only just racked the balls when Adam's voice reaches me. "Don't expect me to put out just because you bought me a drink."

"Damn, I was really hoping that'd work."

With a grin, he grasps my hand and pulls me in for a one-armed hug with a slap on the back.

"You ready to get your ass handed to you?" he asks.

I snort and turn back to the table, grabbing my pool stick. "You've been gone too long. Your memory is all foggy and shit."

"Why don't you put your money where your mouth is? Loser buys drinks all night *and* dinner. I'll even let you go first."

"Hope you brought enough cash with you," I say as I break, calling out stripes after three have found their way into different pockets.

"Well, fuck."

I smile at the table and take my next shot. "So what's with the sudden trip here? Thought you weren't coming home till Christmas?"

"Yeah, well. Some shit's going down at my parents' shop."

After missing my last shot, I step back and let him move in. "What kind of shit?"

He doesn't answer until he's made two shots, missing the third, and turned the table over to me. "Business has been slow, I guess. I just don't know how long it's been that way for. And they're not telling me jack, but it's got my mom all freaked out."

"So what's your plan? Busting in during the middle of the night and going through their books to find the dirty secret?"

He shrugs. "I wasn't planning a five a.m. break-in or anything, but yeah. Something like that." He takes his next turn, and effectively takes the spotlight off himself and puts it right back on me. "You talk to Cade yet?"

Sunday night, after I left Tessa's, I called Adam. Filled him in on how shitty a job I'd done at the whole staying-away-from-her thing. And, just like I knew he would be, he was all laughs and virtual pats on the back. And then he told me to get my head out of my ass and tell Cade. Problem is, I like my balls a little too much to deal with that right this second.

Leaning against the wall, I grab my beer off the high table and take a healthy swig. "Nope."

"You're only delaying the inevitable and making it that much harder on yourself."

"I just . . . I'm already going to be dealing with my parents around her and Haley this week. I don't want to deal with her overbearing, overprotective brother on top of it all."

When I glance over at him, his eyebrows are nearly up to his hairline. "Since when do you bring a girl—or anyone, for that matter—home to meet Mommy and Daddy Dearest?"

"Since I'm a goddamn idiot, that's when." I take another swallow of my beer, then set it back down before heading over to take my shot. "I asked her to come for Thanksgiving. Because I've clearly lost my fucking mind."

"Well, holy shit."

"What?"

"I mean . . . I honestly thought this day would never come. My baby's all grown up," he says in a falsetto.

Laughing, I say, "Shut the fuck up. I don't even know what that means."

He levels me with a stare. "Really."

"Yeah, really, so stop with your Dr. Phil bullshit and just say what you want to say."

He waits until I pull the cue back to take my shot before he says, "You're in love with her."

I scratch and spin around to face him as he laughs. "What the fuck."

"You gonna deny it?" he asks with a raised eyebrow.

I open my mouth to do just that, then snap it closed because the words won't come. Jesus Christ, *am* I in love with her? Is that why the thought of spending all this time with her doesn't send me into a blind panic, why words like *spend Thanksgiving at my parents'* didn't break me out into a cold sweat?

When I don't say anything, he continues, "Come on, man. You've always had this weird protective streak when it came to her. You were nearly as bad as Cade was. You just needed to fuck your way through anything that had two legs and the right parts in between before you actually acknowledged it. It's not really that much of a shock, is it?"

But it is a shock, because I never saw this coming. Not in a million years.

I think back to all the times Cade and I had roughed up some asshole who tried to talk shit about Tessa in the locker room in high school, about the rage that coursed through my body when I found out Nick bailed on her after knocking her up . . . how I wanted to find him and beat the living hell out of him. How it felt to know she was searching for some guy on a goddamn website and the answering pang every time she went out with one of them. How it felt when she went out with that boring-ass orthodontist right under my nose.

Blowing out a breath, I grab my beer and swallow the rest. I set it down with a heavy clank. "I'm fucked."

"That you are, my friend. You also owe me drinks and dinner. Pay up."

TWENTY

tessa

"Baby, you need to hurry up. Cade's gonna be calling any minute," I yell down the hall to Haley.

"Coming, coming!" She runs into the living room and dives on the couch just as the call comes in. Having done this a hundred times, she already knows how to accept it. Her smiling face is close to the camera on my laptop, and when Cade's face pops up, he smiles, too.

"Hey, short stuff. Has your head gotten bigger?"

Haley falls into a fit of giggles, and with a smile, I leave them to their talk while I go change into some yoga pants and a loose long-sleeved shirt, thankful for a few minutes of solitude. This week has been nerve-racking, my thoughts constantly swirling around the conversation Paige and I had over dinner and the barrage of feelings toward Jason I'm suddenly all too aware of.

I never thought it would happen like this. I always figured

that when I fell in love with someone, it would be a slow, gradual process, like scattered snowflakes accumulating on the already-warm ground. It would take a while for anything to stick, for anything to grow, and when it did, it would be steady and consistent.

I didn't think it'd hit me like a frickin' avalanche, burying me under all these conflicting feelings I have. Worry and anticipation and intrigue and excitement and, yeah, love.

Maybe it's because I've known Jason for so long . . . I know exactly what kind of person he is, his good points and bad points, and really the only thing missing between us was the physical intimacy, and that's obviously not an issue any longer. Our chemistry is off the charts.

Really, I should've seen this coming from a mile away, yet I was still knocked on my ass.

I've never been more thankful that we've had a legitimate reason not to see each other for a few days, because I've needed the space to sort through everything in my head. We've talked on the phone every night and texted throughout the days, but both of our schedules are hectic because of the upcoming holiday, so that makes any visits nearly impossible. I had clients trying to squeeze in, wanting to get their hair touched up for whatever family gatherings they were traveling to, so I've worked late every day this week. Thankfully, Becky was able to pick up Haley from Melinda's and stay with her until I could get home. I hate twelve-hour days, not just because they're exhausting, but because I feel like I see my daughter only long enough to get her ready for school in the morning and then to put her to bed at night. I miss her.

I walk out into the living room and see Haley holding up a drawing she made of everyone sitting at a table for Thanksgiving, a giant, deformed turkey placed right in the middle. "There's me and Mama, and that's Jay," she says, pointing out each of us. "The empty chairs are 'cause I dunno what his mommy and daddy look like, so I didn't draw them, but I'll finish it after we see 'em."

"That's great—wait, after you see them? When will you see them?" Cade's normally smooth voice has gone tense, and I blow out a breath, knowing this is going to be a topic he covers repeatedly and in great detail with me until I give him exactly as much information as he wants.

I knew going into this thing with Jason that Cade would take issue with it. He, of all people, knows exactly what kind of shadows mar Jason's past, and combine that with how needlessly protective of me he is, he's going to be like a volcano ready to blow.

Haley talks more about our plans for Thanksgiving, and Cade answers appropriately, though I can hear the strain in his voice. When they're done, Haley blows him a kiss and slides over for me to take my turn.

I sit down in Haley's spot, sighing because I know what's coming. "Hey."

"Is she still there?" he asks.

Oh boy. If he wants to make sure Haley's out of earshot, this is going to be worse than I expected. I glance over at Haley, who's admiring her picture, and say, "Go brush your teeth, baby, and then pick out what book you wanna read tonight, okay?"

Once she's out of the room, I turn back to my computer screen with raised eyebrows. "Yes, Dad?"

Cade's jaw clenches and his nostrils flare, and for the first time since he moved, I'm glad five hundred miles separate us. If he was here with all this happening, it wouldn't be pretty. "Jase? Really, Tessa?"

I narrow my eyes at him, my anger starting to show itself. "Jason, your *best friend*? That Jason? Yes, really."

"Jesus Christ," he mutters as he scrubs a hand over his close-cropped hair. "I fucking *knew* this would happen. What the hell are you thinking?"

Now my hackles are up, and I'm irritated that I have to defend his best friend to him. "What do you mean what am I thinking? I'm thinking he's an amazing guy who's always here to help whenever I need him—who you made *sure* was here to help after you left, by the way. Let's not forget that." Cade just glares at me, so I continue on, "I'm thinking that he plays with Haley and lets her dress him up and *loves* her. I'm thinking that he makes me feel stuff I haven't felt in a long time."

"Yeah, I bet he does," he says dryly.

"What the hell is that supposed to mean?"

"You know exactly what it means. Tessa, you know as well as I do what kind of history he has. You know he's not the kind of guy who sticks around after he gets what he wants. He's not like your orthodontist—"

"Who bored me out of my mind."

He continues as if I never spoke, "He's not sure and he's not steady and he sure as fuck isn't the right kind of guy if you're looking for someone for the long haul."

"Well." For a minute, that's the only word I can muster up, left speechless after Cade laid out just exactly what he thinks of his best friend.

And then I get mad.

Not just at him, though, but at myself, too. Because those were the same thoughts I had a dozen times before I decided to try this thing with Jason. And, really, when was the last time anyone believed in him and didn't hold his past over his head? When anyone thought he was more than just the sum of his past indiscretions? How would I feel if everyone did that to me? That the first thing they saw when they looked at me was a giant sign with bright red letters that said PREGNANT AT SEVENTEEN? And yet that's exactly what we've been doing to him. The people in his life who are supposed to care the most about him.

"Well," I say again, "it's nice to know exactly what you think of your best friend."

"Don't play that card. As a best friend, he's all I could ask for. As the boyfriend to my baby sister? *Fuck. No.*"

"Lucky for me, you don't get a say."

"Tessa . . ." The warning in his tone makes my temper flare even more, and I stiffen.

"Oh, get off it, Cade. You don't get to run my life from Chicago any more than you got to run it when we lived under the same roof. You need to back off. This is *my* life, and I intend to live it how I want to, with or without the approval of my big brother."

He's quiet for a minute, his arms braced on his knees as he leans forward and stares at the screen. He's pissed, more than I've seen him in a long time, and I get that he's worried. I get it, but this isn't his life.

It's mine, and I made the decision to include Jason in it.

Finally, he says, "This is going to be Nick all over again. You know that, right?"

A disbelieving breath leaves me as I stare at him wide-eyed. He might as well have reached through the screen and slapped me across the face. It's nothing I haven't thought a hundred times before on my own, but hearing it come from someone else's mouth, hearing it come from my *brother's* mouth—the one person who's supposed to be the most supportive of me—is like a knife to the back.

"Fuck you, Cade."

And then I end the call, not having the patience or the mental space to deal with him right now. As if I didn't have enough already on my mind with the dinner at Jason's parents' tomorrow, now I'm going to be replaying this in my head over and over again. Because what Cade said is the exact thing that kept me from pursuing Jason in the first place.

He gave life to the very fear that's been clawing at me from the beginning.

jason

Considering it's the day before Thanksgiving, the library is surprisingly full. I sure as hell don't want to be here, but the group project we were given at the beginning of the month is due next week. We've been here for two hours, and through that entire time, Kristi has tried to stick herself to my side, despite there being two other people in the group. The project is to design and code a website with integrated e-commerce, and while I could've breezed through this on my own in about two days, I'm forced to slow down and take into account the ideas of everyone else on my team. Such a waste of time.

"Jason, can you look over my code? I can't figure out the problem . . ." Kristi leans closer to me, her hand on my arm, and I have to physically restrain myself from rolling my eyes at her blatant attempt at flirting.

The thing is, I can't even fault her for it. Because last year, I would've been all over it. In fact, I probably would've taken her to a darkened corner in the library and figured out what kind of panties she's wearing.

Now, though, I'm only too glad my phone buzzes in my pocket, saving me from her desperate clutches. Seeing that it's Cade, I slip away from the group and walk toward the front, where more people congregate and radio silence isn't enforced as heavily.

"Hello?"

"When the fuck were you planning on telling me?"

I cringe at his harsh tone, the words spat into the phone, and press my thumb and forefinger to my eyes. Blowing out a deep breath, I say, "I take it you talked to Tess."

"What part of 'keep your fucking dick in your pants' did you not understand?"

"Look, man, I know you're pissed, but it's not—"

"You're fucking right I'm pissed. You told me I could count on you. That you wouldn't let anything happen to them. I left there and *against my better judgment* trusted you to look after them."

"Hey," I snap loudly and get shushed around me. Lowering my voice, I turn and walk through the first door into the lobby. "I *do* look after them."

"I know how you are with women, and I have a real hard

time with the idea that you were looking after Tessa with more than the head in your pants."

"I get it, Cade. You're pissed. But you're going to have to—"

"You were there the whole time she went through all that shit with Nick, and you still did this. You're no better than him."

My spine straightens, and I say harshly, "The fuck I'm not."

"What, you gonna try and tell me she's different?"

"She *is* different."

"So she's the one who will finally stick? Not fucking likely." He scoffs, and the sound grates on my already-frayed nerves.

Anger boils, hot and steady through me, and I'm ready to bite his fucking head off, set him straight once and for all, when something occurs to me. "Did you say this same shit to Tessa?"

"Hell yeah, I did."

Working hard to keep my voice steady, I ask, "Did you talk to her in a reasonable manner or did you throw around this bullshit with her like you're trying to do with me?"

His silence says all I need to know, and despite spending the last several minutes listening to him give me a verbal beatdown— having him interrupt me at every turn and shutting me down— knowing he did it to her is what really sets me off.

"Listen up, fucker, because I'm not going to say this again. You might be my best friend, but I give zero fucks about that right now. Right now you're just the asshole brother giving my girlfriend a hard time. Tessa is a grown woman and she doesn't need your goddamn approval for anything that goes on in her life, especially the men she decides to include in it. You have a problem with me, you come to *me*, you chickenshit, and leave her out of it. You got me?"

I hang up before he can say anything more, because if I have to listen to another second of his ranting, I'm liable to punch a hole in the wall. Ignoring the stares of people around me, I head back to the table where the group is spread out, make my excuses to leave, and let them know I'll get my part of the coding done and sent to everyone over the holiday weekend.

Right now, adrenaline is pumping through my veins, and I have somewhere I need to be.

Because even though none of what Cade said got to me . . . what if it got to Tessa?

TWENTY-ONE

tessa

I can't shake the feeling I've had since hanging up on Cade. It's sitting over my head like a dark rain cloud, dampening my mood, making me question everything I thought I'd figured out with Jason, and now I'm second-guessing myself. I need to call Paige and talk this through with her, but I know she's working late tonight, so my neuroses are going to have to wait to get the BFF treatment until tomorrow.

Knowing I won't be able to get out of my head unless I force myself to think about something else, I pick up the book I'm in the middle of and try to lose myself in it. I've read the same page three times before I give up and, with a huff, slam the paperback down on the coffee table at the same time there's a knock at the door.

I glance over at the clock, brow furrowed when I see how late it is, and peek out the side window to see who's standing there.

The resulting flip and spin my stomach does would be embarrassing if it weren't so disconcerting. I am in so deep with this, with *him*, I can't see over the hole I've fallen into.

Taking a deep breath, I pull open the door, the words caught in my throat when I get a good look at Jason. His hands are bracketed on the doorframe, his entire body radiating tension. His voice is low, rough, when he says, "Did he get to you?"

And I know immediately who *he* is, which means Cade called Jason, too. The thought sends panic through me, worried that my brother somehow planted seeds in Jason's mind to call this whole thing off . . . to make my fear come true.

He must see something in my face, because he steps over the threshold and into the house, closing the door behind him before he grips my face in his hands.

"Tell me you didn't listen to him, Tess." His thumbs run over my cheeks, almost like the touch is soothing him as much as it is me. "Tell me he didn't make you change your mind about me. Tell me you still want this."

Cade didn't change my mind about anything, which is the scary part. That despite all the warnings he gave me, I'm still ready to dive in with my eyes wide open, heart vulnerable to break.

Jason steps into me, forcing me back until I'm pressed against the wall and he's pressed against me. Leaning in, he nips at my bottom lip. "Give me the words, baby. Are you still with me in this?"

I can't think, my mind a jumbled mess of worries—of what *could* happen . . . if Jason leaves, if he screws up, if *I* screw up—but I push all of those away in favor of what is happening right now. Because this is real. It's not a what-if, not a possible outcome from an imagined scenario. He's really here, standing in front of me even after my brother no doubt tried his hardest to scare him away. He's here in front of me, wanting *me*. He still wants me.

"I'm still with you," I whisper against his lips.

Jason doesn't give me any warning before he captures my mouth with his, pushing through my lips to slide his tongue against mine without waiting for any indication from me. This kiss is a promise . . . a possession, and I love every second of it.

His hands grapple at me, pulling at the too-wide neckline of my sleep shirt until it falls off my shoulder and not stopping until he has the front pulled below my breast. A groaned curse leaves his lips as he descends, placing sharp, nipping kisses down my chest until he gets to my nipple and sucks it harshly into his mouth.

I cry out, my hands flying to his hair as one of his hands reaches for my yoga pants, pulling the side down until half my ass hangs out the back and he has an unobstructed path into my panties. And then his whole hand disappears under the cotton of my underwear, his fingers stroking, back and forth, up and down, until I'm panting and grasping to him for support.

"Come on, baby. Give me one out here." His strokes turn measured, his fingers sliding down to slip inside me, and then stroking back up to circle the wetness around my clit. Faster and faster until I can barely see straight. Breath against my ear, forehead resting on the wall beside my head, he says, "Come on my hand, then I'm going to take you to your bedroom, lay you facedown on the bed so you can muffle your screams in a pillow, pull that pretty little ass up, and fuck you until you come again."

"*God*," I say on a moan, my whole body tightening until it's almost painful, his words and promises only pushing me that much further. "Just . . . just take me now. Now, Jason." I don't even recognize my voice—all throaty and breathless, begging someone to fuck her.

"No, not until you come."

I groan, dropping my head back against the wall, and move my hips against his hand faster, pressing down on his seeking fingers, wanting him deeper, harder, wanting him to take me like he kissed me. With complete and utter possession.

He slides his fingers as deep as he can, curling them inside me, his palm grinding against my clit, and fireworks explode behind my eyelids.

"Fuck yeah," he groans against my neck. "Knew you'd give it to me."

Jason peels the clothes from my body as he walks me backward to my bedroom, and by the time he's kicked the door shut behind us, I'm completely naked.

"Get on the bed, Tess. Just like I said."

I nod, moving until the backs of my knees hit the mattress, not ready to turn my back on him and miss a second of him stripping off his own clothes. He does it quickly and efficiently, and when his boxers are on the floor with everything else and he takes himself in his hand, gripping tightly and groaning, I drop back on the bed, not sure my legs can even support me any longer.

I do as he said in the living room, lying on my stomach, watching him over my shoulder as he walks toward me. He traces a line up both legs with his fingers, then he leans down and bites me right on my ass.

"Hey!" I yelp, then moan as he licks a path straight up my spine, straddling my thighs as he goes. He kisses my shoulder blades, brushes the hair away from my neck, and kisses me there, too.

Then he pulls back and grips my hips, saying, "Lift up for me, baby."

With his legs pressed to the outside of mine, I'm forced to keep my thighs together. I lift up as best I can, helping him guide me into the position he wants me, his cock sliding up and down the length of me, driving me out of my damn mind. "Jason," I groan, trying to push back against him.

"Are you wet enough? I'm not sure you are."

The question is absurd because I can *hear* him sliding through me. I open my mouth to tell him just that when he backs away, and then he grips the outside of my thighs and gives me one long, slow, torturous lick from my clit to my entrance.

"Oh my God . . ."

He moves his face down, the tip of his tongue pressing to my clit as he hooks two fingers inside of me and proceeds to steal every breath from my lungs. I tighten around him, barreling closer and closer to my second orgasm, his answering groan reverberating against me and shoving me the rest of the way over.

jason

This girl makes me lose my goddamn mind. Makes me forget every rational thought I've ever had. Makes me forget about everything but what she looks like under me, what she feels like gripping me, what she sounds like when she calls out *my* name.

I grab a condom and roll it down my cock, groaning at the sight in front of me. Tessa's on the bed, just like how I wanted her. Facedown, ass up, looking back at me with heavy, lust-filled eyes, and I fucking love that I'm the one she's looking at like that.

That, despite whatever bullshit her brother fed her, I'm still the one she wants.

Climbing on the bed, I straddle her thighs again, holding her hip with one hand and guiding myself to her with the other. I push forward, watching how she opens around me, how she swallows my cock whole, and I can't stop the groan when I look up at her face and see the reflection of hunger there.

I want to pound into her, fuck her so hard she forgets her own name. Forgets every other man who's had the pleasure of knowing her this way. Until she remembers only *me*. Until she wants only *me*.

"Do you know how perfect you feel around me?" I slide nearly all the way out, then push into her deep and slow, watching with satisfaction as Tessa grips the comforter tighter in her hands. She lifts her ass higher, silently begging me for something more. "You need it deeper, baby?"

I smile at her answering groan and grip her ass, lifting up and opening her as wide as I can with her legs pressed together. Then I repeat the slow, deep slide, pushing in as far as I can go and listening for her answering gasp. When she gives it to me, I move faster, thrusting into her with enough force to move her forward on the bed. Reaching up, I grab her hand and pull it away from the bedding, not stopping until it's behind her back, her body twisted under me, her breasts bouncing with each forward thrust of my hips. Her face is slack, her lips parted and her eyes fluttering closed at every push into her. Holding her wrist with one hand, I slide the other to her mouth, brushing my finger against her lip.

"Open up, baby. Suck it."

She complies immediately, her mouth opening to accept my

finger, her tongue slipping out to brush over the tip. I groan as the soft, warm wetness of her mouth surrounds my finger, pumping my hips into her faster, harder, not able to control myself anymore. Pulling my finger from her mouth, I trail it down her chest to her exposed breast, swirling the wetness around her nipple, and smile when she moans, her eyes fluttering closed, her pussy pulsing around me.

"That's it, pretty girl. Give me another."

Tessa's always been beautiful—even before I accepted this pull toward her—but now? Here, tonight, when she's laid out in front of me, her mouth open on gasps from feeling me inside her, her eyes locked on me as I push her exactly where she needs to go?

It's too much, and when she lets out a choked gasp, her eyes rolling back in her head as she comes around me, I let go and fall with her.

TWENTY-TWO

tessa

Despite having been here a few times before, the looming sight of Jason's parents' home as we pull up never fails to impress. It sits a ways back from the quiet suburban street, set apart from the equally impressive houses on either side of it. While I've always thought we lived in a nice neighborhood, when compared to this, we might as well be living in a cardboard box under a bridge.

A housekeeper—Magda, I'm told—greets us at the front door and takes our coats, all while Haley stands next to me, her mouth gaping like a fish. "Wow," she whispers. "Is this really *one* house?"

"Afraid so, shorty." Jason pats her on the head, ruffling her hair and making her giggle and duck away from him. At my silence, he turns to me and grabs my hand, giving it a light squeeze. "It's no big deal. This is them, remember? Not me."

And the thing is, after last night, after Jason coming to my place even when Cade called him to try and scare him off, I'm secure in the fact that he's here, with me. Maybe not for the long haul, but for the foreseeable future. And for now, that's enough.

What I am worried about, what kept me up most nights this week, is his parents' reaction to Haley. She doesn't deserve any of their prejudice, and I'm not going to be held responsible for my actions if they say anything remotely rude to her.

When I give Jason a nod, he smiles *my* smile—the one that's mine alone—and leans in, giving me a light kiss on the lips. A throat clears to the left of us just as he's pulling away. Jason's mom stands a few feet away, looking like she just stepped out of a fitting room at Neiman Marcus, complete with a personal shopper to dress her. I don't know, maybe she has someone on staff who lives in her closet. Her dark hair is pulled back in a tasteful twist, something I've done a hundred times for mothers of the brides. Her makeup is subtle but flawless, her pale pink lips pursed as she appraises us. She's wearing a button-down silk shirt with a pencil skirt, her heels something I'd never wear while walking around my house, and under her assessing gaze I feel out of place in my knee-high boots and frilly skirt, the vintage sweater I snagged at the thrift store feeling exactly like I spent three dollars on it.

"Mom." Jason's voice interrupts my thoughts, allowing me to swallow my insecurities. At least for a moment.

"Hello." She comes forward, and instead of hugging Jason like I would expect from a mom—that's what mine did anytime we came and went from the house, no matter if she'd seen us thirty minutes prior—she holds out her hand for me. "It's nice to see you again, Tessa."

I reach for her hand, returning the limp handshake. "Thank you for having us, Mrs. Montgomery. I hope it wasn't too much trouble."

"No problem at all. We're glad Jason decided to bring some-one home for once."

I slide my eyes to Jason, watching as his jaw clenches, but he doesn't say anything. Holding out the casserole dish I brought, I say, "I wasn't sure what I should bring, and Jason wouldn't tell me. I hope this is okay. It's green bean casserole."

She takes it from me, her lips twitching, and it's as close to a snarl as she'd show company. "How . . . lovely. Thank you. I'll give this to Megan to reheat."

"It's Magda, Mother, and you know that."

"Yes, well," she says as she turns away, expecting us to follow after her. "Your father is in the sitting room along with Charles and Steven and their wives. I'll be in after I drop this in the kitchen."

As soon as she's out of earshot, I whisper, "Well, that went well. I bet she's dumping it down the garbage disposal as we speak."

Jason laughs, grabbing my hand and giving it a squeeze. It looks like he wants to offer more physical reassurance, but Haley's no longer preoccupied with staring wide-eyed at the entry-way, so he just grabs her hand, too, and leads us toward the *sitting room*. Seriously, who has a sitting room? Where I come from, it's a living room or a family room, though I'm sure they have both of those, as well. And probably a study. And a library. And a wine cellar. I'm actually surprised there wasn't a moat around this castle.

"She wouldn't dump it. Her manners are too ingrained for that."

"Could've fooled me," I mumble as we walk down a long hallway. The walls are dark burgundy, adorned with pieces of art that are no doubt original—and that no doubt cost more than my annual salary. The long corridor is broken up with several antique side tables, all decorated with fresh flowers. I'd never really given much thought to how Jason views our home. It's older; the only room recently redone was the kitchen just before my mom died. Otherwise, it's faded and cozy, with furniture I remember from when I was in middle school. I have too many other things I'd rather spend any extra money on, and it's never really bothered me that we didn't have the newest or the nicest.

Being here, though, seeing the space he grew up in, the kind of space he's accustomed to, I can't help but wonder if it's bothered Jason.

WHEN PEOPLE TALK about a formal dining room, *this* is the kind of room they're talking about. A dark wood table that must seat at least sixteen takes up the majority of the room. A crystal chandelier hangs from the ceiling, the lights set just brightly enough so we can see clearly. A crystal goblet and too many pieces of silverware are set out in front of each of the ornate wood chairs, and this is just like that restaurant Greg took me to. Too rich, too stuffy, too much.

"Just a house," Jason whispers in my ear as he squeezes my knee, drawing the sharp eyes of his father.

Mr. Montgomery is sitting at the head of the table, and though he hasn't done anything outwardly to show his distaste, it still seems like he's looking down at us. Since we arrived, his attention hasn't strayed far from me or Haley, even while deep in talks with Charles and Steven—two of the partners at the firm, I found out. His gaze is unnerving—not because it's creepy, but because it's calculating, and that's almost worse.

The serving staff—seriously, who has a serving staff?—come sweeping into the room shortly after we've been seated, placing artfully adorned plates of what I guess is some sort of Thanksgiving food in front of us. The portions are minuscule, and if Cade could see this, he'd have a coronary. There's a time and place for fancy food, but Thanksgiving isn't it.

The thought of my brother brings a pang to my chest as I remember the things he said last night . . . remember how I ended the call. I know he's just looking out for me, making sure I don't get hurt, but his words still stung. Especially when they unearthed the fears I tried hard to bury before walking into this with Jason. I need to talk to him, try to get him to understand.

Because even though I'm a grown woman raising my daughter and I don't *need* his approval, I would like his blessing.

Haley tugs on the sleeve of my sweater, and I lean down so she can whisper in my ear. "Mama, I don't like any of this stuff." She wrinkles her nose in disgust.

I breathe out a laugh, because I don't much like any of it, either. "Just eat what you can, baby. You like turkey."

"But it's got that yucky red sauce on it."

"We can scrape it off. And there's my casserole. And these are mashed potatoes . . . I think." I gesture to the white mass that's been piped out in the shape of a rose . . . or something.

"Oh dear, is the meal not fit for a child?" Mrs. Montgomery speaks from across the table, and though her words sound contrite, her voice is anything but. "It's just we haven't had one here for so long . . ."

I straighten in my chair and wave a hand. "No, no, it's fine. Thank you again for having us."

She gives me a tight smile, her eyes darting between Jason and me, and I want to shrink down, hide myself away. I don't belong here . . . don't fit in. I feel like his parents are just waiting for my daughter to start a food fight or burp at the table—something where they can point and say, "See? Why would you want to get involved with someone like that?"

Neither of them have been outright rude to me or Haley, but it's pretty easy to pick up on the subtle cues, the unspoken judgments, and I hate every minute of it.

But not just for me, because Jason's not exempt from the misery. He's trapped in talk of work with his father and the other partners, and if the death grip he has on my leg is any indication of how it's going, he's going to need more than the single glass of bourbon his father poured him.

Conversation around the table is focused mostly on the state of the company, and after scraping as much of the "yucky red sauce" off Haley's turkey as I can, I slice into mine, hoping I can eat enough of this to be acceptable.

"So tell me, Tessa, are you a student, as well?" Conversation lulls with Mrs. Montgomery's question, and I smile and swallow the bite of food in my mouth.

"No, actually, I'm a hairstylist."

It's subtle, the way her hand stills as she brings her glass of wine to her lips, but I see it. I also see the way her eyes flit to my hair, to the purple streaks I was so worried about and now sort of wish they weren't just streaks, but that I just had a solid mass of purple hair for her to look at and judge. "A hairstylist . . ."

"Yes."

"Well . . . how nice for you." If the tone of her voice is anything to go by, she doesn't think it's nice at all. "Though I suppose you did have to jump into something rather quick—anything you could get, really—having Haley so young."

Jason stiffens next to me, and I reach over and squeeze his knee, much the same way he's done to me. Little does he know, this isn't the first time I've received this kind of treatment. People think just because I'm a young, single mom, I'm an open target for their judgments. I had to learn pretty damn quick how to deal with them.

"Actually, it's what I've wanted to do for a long time, well before Haley came along. And I'm good at it, so . . ." I shrug and take a small sip of my wine, effectively shooting down any more conversation.

Or so I thought.

"Surely we have an opening for something at the company. Lawrence? Isn't there a position open in the mailroom? Or perhaps a receptionist?"

Before Jason's father can reply, I give a tight smile and say, "I appreciate the offer, but I'm not looking for another job. I'm happy where I am."

"Well, yes, but surely this would be a bit more . . . prestigious," Mrs. Montgomery says.

I bite my tongue to stop myself from saying the myriad of retorts I want to throw at her. Instead I say the most polite thing I can. Which probably isn't very polite at all. "Perhaps to you, but I like where I am. I don't much care about prestige or how my career will look to other people or how much money I could make, because I'm happy there."

Everyone around the table goes completely silent, their faces showing shock—no doubt at my answer rather than at the person their shock should be focused on. I want to sink in my chair until I slide right under the table, mortified that I couldn't keep my mouth shut for two seconds, whether these snobby people pissed me off or not. And then I glance over at Jason and see the smile that takes up half his face as he looks down at his plate of art, and I pull my shoulders back and sit up a little straighter.

After only a couple seconds of awkward silence, conversation starts up once again around the table, and Jason's pulled back into talk of the company, the smile slipping off his face. For the first time since he told me about his parents' ultimatum, I can empathize with him. As his mother proved, a job less than satisfactory in their eyes just isn't acceptable. And for him, the only child to carry on the Montgomery name? I can't even imagine their reaction to him telling them he wanted to design websites for a living instead of carrying on in the footsteps of his father and grandfather. I'm not even part of the family, and his mother wanted me to switch jobs, pushed something else on me, just so I could have their business name attached to it, despite the fact that I'm happy where I am.

I glance over at Jason, seeing his tensed jaw, his stiff shoulders, and I'm finally getting a small glimpse into what, exactly, it means to be a Montgomery. I hate that he's subjected to their impossible standards—that his parents can't just accept who he is and support him.

jason

"So, Jason, are you ready to start shadowing your father in the new year? You've got some big shoes to fill in the next few years," Charles says.

It's just the four of us in my father's study, the women having congregated in another part of the house, my mother dragging them off to show them some stupid-ass society thing no one gives two shits about, least of all Tessa and Haley. Even though I'd like nothing more than to get trashed, I switched to water an hour ago so I could drive us home as soon as fucking possible. I need to get out of this house. I can't *breathe*.

The other men all hold their crystal tumblers with their favored liquor, smoking my dad's cigars as they bullshit about topics I give zero fucks about. It's like looking into the future, seeing what my life will be like twenty years from now. It makes me want to jump out the fucking window.

Clearing my throat, I say, "I'm certain he'll make sure I have the ropes down."

"Of that I have no doubt." Charles studies me for a minute, Steven doing the same thing. "There are some things we *do* have doubt about, though."

I raise my eyebrows, knowing I'd hear about this at some point before I stepped up at the company. "What's that?"

Instead of answering, he says, "Tell me about Tessa."

Immediately, I'm on edge, my shoulders rigid as I study him. I have no idea what he's playing at, but I also have no doubt it's something I'm not going to like. "What about her?"

"Is it serious?"

"I don't see how that's any of your business."

My father clears his throat loudly, but I don't even glance over at him, my focus intent on the Armani-wearing dickhead in front of me.

"It is, actually."

"Care to clue me in on how the hell you figure that?"

He leans back in his chair, resting one of his ankles on the opposite knee. "Come January, when you officially start the transition into Montgomery International, every facet of your life is going to be under the microscope, available for public consumption."

"Oh good, and here I thought it was just my life ending in January."

As if I never spoke, he continues, "You haven't exactly been discreet in your . . . extracurricular activities. Perhaps it's time you settled down, set people's minds at ease."

The water I just took a drink of goes down the wrong tube, and I cough, my eyes bulging. "Excuse me?"

He appraises me with cool eyes. "Our clients have come to expect a certain . . . family aspect when they come to our firm. Your grandfather started it in that vein, and your father has made sure to nurture that image."

"You mean lie about that image . . ."

He stares at me for a long moment, then says, "The other partners have expressed their . . . concerns about your lifestyle. But, well, maybe you settling down with a family isn't so far off . . ." he says with a nod in the direction of the room we left all the women in—Tessa and Haley included.

Normally, even the mere mention of this would've sent me packing, hives bursting out on my skin. Having a front-row seat to the shitshow marriage my parents have, I had no desire to jump into it quickly. Or ever.

Except now, the thought of it being with Tessa doesn't strip all the breath from my lungs like it might have only months ago.

Instead, the thought that they'd—these greedy fuckers who think only about the company, not the lives of the actual human beings there—use her, bring her into my life, and force us together for nothing more than the image of the company pisses me the fuck off. Setting down my glass, I stand. "I hate to burst your bubble, Chuck, but that's not going to happen. Don't insult me by asking again."

And then I turn around and walk out, off to find Tessa and Haley and get them both as far from this life as possible.

TWENTY-THREE

jason

My hands grip the steering wheel, my knuckles white under the pressure, and I'm still stewing over what transpired more than thirty minutes ago. Charles's attempt to subtly suggest I put a ring on Tessa's finger to appease the partners—just to appease the fucking *partners*—was so thinly veiled it would've been funny if it weren't so goddamn insulting.

It's clear everyone at that company thinks I'm in their pocket—no doubt a result of my father's cockiness—that I'm their fucking puppet to work and twist how they please.

I should've seen it coming, though. I *knew* something like that was going to happen, that they'd find a way to get their claws in the one part of my life I want to keep for myself, the one part I should've left locked away. I shouldn't have invited Tessa and Haley tonight . . . not because I don't care about them, but because I do. I care about them too much to let my toxic family work their way between us. I should've gone to the damn thing by myself and kept them out of it—Tessa had an awful time, Haley not much better. And all it did for me was get the fucking bloodhounds on my ass for something I'd never give them.

I'd never give Tessa or Haley up to them.

The car is filled with silence on the way back to Tessa's place, Haley having fallen asleep about two minutes into the ride. Tessa hasn't uttered a word, either. And I'm not sure if she can tell something is going on with me, or, worse, if my mother said something to her while they were off in another part of the house. Something worse than telling her that her job wasn't good enough like she did at dinner. I hope to God my mother didn't say anything remotely similar to what Charles cornered me about.

All the possibilities twist my stomach, making regret sit heavy on my shoulders. I don't want her to know anything at all about what was said to me, don't want her to think I'd ever use her that way.

When we pull up to the house, Tessa gets out without a word, going back to get a still-sleeping Haley. I meet her there and pull her to me, pressing my lips to her forehead. I don't want to talk about anything that happened tonight, but I hope this is enough to show her it's not her I'm upset with. Luckily, her arms circle my waist, returning the hug, and I let out a breath of relief.

She pulls away to get Haley, but I reach around her to open the back door and say, "That's okay; I've got her." I unhook Haley's seat belt and pull her limp form from the car, following behind Tessa as she unlocks the door and holds it open for us.

Haley's head is resting on my shoulder, and whether consciously or not, she has my shirt clenched in her fingers. I've fallen so fucking hard for this little girl. The thought of having this every night, of tucking her in and reading her bedtime stories and building snowmen with her followed by taking Tessa to bed and then waking up next to her every morning doesn't fill me with anxiety and fear and panic like I would expect it to—or would have expected it to only a few months ago. Now, I finally get what kind of family my grandpa was talking about when I was younger . . . when I couldn't understand it because my parents never showed even a morsel of love. Now I *want* it. It's too soon and I'm too young and this is completely the opposite of everything I thought my life would turn out like, but I can't deny the truth.

I want them. Every day.

I just want it on my terms and not because it would look good to the fucking partners.

Tessa

Haley barely wakes as I try to get her changed from her fancy dress into her pajamas. With absolutely no help from her limp form, I finally get her tucked into bed with a kiss on her forehead, and slip out of her room.

I think she was under the impression tonight was going to be like going to a real-life tea party, but I could see the disappointment on her face as the night unfolded and she was bored out of her mind, having to interact with people who were unlike any she'd met before. She behaved like an angel, though, despite the situations we were put in, despite the barbs thrown my way. I only hope she wasn't aware of any of them.

I've never been ashamed of what I do for a living or the fact that it supports me and my daughter—why should I be? And I resented the hell out of it when Jason's mother put down my chosen career with little more than a raise of her eyebrow. My mom was long gone when I decided to go to cosmetology school, but I like to think she would've been supportive of it—hell, she would've been supportive if I said I wanted to go to clown school, if that's what made me happy. Seeing how it unfolds in another family, witnessing firsthand the sort of pressure and expectations Jason's held up against breaks my heart for him.

No wonder he feels hopeless and trapped under impossible standards.

Something happened tonight—something besides what transpired over dinner—but it's clear he doesn't want to talk about it. He was quiet the entire car ride, and I didn't want to interrupt his thoughts. I can't imagine what sort of mental letdown he has to go through every time he leaves his parents' house . . . and he has to do it every single week. I wonder if they berate him for his college career . . . for his choice in university or the amount of time it's taken him to complete his degree. I wonder if they do it with any sort of subtlety or if they just put it all out on the line when there aren't other people around to serve as buffers. I wonder how often they do it—if it's a weekly or monthly occurrence.

I wonder how the hell he puts up with it at all, because I lasted one sentence from his mother before I snapped, barely reining myself in enough to deliver a semi-appropriate response. If I had to listen to it week after week, month after month, year after year . . . I probably would've told them to go screw themselves a hundred times by now.

Once I get out into the living room, I find Jason sprawled out on the couch, his head resting back on the cushion, eyes closed, and it kills me to see his normally outspoken personality reduced to silence and resignation.

His eyes stay closed when I climb onto the couch, straddling his lap, his hands sliding under my skirt to palm my bare thighs.

"I'm sor—"

I kiss his apology away—not wanting it, not needing it—and sweep it aside with my tongue as he groans into my mouth. His hands tighten against me, pulling me flush to him, and if this is what it takes to get back the Jason I know—*my* Jason—I'll give it to him a hundred different times.

He slides his hands up my thighs, slipping them under the satin material of my panties until they palm my ass. With my fingers locked in the unruly strands of his hair, I guide his head down when he pulls away from my mouth, holding him to my neck as he nips and licks, as he leaves long, lingering kisses across my collarbone. Then his hands are on my waist, sliding up and under my sweater, and I lift my arms for him to take it off. His eyes flit to every part of me that's uncovered, thinly disguised want in his eyes. He doesn't bother to remove my bra, too impatient, and instead just pulls the cups down before he sucks a nipple into his mouth.

His name is just a breathy sigh on my lips, and his answering groan vibrates against my skin, causing me to arch farther into him. He pulls me closer, gripping my hips and pressing me against the hard ridge of his erection, still confined in his pants. With fumbling fingers, I reach down and undo the buttons on his shirt, then spread it open, my hands roaming up and down the contoured ridges of his chest and stomach. When I slip the button of his pants through the buttonhole, then lower the zipper, I don't pause as I reach inside and pull him out of his boxer briefs. I revel in the moan he gives me when I stroke him firmly, my thumb circling the head.

"Jesus, Tess," he says as he reaches up to cup the back of my neck, pulling me forward to kiss him while I work my hand up and down his length. He pulls back, resting his forehead against mine as he looks down and watches the way he slips through my fist. "You feel how hard you make me? How much I want you?"

His words and the evidence of his want gripped tightly in my hand are powerful drugs. The knowledge that he's thick and hard because of what I do to him makes me feel sexy . . . wanted. And when Jason struggles to reach under him and pull out his wallet, retrieving a condom with quick fingers, I know this need isn't one-sided. He wants this just as badly as I do. He rolls the condom down his cock, then reaches for me, pushing my panties to the side so he can stroke me until I'm clinging to his shoulders, panting against his neck, and rolling my hips in hopes of feeling him fill me with more than his fingers.

He takes my unspoken plea, lifting me just enough, holding my underwear to the side so he can slide inside me. And when I sink down on him, taking him all the way into my body, watching him watch me through hooded eyes, I can't get over how different this is with him. All of it—the butterflies and the antic-ipation and the constant, aching need I feel around him . . . It was something I didn't expect, something I didn't count on, but it's undeniable. This connection between us—both how new it is with him, and how *easy* it is, like we've had years to learn each other's bodies—is exhilarating and I want to grab on with both hands and never let go.

His hands grip my hips, urging me to slide back and forth against him, the pressure against my clit exactly what I need to get me higher and higher. He leans forward, licking around one of my barely exposed nipples, and the urgency of our encounter only amps up my desire for him.

I've never had this burning need with anyone else before. Never had that all-consuming want that wouldn't be sated until I had the other person. Needing to have someone so much I couldn't take the time to remove my boots. Couldn't even bother to slip off my panties, instead just moving them to the side because I needed him inside me immediately.

It feels illicit and naughty and unbelievably intimate.

That I can be this bold with him, that he takes everything I give, every moan and plea, every sigh, and doesn't hold back with me, either, is unparalleled.

The revelation combined with the way he grips me, pants my name over and over again as he reaches his peak and holds me to him like he never wants to let me go has more than just my body spinning, free-falling over the cliff.

My heart decides to jump off, too, uncaring of any consequences.

TWENTY-FOUR

tessa

Jason's harsh breaths blow across my skin, my head resting on his shoulder. He places a single, soft kiss on the place where my shoulder meets my neck, and I can't help the shiver from rolling through my body.

The realization I've just come to settles over me—that my heart took the leap for Jason, despite doing everything in my power to protect it. To keep it safe. None of it matters. All my careful planning before Jason, my avoidance and distractions were useless. Because I'm lost to him.

I don't want to let go of this feeling.

I want to run away as fast as I can.

I've been here before—or I thought I was, anyway. Young and in love, though I realize now I wasn't ever in love with Nick. Because this—whatever this is that I feel for Jason—is a thousand times more powerful than anything I ever felt for Nick.

And I'm terrified.

I'm terrified of what this means for our future. For my and Haley's future. What Jason would do if he knew . . . Would he panic? Flee? Would he push me away or pull me closer? Everything I've known of Jason for most of my life says the former, but everything he's done in the past several months points to the latter. I wish I could be sure, that I could know what he's feeling. If he's in this with me or if I'm *his* distraction.

Jason's hands move down to my ass and hold me tight against him as he stands with me still wrapped around him and walks us down the hallway to my bedroom.

"Wait, our clothes . . ." Because *that's* what's important after the realization that I'm in love with this man.

"I'll get them," he says as he lays me down on the bed, kissing me before pulling away. He quickly rids me of the rest of my clothes, unzipping my boots and pulling them off, then doing the same with my skirt and bra. "Be right back."

I unabashedly watch him as he walks away, carefree in his nakedness. And when he's out of sight, my worries and fears compound a thousand times into something that eats away at me. Despite my revelation, or maybe *because* of it, I can't stop thinking about what I realized on the ride home from his parents' house— that Jason's never invited me to his place. Is it just because he's being a guy about it, unaware of how it may seem to me that he's never once had me over there? Or is there something more to it? Is he trying to keep that part of his life separate from this? From *us*? Is it a clue that he's not invested enough in this to show me something as simple, but deeply personal, as where he goes most nights?

And then a part of me I try very hard to keep pushed down rears her head, wondering if he's brought other girls there . . . if they know the color of his walls, the smell of his sheets. And I ache, thinking that dozens of others might know this about him, when I haven't even gotten a cursory invitation.

It barely registers when Jason slips into bed behind me, his arm reaching around my waist and pulling me back against him. My body wants to sigh at how right, how *perfect* it feels to be pressed up against him like this, but my mind won't shut off. It keeps spinning, images of a thousand faceless girls in an imagined bachelor pad flitting through until I can't stop the words from spilling out of my mouth. "You know I've never seen your apartment?"

Jason's hand stills on my stomach, and it's not until he freezes behind me that I realize he was brushing his lips back and forth over my shoulder. I close my eyes against what I fear is coming. This is when it'll finally be too much for him. When he'll start retreating, pulling away from me, all because I wanted to see where he lives.

And then he laughs. Puffs of air blow out against my skin and his chest shakes against me.

"What the hell are you laughing at?"

"You." He presses a kiss to my shoulder, then pulls me tighter against him. "I have no idea how your mind works. In the span of five minutes, how did you go from coming so hard I had to press my hand over your mouth to keep your scream from waking up Haley to wondering what my apartment is like?"

I don't know how to answer that, so I just shrug. And I can feel the way the smile he had pressed into my skin slowly fades away, and then he props himself on his elbow so he can peer down at me. "Wait, does this really bother you?"

His brow is furrowed, his eyes flitting between both of mine, and I breathe for what feels like the first time in five minutes.

With a nod, I say, "Yeah." Glancing between his eyes, I see the genuine confusion there, and sigh. "So I take it this was a boy thing?"

"What was a boy thing?"

"You not inviting me over . . ."

"I don't know what you mean by 'boy thing,' but if it's me being a dumbass and not thinking you'd even want to be there in the first place, then yeah."

I stare up at him, trying to read his expression. He looks contrite and sincere, but the part of my brain that wove all those detailed exploits in his imagined apartment isn't pacified yet. "Did you . . . I mean, have you ever had anyone, you know, other girls or whatever, there? At your place?"

When the smile slowly spreads across his face, I want to reach up and slap it off, shove him in the shoulder and push him off me, then off the bed altogether, because I'm embarrassed that I've been reduced to this kind of insecurity. It's something that doesn't happen very often, and for that I'm thankful, but with a rap sheet like Jason has, it was inevitable.

"You're jealous," he says with a grin.

"Shut your face, I am not."

"You are." He huffs out a disbelieving laugh. "I can't believe it."

"Well, you shouldn't, because I'm not." I jerk away from him, rolling over and curling away from him and his stupid face and his smiling eyes.

"Aw, come on, baby, don't be like that. It's cute. It's *nice*. I don't think anyone's ever been jealous about me before."

"I can probably name twenty girls off the top of my head who've been jealous when it comes to you."

"Okay, let me rephrase that: no one who's important to me."

I turn my head and peek at him again, my chin pressed to my shoulder, and wait for him to continue.

"No, no one's ever been there, unless you count Adam or Cade, and believe me, I don't. They don't smell nearly as good as you do." He slides over closer to me, fitting his body against mine again as he presses a kiss to my neck. "Is this the cold shoulder? I'm new to all this, so I'm not so good at picking up these subtle hints. If you're pissed at me, you need to just come out and tell me."

I look up at him, all messy hair and whiskey eyes, and I realize he's being completely and totally honest with me. I release a deep breath and lift up to kiss his lips. "I'm not pissed. I wasn't ever pissed, just . . . uncertain, I guess."

His once-playful eyes turn serious as he reaches up and brushes his thumb over my lower lip. "You don't need to be. It's just you, Tess." He leans down and kisses me, slow and deep, his tongue sliding against mine before he pulls back, his mouth brushing against mine as he repeats, "Just you, baby."

THE SOUND OF deep, rumbling laughter wakes me, and I stretch, reaching back automatically, even though I already know I'll come across just cold sheets and an empty bed.

After our talk last night, after I exposed the first crack in my armor, Jason proceeded to kiss and lick every inch of my body, as if he was trying to prove his words to me. Prove to me I was the only one. I think he was worried that I suddenly felt like that because of the rushed and hurried way he'd taken me on the couch, afraid I'd think I was just like all the others who came before.

Little did he know that was the exact moment I realized I'm in love with him.

I take a deep breath, absorbing my thoughts, smiling when it doesn't send me headfirst into the panic it did yesterday, though the flutters in my stomach are still there and no doubt will be for a while.

I push back the covers and pull on a pair of yoga pants under the oversize T-shirt I slipped into last night before finally falling asleep pressed against Jason. When I step out into the hallway, I hear the laughter again, only this time I'm aware enough to realize it's not Jason's normal laugh, but an exaggerated, deep, and haunting one followed closely by a higher-pitched, softer laugh attempting to mimic the original.

"That's good, but do it deeper. Like this," Jason says, then proceeds with the maniacal laugh again. "From your belly, shorty. Make 'em think you're crazy evil."

My perfect, angelic daughter who dresses up in tutus and has tea parties with her teddy bears does as Jason instructs and lets out a perfect replication of his evil-villain laugh, and I can't help the smile from spreading across my face. Quietly, I creep down the hallway and through the living room, peeking around the corner and into the kitchen, where they sit at the island, way more donuts than the three of us could reasonably eat spread out in front of them. Haley's arms are around the pile perched on the plate in front of her, like she's protecting them from all the trolls roaming around the house.

"There, now you've got it! Make sure everyone knows whose donuts these are."

She lets loose another laugh, growing louder each time until her head is tossed back, and I don't know whether to laugh or cry at this sight. This is everything I've been striving for for so long—someone to take the occasional early-morning shift so I could sleep in an extra hour. Someone to laugh with Haley, have fun with her, and do things with her I don't. Someone to take her out at 6 a.m. for a donut run just because she no doubt begged for it . . . just because it would make her happy.

Jason laughs along with her, both of them cackling like crazy lunatics, and I want to go over and smother them both in kisses, squeeze them until this bubble of euphoria has a way of escaping my body. I want to have mornings like this . . . forever.

With them, I want forever.

TWENTY-FIVE

jason

I could get used to this.

All right, so the 5:30 a.m. wake-up call can go fuck itself, but other than that, I'm totally on board with this whole thing. I didn't even mind going out in the cold-ass weather to get Haley donuts, because when she bats her eyelashes and pouts that bottom lip, I'm pretty much a slave to whatever far-fetched request she has.

After creeping on Haley and me in the kitchen while I was teaching Haley the art of the evil-villain laughter, Tessa went off to shower while her daughter coerced me into a game of hide-and-seek. On all four of her turns to hide, she's hidden in the same three-foot vicinity, and each and every time, I spend a solid five minutes pretending I don't know exactly where she is, and I can honestly say there's nowhere I'd rather be.

It's my turn to hide now, and I'm flattened against the wall behind the heavy cloak of the curtains in the living room. Haley's calling out for me, trying to get me to respond, talking to herself as she goes to every place I've already hidden to check if I'm there again. Her footsteps get closer to me when a weird, repetitive ringing-slash-beeping sounds, and she freezes before running over to the coffee table where Tessa's laptop is perpetually set up.

"Uncle Cade is calling! Jay! Can I answer, can I answer, *can I answer?*"

I don't have to see her to know she's jumping up and down, waiting for my response. Of course Cade would call while Tessa is otherwise occupied. I pause for a second, wondering if maybe it would be better for Haley to wait and answer when her mom is out here, but then decide *fuck it.* I'm here, for however long Tessa will have me, and it's about damn time Cade got on board with that. Coming out from behind the curtain, I say, "Yeah, go ahead."

She startles and spins around with a gasp. "*Ohh*, good hiding place! I'm gonna hide there next time!" Then she goes to the computer, sitting down and accepting the call.

"Uncle Cade!" she yells at the laptop, her face so close to the screen I'm sure Cade can count exactly how many teeth she has.

"Short stuff! How was your Thanksgiving?"

I watch as Haley's face dims, her shoulders slumping and the corners of her mouth bending down into a frown, and something twists in my gut. I hate that she had to be there at all, and if I had to go back and do it all over again, I would've told my parents I wasn't able to come and just had Thanksgiving with Tessa and Haley here at their house.

"Not fun. But Jay's house was so cool, like a zoomeum."

"Museum," Cade corrects and Haley nods.

"Yeah, like that. It was real boring and the food was yucky. I like your mashed 'tatoes *way* better and I wish you could've been here because I miss you."

"I miss you, too, short stuff."

"But Jay's here now and he took me to get donuts this morning and I got *five*!" she yells, extending her hand toward the screen to illustrate exactly how many she means.

"Wow, that's a lot of donuts. You have a bellyache yet?"

She falls into a fit of giggles. "I didn't eat them *all*, silly. I'm gonna save some for later."

"Probably a good idea." Cade clears his throat, and then says, "Is Jase there now?"

"Yeah, he's hiding in the curtains."

"Why's he hiding in the curtains?"

"Well, he's not anymore. We were playin' hide-and-seek."

"Ah, well, that makes more sense. Do you think I can talk to him for a minute?"

Haley shrugs and says, "Sure."

"Will you go draw me a picture? One I can hang on my fridge?"

She nods vigorously. "What do you want it of?"

"Anything. Surprise me."

She doesn't even wait until he's finished talking before she shoots off the couch and runs down the hall to her bedroom. With a sigh, I run my hand through my hair, then take a seat at the spot she vacated.

"Hey," he says when he sees me come on screen.

I return the greeting and brace my forearms on my knees, waiting for him to speak. I sure as shit don't have a lot to say to him, considering I said all I needed to the other night.

"Where's Tessa?"

"In the shower."

He sighs and nods. "I see my lecture did absolutely nothing." His voice isn't harsh like I would expect it to be; it's resigned, and that's almost worse.

"Actually, it did a lot. Just not what you wanted." I scrub a hand over my face, then drop it and stare right at him. "Look, man, I know I wouldn't be who you picked for her if you could, but you can't change it. I'm here and we're together, and there's nothing you can do to stop that. I'm sorry I didn't talk to you about it, and that's on me. But it's happening whether you like it or not. So you either need to get on board with it, or you need to stew quietly to yourself, because you're never cornering her about it again, got it? Support her . . . support us, or shut the fuck up about it."

He's quiet for a minute, then says, "My niece better not be within earshot."

I snort and roll my eyes. "Yeah, that took one poorly timed f-bomb with Haley around—which she, of course, repeated . . . while at day care—for Tessa to make me aware of the rules in no uncertain terms."

He smiles a little, no doubt at the thought of Tessa's tiny frame unleashing a verbal beating over my teaching her daughter the f-word. Then he sobers and looks at me, really looks at me, and I shift uncomfortably, not liking being under his scrutiny. I prefer straight-up phone calls instead of this video bullshit, to be perfectly honest.

"Never thought when you were giving me all that shit about Winter that it'd happen to you, too."

It's on the tip of my tongue to deny it, but I can't. I don't want to. Because it's the truth.

"She's good for you," he says.

With a single nod, I agree. "She is."

"She's *too* good for you."

"I'm not denying that, either."

"Good, remember that and we'll be okay. But listen, jack-ass . . . don't think this talk gets you off the hook. Don't think I won't kick your ass totally and completely if necessary. You need to be good for her, too."

I blow out a breath, the weight of his words sitting on my chest, reiterating what I already know. What I already feared from the start. "I'm trying."

tessa

When I'm done with my shower and I've gotten ready, I walk out to find Jason helping Haley make out her Christmas list.

"S-h-e-t-l-a-n-d," he spells out, pausing between each letter while Haley dutifully copies them down on her list. "P-o-n-y."

I snort as I walk in and pull out a stool on the opposite side of the island from them. "I hope you're footing the bill for that one. And for a stable to keep it in."

"Jay's givin' me ideas for my list. Look!" She thrusts the list at me, and I read my little girl's messy pink scrawl, half of her letters the right direction and half of them backward.

With raised eyebrows, I look over at him. "An actual tea party?"

"Yeah!" Haley says at the same time Jason asks, "What's wrong with that?"

"In London?" I say, pointing to the line where she jotted *London tea party* on her list.

He shrugs. "What was I supposed to do? She wanted ideas, and she loves tea parties . . . Seemed like kind of a no-brainer to me."

I laugh, handing the list back to Haley as I shake my head at Jason. "You are ridiculous, but I lo—" I choke on my words, stopping myself just in time from making my epiphany from last night known. It's too soon, too much, and would no doubt send Jason packing in a heartbeat, despite the fact that we've known each other for so much of our lives.

"But you what?" he asks with a smile.

I clear my throat, and brush invisible crumbs off the counter. "But I'm not letting you help Haley with her lists anymore unless you're buying everything on there for her." It sucks as far as cover-ups go, and by the look he gives me, the way his eyes narrow ever so slightly, I know he doesn't buy it. But, thankfully, he doesn't push.

"Well, what do you usually suggest she puts on it?"

"Um, Barbies. Games. A new tea party *hat*. Things that won't put me out of house and home."

"Ah, that makes a lot more sense."

"Jay, how do you spell *carousel*?"

He holds up his hands and looks at me. "That's all her. I had nothing to do with it."

I laugh as my phone buzzes on the counter with an incoming text. Picking it up, I see Cade's name, and my heart drops, memories of the last time we talked making my palms sweat, a knot forming in my stomach. Holding my breath, I open my text messages and read the latest from my brother.

I'm sorry. I was out of line w/ everything I said. If he makes u happy, it makes me happy. Love u

I expel the breath I was holding, like a weight lifting from my shoulders, and I don't realize until that moment exactly how much Cade's opinion matters to me. And while it's not unusual for him to admit when he's wrong and say he's sorry, normally he stews on it for a week, letting everything fester before he says anything.

"Everything okay?" Jason asks, pulling me out of my thoughts.

I turn the phone to him, showing him the text. "You wouldn't know anything about this, would you?"

He reads it as I watch his face, seeing a satisfied smile before he wipes it away quickly and then offers me a shake of his head. "Nope. Glad he apologized, though."

"Mhmm," I say, but I don't believe him for a second. And the fact that he talked to Cade about it, somehow made him see how much it hurt me that he wasn't accepting of whom I chose to invite into my life, makes me fall all the more for him.

This time the buzzing of a phone comes from Jason's, and he pulls it out of his pocket, quickly reading the text and replying. "I need to run home and do some homework for class. I've got a group project due next week. And Adam wants to get together tonight."

"Adam's in town?" I ask.

"Yeah, flew in last minute. Something's going on with his parents' shop, but he's not sure what." He finishes his text and pockets his phone again before leaning forward, elbows braced on the table. "Can I see you tomorrow?"

I smile and roll my eyes, but even as I do that, my stomach flips. "Since when do you ask?"

"You're right. I just show up."

"All the time."

"You love it."

Afraid I'm going to let something slip, I keep my mouth shut and offer him a smile as he moves to stand.

"Hey, shorty, I gotta run. Thanks for making me get donuts this morning." He ruffles her hair, then drops a kiss on her head before he walks over to me. With a question clear in his eyes, he darts a quick glance to Haley, then back to me, silently asking if he can kiss me.

In response, I tip my chin up, waiting for it, and he doesn't disappoint. The kiss he gives me is much less chaste than the one he pressed to Haley's head, and I have to force myself to keep quiet, to kill the moan in the back of my throat before it can escape. After several moments, he finally pulls back, dropping a couple quick kisses on my lips.

And then Haley interrupts, reminding me why it was a good idea to hold back that moan. "Why do you sleep on the couch so much, Jay? You Mama's boyfriend now?"

I inhale wrong and sputter a cough, looking at Jason with wide eyes while he looks back at me with something close to amusement. Taking a deep breath, I say, "Um, does that bother you? Jason sleeping on the couch?"

She shrugs, going back to drawing a sleigh and reindeer on her list. "No, but is he?"

"Is he what?"

Haley sighs, her eyes rolling toward the ceiling. "Your boyfriend. Hannah at school says that Tommy is her boyfriend, and that's fine with me, because I like Brandon best. I'm gonna marry him."

"Whoa, whoa, whoa," Jason says, all humor gone from his eyes. "I don't like the sound of that. Who is this little punk? Do I need to have a talk with him?"

"About what?"

"About keeping his hands to himse—"

I stop him with my fingers on his arm, shaking my head. As much as I love his protective response, I don't think we need to take active measures to make sure a four-year-old boy has honorable intentions toward my daughter.

"So is Jay like Tommy is to Hannah? Is he your boyfriend, too?"

I stare at her for a beat, trying to buy myself time. Jason and I never talked about this, haven't had a chance to really define whatever this is between us. And despite letting Jason kiss me in front of Haley, I hadn't been prepared to answer questions about it. I never thought she'd actually ask outright, demand a definition of this tentative relationship Jason and I have. But now I have to give her one.

Taking a deep breath, I say, "Yes, he's my boyfriend."

"Yes!" Haley hisses and throws both arms in the air. "This means donuts every morning, right?"

With a laugh, I shake my head. "Maybe if you're lucky you can get them once a week."

She's pacified with that and quickly goes back to working on her drawing just as Jason bends down, his lips at my ear. "I'm your boyfriend, huh?"

Before I admitted it to Haley, I worried about what Jason would say, worried about how he would react to hearing that inconsequential word in regard to himself. But from the teasing lilt to his voice and the smirk I see on his lips when I turn to face him, I realize my worries were unfounded.

Leaning in, I press my lips to his ear and whisper, "Somehow, I don't think 'guy I have hot, amazing sex with' is an appropriate title to tell my four-year-old."

Jason laughs out a groan, then kisses me again. "Tomorrow night, I'll continue on that streak." Then he straightens and grabs his coat before slipping it on and heading to the door. "Later, my lovely ladies. I'll bring popcorn tomorrow night. You have *Tangled* ready."

Laughing at Haley's squeal of excitement, I stand and go to grab a notepad and pen out of the drawer. Since I had yesterday and today off for the holiday, I have to work tomorrow, so our usual weekly Saturday-morning grocery shopping has to get done today. Clicking the pen on and off, I think about what I want to make this week for dinners, having been trying to get in the habit of having something at least semi–planned out so I don't have to always resort to frozen food. It's worked well so far, a routine making it easier to not feel so overwhelmed.

As I walk over to the fridge to peer inside, a bright pink Post-it note on the counter catches my eye. Two words are scrawled in Jason's handwriting—*Anytime, baby*—and I pull the tiny note from the counter, confused. Until I see what lies underneath it.

And then my heartbeat falters for a moment before speeding into a gallop, because there, under the bright pink square, is a single metal key.

A key that no doubt unlocks Jason's apartment.

With shaky hands, I grab my phone and snap a picture of the note and the key, sending it in a text to Jason.

You wouldn't happen to know anything about this, either, would you?

His response takes a couple minutes, and I'm biting my nails the whole time, one eye on Haley as she occupies herself, the other staring at my phone, waiting for the screen to light up. And when it does, when that simple, four-letter word comes through, followed almost immediately by another text from him, I can't stop the smile from overtaking my face.

Nope.

Better use it, tho.

TWENTY-SIX

Tessa

There should've been speed bumps on the road by now. Hiccups or hang-ups or giant, gaping potholes in this relationship Jason and I have fallen into. And yet, there haven't been. Not one, and that actually worries me more than if there'd been a dozen.

It's been two and a half weeks since Thanksgiving. Two and a half weeks since the night I knew I'd fallen head over reluctant heels in love with him. Two and a half weeks filled with secret sleepovers and movie nights and sex and laughter and watching the man I love play dress-up with my daughter just to see her smile.

And even though I know it's not healthy to focus on what could possibly go wrong in a relationship, I still can't stop feeling like I'm waiting for the other shoe to drop. Perpetually on edge, anticipating a hiccup that hasn't come. I should be relieved. I should be counting my blessings and thanking God that there *haven't* been any issues. Even the situation with Cade was cleared up quickly, and I haven't heard a negative peep out of him since his apology.

"Hey, what's got you thinking so hard over there?" Paige asks from across a table in the mall food court. Normally, I wouldn't be caught dead out here this close to Christmas, but it's a week-night and Jason and Haley had special, secret plans that I was told were none of my business, so Paige and I hit the mall to get in some holiday shopping.

I shake my head, twirling a bite of my lo mein onto my fork. "Nothing."

"Liar," she accuses with a jab of her fork in my direction. "Now spill. What's going on? Jase not able to get it up anymore? Your lady business feeling a little neglected?"

"Paige!" I hiss, darting a gaze around and seeing an older woman sitting off to the side of us, looking affronted as she purses her lips and shakes her head. "Would it be so difficult to censor yourself just a little while in public?"

She snorts. "I don't censor myself, ever. And if people over-hear"—she raises her voice and stares pointedly at the old lady—"it's their own damn fault for eavesdropping in the first place."

"Oh my God." I drop my head into my hands, feeling my face flame.

As if the entire exchange didn't even happen with the poor, scarred older woman, Paige says, "So, seriously, what's up? Is everything okay?"

And that's why I love her, why she's my best friend. She can go from funny and carefree and completely inappropriate to car-ing and concerned in a second flat.

Sighing, my shoulders sag. "I don't know. Nothing's wrong. And that's kind of the problem."

She raises her eyebrows. "Nothing is wrong and that's the problem," she repeats. "I'm gonna need a definition of that from the Tessa Dictionary, please."

"I just . . . I don't know. I was anticipating this thing with Jason to be full of complications, and it's been . . . easy. *Too* easy."

"Honey, that's not a bad thing."

"I know it's not a bad thing. I just can't stop from waiting for the other shoe to drop."

"Are you waiting for him to screw up?"

"No . . . Yes . . . I don't know." I sigh, my shoulders dropping as I stare at her. Her face is completely free of scrutiny, and I know whatever I tell her will stay in the vault. Whatever I tell her will be accepted without any kind of judgment. I can bleed in front of her, show her all my ugly insecurities, and she'll take it all in stride, not blinking an eye as she soothes my fears. "He's new to all this, you know? Me, I've done the relationship thing. But him? His longest relationship lasted about two hours. What if I'm just, I don't know, practice?"

"If you're just practice, that boy is an amazing actor and needs to go to Hollywood to get started on his journey toward an Oscar. He's into you, Tess. Like, really, really, *totally-head-over-heels-in-love-with-you* into you."

"What?" I'm shaking my head, rejecting her answer. "No. I mean, I know he's into me. I get that. But he's not in *love* with me." And then I think back to the shiny metal object he left under the bright pink Post-it note I may or may not have kept and tucked into my nightstand drawer. Did giving me a key have as much meaning to him as it did to me, despite trying to stop myself from reading too much into it?

"Okay, what's with the face? What were you thinking about just now?"

Worrying my lip, I glance up at Paige, knowing she's going to be furious with me for keeping this from her for so long. "He, um, he sort of left something at the house the day after Thanksgiving."

"What, like a stash of condoms?"

I huff out a laugh and shake my head. "No, not condoms. He left a key."

Her eyebrows furrow, and she leans back in her chair. "The key to your place?"

"Nope, the key to his."

"He *what*?" she screeches and bolts forward in her seat. "Hold the fucking phone." She slams her hand on the table with every word. "He gave you a *key* to his *apartment*—two fucking weeks ago, mind you—and *you didn't tell me until right now*? That's it." She sits back, directing her pointed stare at me as she crosses her arms against her chest. "Your BFF privileges are revoked."

"I know, I know." I lean forward, trying to reach across the table to tug her arms away from where they're held tightly against her. "I'm sorry. I wanted to tell you right away, but I was kind of worried it was a fluke, you know? Like, maybe he didn't really mean it and he'd take it back when he came to his senses."

"Has he?"

"Has he what?"

"Come to his senses and taken the key back."

"No. He just asks when I'm going to get around to using the damn thing."

"Well," she says as she finally removes her arms from their prison against her chest and leans toward me, "looks like you need to make a surprise trip soon."

TWENTY-SEVEN

jason

I walk out of my last undergrad class . . . ever. All the other students around me hustle out of the building, excited to get on with their winter holiday plans. Meanwhile, my feet are dragging, my steps slow and shuffled as I force myself away from the one place that was *mine* for the last five years. Too long? Maybe . . . probably. It was something I did to put off the inevitable, but something I loved nonetheless. My grandpa understood it; my parents tolerated it. But it was mine and mine alone, something my parents couldn't touch. Or I didn't think they could, anyway.

And now, the days are ticking down to a future I don't want, a future I can't stop. Two short weeks, and I'll be walking the path my father set out for me, following behind his footsteps to take over a company that no longer resembles the one my grandfather started, all because I'm standing by a family who hasn't ever stood by me.

The whole scenario makes me want to jump off a bridge.

I pull out my phone on the walk to my car, calling the one person I know can take me out of my shitty mood. Tessa answers on the third ring. "Hey, are you done?"

"Yep, I'm officially done with my undergrad."

"You actually don't sound too happy about that."

A humorless laugh slips out. "What's there not to be happy about? In a couple years, I'll be making six figures, wearing a suit every day, eating at expensive restaurants, and flying all over the world running a multimillion-dollar company while shitting all over people to make sure my pockets are lined. Sounds stellar."

"Jason . . ."

Not liking the concern I hear in her voice, I cut her off. "Can I come over tonight?"

She lets me change the subject, not pushing me on what she's already said a hundred times over the last two months: that I should just tell my parents I don't want any part of it. That I want to do my own thing. But I already know exactly how that conversation would go—it'd be the last one I ever had with them.

"I have to work late tonight."

"I don't care if it's midnight."

She laughs. "Okay. I'll text you when I'm done, and you can meet me at home. Becky's watching Haley tonight, so I'll let her know you're stopping by in case you get there before me."

"Sounds good. See you in a couple hours, baby."

We disconnect the call, and I continue on my path straight for my apartment. I have roughly six hours until Tessa will be at her place. A lot of hours to try and forget about what's going on in my life right now before Tessa can distract me.

I'M ON MY second beer, having decided I had enough time to drink a couple and allow the effects to wear off before I need to go to Tessa's, when there's a knock at my door. I glance at the time, hoping Tessa figured out a way to slip out of the salon and surprise me. I've been waiting for her to use that fucking key I gave her for two weeks. And the thought of her showing up here, unannounced, doesn't even break me into a sweat. All I keep fantasizing about is her using it on the nights I don't stay at her place and waking me up with her lips around my cock.

I stand with a groan and adjust myself, tossing my game controller on the couch before walking to the door. A quick look out the peephole dashes any hopes of my girlfriend—fuck, it feels weird to say that—giving me an afternoon quickie. And the person on the other side of the door effectively deflates any stirrings of a hard-on I had.

Opening the door, I meet the cool, appraising eyes of my mother. "Hey, Mom. What brings you to my awful neighborhood?" I ask as I lean against the doorjamb. In truth, it's a great location, but it's not brimming with doctors and lawyers and CEOs. With multimillion-dollar homes and five-acre estates. It's a nice, middle-class neighborhood, and the one place I could get my parents to concede to when I moved out of the dorms after freshman year.

She sniffs as she walks past me, all prim and proper in her pressed suit, her hair up in some kind of twist, handbag that no doubt costs as much as my monthly rent hanging in the crook of her elbow. "I can't stop by and see my only son without a motive?"

"Well, you never have before, so . . ." It's the truth. In the four years I've lived here, neither she nor my father has ever graced me with their presence. My grandpa used to come here sometimes, before he died, but not my parents. Never them. I walk past her, down the long hallway and into the kitchen. "Wasn't exactly expecting company." I open the fridge and gesture inside. "I've got beer and water."

"Nothing, thank you." She looks around, taking in the plain white walls, the distressed leather couch, and an entertainment setup to rival that of a sports bar. No chandeliers hanging from the ceiling or fifteen-thousand-dollar pieces of art adorning my walls. My place is nice, and I love it, but it's not the mansion I grew up in—far from it—and I can tell she's looking down her nose at it. Just like everything else in my life.

"Yeah, well, if you don't mind, I'm kind of busy . . ." I gesture vaguely to the space around me, hoping she gets the hint and leaves.

"Doing what?"

No such luck. Shrugging, I say, "Fucking around."

She looks affronted, her eyes going wide as she places a hand at her chest. "Jason, watch your mouth."

I bark out a laugh and shake my head. "Nope, sorry. You can pull that at your house, but not mine. And you don't own me quite yet, so if I want to spend the afternoon playing video games and coding a website for fun, I can. Now what do you need, Mother?"

She smooths a hand over her impeccable hair, not a strand out of place, and asks, "How's Tessa?"

The question startles me, halting my steps. Not because I don't want her asking about Tessa, but because she never would.

Not without an ulterior motive. My voice is laced with heavy skepticism when I ask, "Why do you want to know?"

She tsks and shakes her head. "Always with the suspicion."

"For good reason."

Undeterred by my tone, she continues, "You two seemed cozy at Thanksgiving."

"Where are you going with this?" I lean against the wall in my living room, arms crossed against my chest as I wait for her to finally say what she wants to say.

"I understand Charles discussed the . . . concerns of the partners with you."

"The concerns that I'm a glorified playboy? Yeah, he might've mentioned it."

"He also mentioned something else, didn't he?"

My slightly buzzed brain finally picks up on where she's going with this. Pushing away from the wall, I clench my jaw. "No."

"He didn't mention anything else?"

"He did, and the answer is still no."

She heaves a long-suffering sigh. "I don't understand why you're being so difficult about this. It could be the answer we've been searching for . . . finally put the partners' unease to rest."

"I don't give a shit what *the partners* think of me. If they're uneasy with me, that's not my problem. It's you two who are so insistent on putting me in this position. I would be just as satisfied working in the mailroom, like you not-so-subtly suggested for Tessa. I'm not dragging her into whatever bullshit you have worked up in your mind."

"But she and Haley are perfect, Jason. Already a built-in family. We thought this would take years to coax, and then it fell right into our laps."

My blood runs cold, my entire body stilling when her words sink in. "What do you mean, you thought this would take years?"

"Maybe now isn't the best ti—"

"What did you *mean*, Mother?"

She leans forward on the couch, her purse resting in her lap like a shield. Clearing her throat, she says, "Well, of course your father and I have a future we'd like for you to consider."

Of course they do. They've always had a future planned out for me, for as long as I could remember. Whereas my grandpa always encouraged my interests, encouraged me to pursue my dreams, the two people who were supposed to support me unconditionally encouraged me only if it had the desired impact on what they wanted for my life.

I barely resist the urge to punch a hole through the drywall behind me. "A future where I'm married to a girl of your choosing who's popping out at least one heir, am I right?"

"But don't you see? Now that doesn't have to happen. It can be someone you've chosen. All the better that it'll fast-track the family portion, at least in the partners' eyes. Of course, I'll have to . . . finesse the truth of Tessa's history with the girls at the club, just to make sure she's accepted, you understand."

And I do. I understand every word that comes out of her mouth, because it's some version of the same thing I've heard my entire life. It's then that I realize this is never going to end. None of it. They'll always have a stake in my life, always pull the strings whenever they get the inkling, whenever they think I won't fight back. And the thought of them doing this to Tessa and Haley . . . the thought of my parents tainting the two most vibrant and beautiful women I know, the two girls I love most in the world, bleeding their toxic nature into them . . . No. It can't happen. I won't *let* it happen.

Quietly, calmly, I say the words that will get her off my back. The words that will make sure Tessa and Haley stay mine and mine only. "There is no me and Tessa, Mother. There's nothing there for you to build into something it's not. There's no wedding bells and no built-in family coming my way."

"But . . . but you invited them for Thanksgiving. Surely it's serious. I've never once met a girl you were seeing."

A bitter laugh escapes my mouth. "Like I would willingly bring someone to meet you two? I invited her because she didn't have anywhere else to go. That's it." I step toward her, not caring that I'm towering over her as she sits perched on the couch, and I'm finally pleased to see a crack in the facade she wears all the time. And then I say whatever I have to so I can keep the only pieces of light in this life my parents are bound and determined to orchestrate for me. "Let me repeat it for you, so you can run off and tell my father and the partners: There is no me and Tessa. She was there to scratch an itch, and I let her. That's it. I learned a long time ago not to get involved with anyone. She's no exception."

TWENTY-EIGHT

tessa

Paige's words ring through my head as I take the elevator up to the third floor, the surprise trip she urged me to make showing up sooner than I expected. With Becky watching Haley until after nine—when my shift was supposed to end—and a cancellation for a cut and full foil leaving me a huge chunk of my evening wide open, I have time to kill. And after talking to Jason earlier, I know exactly how much he could use a little distraction.

I repeat my mantra since leaving the salon—*this isn't a big deal*—over and over as the elevator slowly climbs to my destination. Jason left me his key because he wants me to use it. In fact, he's asked me repeatedly *when* I'm going to get around to using the thing. With this in mind, I take determined steps toward his door—317—but hesitate when I finally get to it. I don't even know if he's home, if he came here after talking with me earlier this afternoon, or if he's out with friends, trying to forget what awaits him in a couple short weeks. I don't know if I should knock and wait for him to answer, or if I should go ahead and use the key he gave me. But then I figure it would sort of defeat the purpose if I came all this way and just knocked, waiting for him to answer.

I imagine a hundred different scenarios if I were to use my key and let myself in, just like I've done every day since finding it under that bright pink Post-it note. Where he's in the shower and I strip naked before walking in behind him and wrapping my hand around his length, stroking him into a frenzy until he spins and takes me right there against the shower wall. Where he's sitting on his couch, watching TV or playing a video game, and I surprise him by licking, then biting his earlobe like he loves before I walk around the couch and straddle him, rocking against him until we both get off.

With renewed urgency, I finally slip the key into the lock, holding my breath as I twist it and turn the knob, pushing through into his space. His building isn't what I'd expect, having seen where Jason lived for eighteen years, but it's exactly what I'd expect knowing just *Jason*. It's nice, but not ostentatious, a solid brick building with large balconies and a small outdoor pool and clubhouse. I passed a tiny gym with only a couple machines on the way to the elevator. No sprawling indoor pool. No Jacuzzi. No on-site spa like I would expect from someone coming from the wealth Jason has available to him. His parents probably shit a brick at the non-extravagant conditions he's living in, and I smile at the thought— his subtle way of giving them the finger, of keeping some of the control he's so desperate for when it comes to them.

I take gentle, tentative steps down his hall, the plush carpeting under my feet muting the sounds of my footfalls. A long corridor leads to what I assume is the kitchen and living room.

No pictures hang on the white walls, but that doesn't surprise me. Jason's a no-frills kind of guy. He'd want everything simple and uncluttered.

The sound of muted voices reaches my ears when I get closer, and for a minute I think it's the TV until I recognize one of the voices as Jason's. A soft, feminine voice sounds next, and my stomach jumps into my throat, fear and uncertainty paralyzing me at why a woman would be alone in Jason's apartment with him. And then I catch the end of something he says— ". . . me and Tessa, Mother." I breathe for half a second as I realize who he's addressing until the rest of what he says registers, and then I'm frozen once again, braced against the wall, but for another reason entirely.

". . . something it's not. There's no wedding bells and no built-in family coming my way."

"But . . . but you invited them for Thanksgiving. Surely it's serious. I've never once met a girl you were seeing."

Jason laughs, the sound bitter and so unlike the man I've come to know, the man I've come to love, and my heartbeat speeds into a gallop, my palms sweating. "Like I would willingly bring someone to meet you two? I invited her because she didn't have anywhere else to go. That's it."

A protest gets caught in my throat, and I press my hand to my mouth while the butterflies in my stomach that have always been present when Jason's around twist and turn and spin like a swarm of hornets. I take a tentative step forward so I can peer into the open space, my tunnel vision seeing only Jason standing in front of his mother, his face cold and harsh and unlike everything I've come to know of him.

And then Jason puts the last nail in the coffin and pounds his point home. "Let me repeat it for you, so you can run off and tell my father and the partners: There is no me and Tessa. She was there to scratch an itch, and I let her. That's it. I learned a long time ago not to get involved with anyone. She's no exception."

That shoe I was waiting to drop just fell from the sky on top of me, a steel-toed boot right to the temple, and even knowing it was coming, even *expecting* it, doesn't lessen the harsh blow. I gasp in disbelief, hurt and anger warring inside, and how did I not expect this exact scenario? Somehow I thought he'd get spooked, run when it was getting too serious. And even though I worried about it, I wasn't actually prepared for all my doubts to get thrown back in my face.

I wasn't prepared for him to discard me so easily.

jason

As soon as I say the words to my mother, I want to take them back. I hate saying them, the lies sitting bitter on my tongue, but I won't give Tessa and Haley to her, not like this. Not to simply please a group of old men I give zero fucks about. Not just for appearance. My parents are getting my *life*, they don't get the reason it's worth living, too.

A choked gasp sounds from off to the side, and I whip my head toward the noise, my back going rigid to see the one person I was trying to keep away from all this staring at me like she doesn't even know who I am. She's bundled in her bright pink coat, a wool beanie pulled down over her head, and I want to kiss her and tell her to get the hell out of here because she doesn't belong anywhere near the woman who's spent the last twenty-four years slowly sucking the life out of me.

Tessa opens her mouth to say something, but snaps it shut, her jaw clenching and eyes narrowing. She throws something in my direction before spinning around and walking back down the hall, the door banging open against the wall in her rush to leave.

"Tessa, wait!" Without thought to my mom still sitting there witnessing this, I hurry after Tessa, past my apartment door and out into the hall, watching as the elevator doors start to close on her red, furious face. I sprint the last few feet, sticking my arm in to keep the doors from closing, then slipping inside. She's braced against the back wall, her expression livid, and I'm glad she's pissed as hell. I can handle that more than I can handle tears. I step toward her and reach out for her hand.

She jerks away like I burned her. "Don't you *dare* touch me. You lost that right about three minutes ago."

I shake my head, forcing my hands to my side so they don't reach for her again. "No, baby, you don't understand. Just let me explain."

She laughs, and even I can admit how lame it sounds. "Explain what? Your words were pretty clear back there, and I don't think I missed much." She shakes her head, looking into my eyes like she's searching for the truth. "I can't believe I fell for it. I really thought you'd changed."

"I *did* change—"

She holds up her hand, stopping me as she says, "Save it, Jason. When this whole thing started, when you *pushed* this thing between us, you knew exactly what I was looking for. A man, not a boy. Someone who wanted to be with me and Haley for the long haul, someone who was mature and knew what he wanted."

"I know, and I—"

She interrupts me again. "I had to grow up way too young, and that sometimes makes it hard to be a twenty-two-year-old, but it's who I am. And it's who I need. I want to be in a relationship with a grown-up, and you're never going to be one, are you?" She shakes her head, taking a deep breath as she closes her eyes for a minute before staring at me again, her jaw set and fire in her eyes. "My car . . . the pipes, and then Thanksgiving—was that all just because you *pitied* me? Well, fuck you," she says with a jab of her finger into my chest. "I don't need your help or your pity. And I sure as hell don't need you."

The doors to the elevator open on the main floor, and she doesn't hesitate as she walks around me and through the lobby, leaving without even a backward glance. Her words, though hurtful and pride-filled, seep into me, and I have nothing to say—no response that will come. All the fire drains out of me, because she's absolutely right. She doesn't need me or my fucked-up family screwing up her life and the life of that little girl I love so much. Because of that, I don't stop her when she opens the main door and steps outside. When she gets into her car and backs up. And I don't stop her when she drives away.

I just let her go, because if there's one thing my mother taught me by coming here today it's that it's never going to end. As long as they're in my life, I'm always going to be a pawn for them, everything in my life nothing more than easily movable pieces, and I refuse to let Tessa and Haley just be pieces in my parents' puzzle. They deserve so much better than that.

Numbly, I take the elevator up to my floor, head hanging in resignation. My door is still open when I get to it, which means my mother is still inside. I walk through, slamming the door behind me, and head to where I know I'll find her. She's sitting primly on the edge of my couch, stiff as a board, and I hate everything my life is because of her . . . because of my father. Yes, they've given me everything I could've ever asked for—except the one thing I wanted more than anything, the one thing my grandfather gave me but took with him to the grave: acceptance.

A glint of metal on the floor catches my eye—the object Tessa threw at me before she left—and I don't have to bend down to retrieve it to know it's the key I gave her.

"Well, as that little situation proved, there is no me and Tessa." My voice is flat as I address my mother. "You can bring the news home to your puppet masters."

"Jason . . ." She hesitates, clearly conflicted after everything she witnessed, but not enough to bottle that shit up. "You're still planning—"

"Don't worry, Mom, I'll be there, suit in place, on January second."

With a nod, she stands. "There's also the holiday party the Friday after Christmas."

"Which I won't be attending."

"It's not optional."

"The fuck it's not. You own me in January. Every day before that is mine. I trust even without a housekeeper to show you, you can find your way out." Even as I say it, I turn around and head into the kitchen. Forgoing the beer I'd had earlier, I pull some whiskey from the cupboard and grab a glass, ignoring my mother as she walks down the hall and the front door closes behind her.

And then I swallow two fingers of the amber liquid, letting it burn my throat, and immediately pour another, content to let the alcohol pull me under.

TWENTY-NINE

tessa

Somehow I make it home, relieve Becky from babysitting, and get Haley to bed before I allow myself to even think about the events of the last couple hours. I can't even say I'm blinded by it, having been expecting it for so long. I just had no idea it would be like this. Admitting to his mom, of all people, that I'm basically a glorified booty call.

I'm lying in bed for forty-five minutes, reliving every word I heard from him, every subtle look in his eyes, before I finally give in and grab my phone to dial Paige's number.

"Hey, girlie. How'd that *surprise* go? Get your lady business all taken care of?"

A choked laugh leaves me, and before I know what's happening, I'm crying—sobbing, really—not able to say anything.

"Oh shit, Tess? What the hell happened?" Rustling in the

background comes over the line, then the jangling of her keys. "Never mind, I'll be there in ten."

The call disconnects, and I let the phone fall to my side, scrubbing my hands over my face. I don't want to cry over this, over him, especially when he discarded me so easily when pressed by his mother, but I can't help it. The tears come unbidden and don't stop until Paige shows up some time later. She takes her shoes off and climbs into bed with me, a carton of double-fudge brownie and two spoons set before me like an offering.

Her eyes are sympathetic when I tell her everything that happened, sparing no details. The compassion that was initially in her gaze is now backed by a flickering fierceness, like she wants to take off and find Jason herself, teach him a lesson, and that in and of itself is priceless. That I have a friend who wants to take a piece out of anyone who hurts me is a balm to my broken heart.

Sometime later, after I've calmed myself enough to stop crying, we're sitting up in my bed, both eating straight from the carton.

"I just don't get it. It doesn't make any sense . . . not with the way he was around you," she says around a bite of ice cream.

"Doesn't matter if it makes sense. He said the words, loud and clear. I wasn't hallucinating."

"No, I know you weren't. But, was it . . . was it maybe something he was saying just to get his mom off his back? I know you've said they're total assholes, making him do shit he doesn't want."

"But what could they make him do? Break up with me? They hate me enough for that, and Jason certainly accomplished it." I shake my head and spoon another bite out of the carton. "No, that wasn't it. But you know what? It doesn't matter. Because this just cemented the fact that deep down he's still a boy. He's never gonna grow up, and that's all I've ever looked for—a relationship with an adult."

"Have you talked to Cade at all? See what he—"

"No. No way." I hadn't even thought about how I would tell Cade this turn of events, especially since he was so against Jason and me getting together in the first place. "How am I going to tell him?" And then a thought I didn't allow myself to contemplate seeps in, and my shoulders sag. "How am I going to tell *her*?" I ask, and Paige knows I'm talking about Haley without my having to say it.

The thought of my little girl's devastation at hearing Jason won't be coming around as much anymore brings a fresh wave of tears from my eyes, and I accept the spoonful of chocolate medicine Paige offers me to help ease the burn in my chest.

IT'S THREE DAYS later before Haley asks about Jason. Three days where I was afforded quiet contemplation—which basically meant I spent three nights crying myself to sleep. I didn't think it through enough before I leapt into this with Jason. He's been a fixture in my life for nearly as long as I could remember, and then, suddenly, he's just gone.

I miss more than the combustible chemistry we had together, more than the intimacy we shared. I miss the guy he came to be over the last few months—my best friend next to Paige. And the loss shatters me all over again.

Once those three days have passed, when Haley finally asks where Jason's been, it becomes an everyday occurrence. Wondering if he'll be by that evening, if he can come over Saturday for a pajama day, if he'll take her out in the snow to play. And I try to fill the void, taking her to a movie on the night she hopes he'll swing by, doing a donut and PJ day, complete with cookies for lunch on Saturday. Making snow angels and snowmen and having snowball fights with her, even though I absolutely loathe the snow, just to see her smile.

But she doesn't stop asking.

And every time she does, my heart breaks a little more.

Not for me, though mine is decimated. But for my daughter. She doesn't understand the mechanics of grown-up relationships, which is why I've always sheltered her from mine, never allowed a man to get too close.

Couldn't really avoid that with Jason, the man who's been in her life since the day she was born, could I?

A week after I broke things off with Jason, Haley and I are in the bathroom at home, her in a bath piled high with white bubbles, some on her face acting like a beard, while I sit on the rug and supervise.

"Do I look like Santa, Mama?"

"Just like him. You need to eat more donuts, though, to get your belly like his."

"Maybe I better have some tomorrow, then."

I laugh, shaking my head as I soap up her hair, trying to make funny shapes with it. It's too thick and heavy, though, and falls down her back before anything can come of it.

"When's Uncle Cade comin'?"

"He'll be here next week, right before Christmas."

"Winter, too?"

"Yep, she's coming, too."

The smile she gives me is blinding, and I'm so glad she has this to distract her, even if temporarily, from the void Jason didn't even realize—or didn't even care—he'd leave.

"What about Jay? He comin', too?"

I guess it's not distracting her like I hoped it would.

Like I've done the last week she's been asking about it, I deflect. "Um, I'm not sure, baby. We'll have to see what his schedule's like."

"How come he's not comin' around as much anymore? It's been *forever*. He said we could build a snow fort."

Despite my broken heart, hearing my daughter's angelic voice say that Jason promised her something—promised and *flaked*—pisses me off, and I work hard to keep my temper under control so she doesn't see it.

"He's been really busy with school and stuff for his parents, I think." That's right, I've been a coward and haven't told her anything about what happened. I haven't told Cade, either, though he's going to know about five minutes after he gets home. He's got this weird voodoo power over me and can always sense when something's off.

"Well, he better get here before the snow melts."

I laugh and pour some water over her head to rinse her hair. "We've got a while till the snow melts, baby. It came early this year."

"Yes!" she hisses, flailing about in the bath and splashing water everywhere.

And just like that, she transitions to talking about something else, her shoulders relaxed and a smile on her face, all contemplation over Jason pushed to the back of her mind.

I only wish it were that easy for me. That the thoughts of him didn't come to me at all hours of the day. That the nights, when I should get a reprieve from him, weren't filled with dreams of what it was like when we were together so I'm forced to wake up with those thoughts fresh in my mind. Memories of his lips and hands on me, of his sweet whispered words crowding my head and heart.

So I can never get a moment's peace from the memory of him.

THIRTY

Tessa

Cade's here for two hours before the drilling starts. He lasted longer than I thought he would, to be honest. I knew it was killing him, though, to know something was wrong but not be able to ask about it—not until Haley was out of earshot, snuggled and sound asleep in her bed.

She's tucked in now, and I'm changed into some yoga pants and a hoodie, ready as I'll ever be to face whatever questioning Cade can throw at me. I know there's no getting out of this conversation with him, and I'm dreading it. Almost as much as I dread the nightly question from Haley about where Jason's been.

I make my way into the kitchen and see Cade in there, opened bottle of beer in front of him and a wineglass filled halfway with red liquid in front of the empty chair next to him.

"That for Winter?" I ask with a nod toward the glass.

"No, she's in the bedroom."

"Ahh, no witnesses for this, huh?"

He ignores my question as I slide into the seat next to him and take a drink of the much-needed wine. Then he dives in. "Where's Jase tonight?"

Taking a deep pull of my wine, I avoid Cade's eyes. "Hell if I know."

He swears under his breath. "What'd he do, Tess?"

I expel a deep breath and shake my head. "It's nothing, okay? All you need to know is whatever we were doing is done. And I really don't need to hear 'I told you so,' all right?"

"How about *I'm going to kick his ass*? Can you hear that?"

I laugh, and think for half a second about actually letting him, because he totally would. "I love you for wanting to protect me, but I'm a big girl, Cade. This is as much on me as it is on him."

He sits back in the chair, his eyes wide. "How the hell do you figure that?"

I shrug, running my finger along the rim of the glass. "I went in with both eyes open, knowing exactly what I was getting into with him, and jumped anyway. Jason was never the idiot in this scenario. That title belongs solely to me."

He clenches his hands against the island. "I'm going to kill him."

Smiling, I put my hand on his arm to keep him seated next to me. "No you're not. You're going to sit here and tell me about your fancy, glamorous life in Chicago to keep my mind off it."

He must see something in my eyes because he relaxes back in his chair and takes a swig of his beer. "It's . . . God, Tess, I can't even tell you how fucking amazing it is. John has me running the kitchen on Oscar's nights off, and I feel like I'm in heaven. Talks are getting more serious about opening another three restaurants. Tentative plans are for Minneapolis, Denver, and . . . here."

I gasp, my fingers tightening on his arm. "Here? Are you serious?"

"Yep."

"Holy shit, Cade."

"I know."

"Does this mean you might be coming back?" I hold my breath, waiting for the answer. And I realize with a start that me wanting him back has nothing to do with lifting the burden he once helped me shoulder. Sometime over the last month, Haley and I really hit our stride, nights going a little smoother, days a little less frantic. It's not perfect—I'm never going to be perfect, and I'm finally okay with that—but it's manageable. And we make a pretty damn good team, just the two of us. No, my excitement is strictly because I've missed having my brother around. And my daughter has missed her uncle.

"I'm not sure. John knows how much I want to be back here, so if I'm ready for it, I can't imagine he'd give it to anyone else. I just have to bust my ass to show him I can handle it."

"That's amazing. Are you glad you did this now?"

"Hell, yeah. It was one of the hardest decisions of my life, but I can't ever regret it, even if I have to be away from you guys."

"We're doing okay."

He gives me a look, the one that says he thinks I'm full of shit.

"We're doing okay, the Jason situation notwithstanding."

"Does this mean you're back to the online douche bags? Gonna call up that dentist again?"

I roll my eyes and take another sip of wine. "He was an orthodontist, and no." I shrug and lean back in my chair. "I'm fine with it being just me and Haley for now. I was so set on finding something I thought I wanted to get my happily ever after, and it blew up in my face. I'm not going to push anything anymore—I did it first with a guy I felt nothing for and then with a guy I knew better than to get involved with." What I don't say, though, is that I still yearn for that—for a connection like I had with Jason, but with a guy there for the long haul, ready to stick it out with me. I know I'm young, but my life doesn't lend itself to quick hookups and shallow relationships.

And my heart never lent itself to that.

jason

I shove pizza boxes and beer bottles out of the way, looking for my ringing phone. I don't even know what day it is. Monday, Tuesday? Christmas or New Year's? Without class to fill my schedule and my parents, for once, leaving me the hell alone, I've been able to just . . . be. I've been able to play *Halo* for five hours at a time, order in pizza and Chinese, and drink beer at noon if I want. No one to talk to, no one to answer to, no one to consider but myself.

It's been just fucking peachy.

I find my phone just as the ringing cuts off, but it starts right back up again, Adam's name lighting up the screen. Falling back to the couch, I answer, "Yeah."

"Jesus Christ, Jase, what the hell did you do?"

"Gonna have to narrow it down, man," I say, even though I know exactly why he's calling. And it looks like my time's up with my other best friend, because if Adam got wind of it, Cade's not far behind.

"I thought she wasn't just a piece of ass for you."

A hundred retorts come to me, sitting on the tip of my tongue, but really what can I say? She *wasn't* just a piece of ass to me, and that's the exact reason I'm not with her right now. Because she meant—*means*—so much more.

When I don't respond, he says, "I can't believe you didn't tell me. I had to find out from Cade—who's on his way to kick your ass, by the way. If my plane got in tonight instead of tomorrow, I would, too."

"Yeah, well, I've kicked my own ass, so your services aren't needed."

"Seriously, man, what the fuck?"

I blow out a deep breath and close my eyes, dropping my head to the back of the couch. "It just didn't work out."

He snorts on the other end of the line. "Yeah, not buying it. And Cade's not gonna buy that bullshit, either."

"I'll worry about that when he gets here. How'd he sound?"

"Like he's ready to rip your balls off and feed them to you. And I couldn't even give you a buffer because I knew jack about it."

I grunt in acknowledgment, knowing I don't deserve a buffer. Whatever Cade sends my way, I have it coming, tenfold.

"Assuming you're still walking tomorrow, let's grab a beer. I'll be there till the twenty-eighth," he says.

"Yeah, sounds good." There's a pounding at my front door loud enough to wake everyone within a three-block vicinity, and I mumble, "Fuck."

"Time's up, huh? Good luck with the beast." And then the line's dead.

I groan, rubbing a hand over my face and dropping my phone

to the couch next to me. I am not nearly drunk enough to have this conversation with Cade.

With a sigh of resignation, I heave myself off the couch and walk to the door, opening it to my red-faced best friend. "Cade, what a pleasant surprise," I say dryly.

He breezes past me, giving me a sharp look as he continues down the hallway and around the corner. When I get to the living room, I find him standing with his arms crossed, looking at the piles of takeout and garbage lying around. "What the hell is all this?"

"Lunch. And dinner. And probably breakfast. Hungry?" I ask as I fall back to the couch, grabbing the game controller from next to me as I prop my feet up on the coffee table.

Cade stalks over and kicks my feet down, towering over me with a glare on his face. "Tessa's been tight-lipped about whatever went down, and I'm taking it from her. I'm *not* going to take it from you."

"Don't have much of a choice, seeing as I'm not telling you shit." I try to ignore him and go back to playing my game, knowing I'm being an epic asshole, especially considering this is the first time I've seen him in six months, but I can't even bring myself to care.

"Jesus Christ, Jase, what the fuck's going on? I thought I'd come over here and find you with two girls in your bed and really have to kick your ass. Instead, I find you looking like you haven't showered in a week."

"Yeah, well . . ." I say with a shrug, avoiding his eyes.

"I don't get it. If you didn't break it off to get with another girl, what's the deal? I know Tessa didn't end it, because she's not doing much better than you are."

The mention of her name is like a punch to the neck, and I'm left struggling for air. "Tessa's doing a hell of a lot better now," I mumble.

"What the hell's that supposed to mean?"

Blowing out a breath, I lean forward and brace my elbows on my knees. "Look, you were right, okay? She's better off without me. And she's sure as hell better without all the family bullshit that's always going to follow me."

He stares at me for a minute, then shakes his head. "If you actually believe that, you're even more of an idiot than I originally thought. Shit, man, did you even listen to yourself?"

"I've done nothing *but* listen to myself for the last week. That's why I'm still sitting here and not at her door. It's for the best."

"Yeah? The best for *who*, exactly? Because from where I'm sitting, you're both miserable."

"She'll be a hell of a lot more miserable if she gets dragged into the bullshit I have to deal with every day from my family."

"You know what? I'm so sick of hearing about your goddamn family. You don't want them to run your life? *Don't let them.* Cut the fucking cord already and grow up."

"You think it's just that easy? There's no compromise with them—it's all or nothing."

"So you'd rather have it be all with them and nothing with Tessa instead of the other way around? And what about Haley? She keeps asking about you every five fucking minutes."

At the mention of Haley, I snap my head to him and take every ounce of frustration he's pouring my way.

He nods. "Yep. Four times just since Winter and I got here."

"Shit." I scrub a hand over my face. "Hey, can you . . . I mean, I got her a Christmas gift. Can you give it to her?"

"You want her to have it? Stop being a pussy and give it to her yourself." He steps a little closer and towers over me. "What are you going to do when Tessa puts up that fucking online profile again? When she goes out with another orthodontist or a lawyer or some other boring-as-hell guy because she thinks that's what she needs?"

And just like always, the thought shoots ice through my veins. It's the same thing that's been on repeat in my mind since I let Tessa walk away—someone filling the place I didn't have long enough. Someone watching sappy chick movies with Tessa or playing in the snow with Haley. Going on Saturday-morning donut runs before spending the day in bed watching cartoons.

And I hate it. I hate every fucking second of it, but I don't want them to be a pawn for whatever game my parents are playing at that particular point in time.

"It's not that easy, Cade."

"Make it that easy. Whatever happened . . . whatever made you end this thing with Tess, it's not unfixable." He turns and walks away, saying over his shoulder, "Pull your head out of your ass and man the fuck up."

THIRTY-ONE

tessa

"All right, bitches, let's get this party started," Paige says as she walks into my bedroom, where Winter sits on my bed, waiting as I try to find something to wear.

"Can't we just stay home?" I ask, turning around to look at her.

"What are you, eighty?" Paige pushes me out of the way while she riffles through my clothes. "We are going to go party. We are going to live it up. We," she says as she spins toward me, pointing her finger in my direction, "are going to *get you drunk*." She turns back around and grabs a few things from my closet before shoving them at me. "Wear that. Your hair looks fabulous, as always. But I need to do something with your makeup situation, because this haggard look you've got going on is not working."

I heave a sigh and toss Winter a pleading glance. She holds up her hands and shakes her head. "Don't look at me. She's *your* best friend. This is why I've stayed away from friends most of my life."

"Well, you're stuck with us now," Paige says as she plops down on the bed while I change into the clothes she pulled out for me. Low-rise jeans and a fitted, open-back long-sleeved shirt. Demure from the front, sexy hellcat from the back. Not exactly the look I'm going for. An oversize sweatshirt and ratty leggings would be a more accurate reflection of my mood.

In truth, though, I could use this night out with them, especially since Cade and Winter leave to go back home tomorrow. The last couple weeks, even with all the excitement of Christmas having come and gone, have been rough. I thought with everything going on that I'd get a reprieve from the constant barrage of Jason-related thoughts. So far, the only time I get a moment's peace is when Haley is there distracting me, and even that's a slippery slope, because she hasn't stopped asking about him.

"Nope," Paige says, cutting me off from my thoughts. "You're doing it again. No thinking about He Who Shall Not Be Named. That's not allowed tonight. Now hurry up, we have shots to do."

Paige pushes me in the direction of the bathroom once I'm changed and goes to work on my makeup while I sit dutifully and let her, hoping all the while she's right. That I'll get some much-needed oblivion courtesy of an alcohol-induced haze.

"PAIGE REALLY LOVES this stuff, huh?" Winter asks from the high table we managed to score, looking toward where Paige is dancing among a sea of guys.

"Yeah," I say with a sigh. My cosmo isn't working as fast as

I'd like it to, and I'm entirely too coherent for my liking. This whole Get Tessa Drunk plan isn't working for shit.

"Cade didn't really tell me much about the whole Jason thing . . ."

"That's because he doesn't know what happened." I take a long pull of my drink. "And I doubt Jason said anything when Cade went over there the other day." When I found out Cade actually went to Jason's to talk to him, I was livid. I reamed Cade up one side and down the other for interfering. The thing that got to me the most was thinking whatever Jason and I had would get in the way of his and Cade's friendship, and despite how heartbroken I am, I don't want their relationship damaged because of it.

"He didn't," she confirms. "Cade's just worried about you. And he'll never tell you that."

"I'm surprised *you're* telling me that."

She looks at me over the rim of her water glass—designated driver, thank God. "Yeah, me, too. But when it's important to Cade, it's important to me." She shifts in her seat and leans toward me a little more, making it easier to hear her over the thumping bass in the club. "He was livid at first, when he found out you guys were hooking up."

I cringe at that term, knowing now that's all it was to Jason when it was never, ever that for me.

She notices my reaction and waves a hand. "When you guys got together . . . whatever. He was pissed, because he didn't want you to get hurt. And, come on, even I knew about how Jason was with girls."

I nod, because I know how he was with girls, too. Everyone does. And I should've listened to that voice in my head that urged me against doing anything with him. Maybe if I had, I wouldn't be sitting in a club I don't want to be in, nursing my broken heart over a nearly empty martini glass.

"Anyway, after a while, he came around." My head snaps up, eyes locking on hers as she nods. "Yeah. It was hard as hell to get him to stop being so fucking overprotective and really *consider* Jason as someone for you and Haley. And when he did? When he finally put aside his big-brother bullshit and thought about who would be the right fit for you and her? Well, he settled down."

"I don't get it . . . He's been like a caged lion the last few days, ready to rip Jason's head off. If he's so cool with us being together, he wouldn't be set on that."

"He wants to pull Jason's head out of his ass, not rip it off. Look, we don't know what happened, but something went down, and from what Cade told me, it's not any other girls."

I snort, not believing it for a minute. It's been weeks since our blowout. Jason's probably made the rounds five times by now. The thought sends a stab of pain to my stomach, the alcohol I've ingested threatening to revolt. So I do what any sane person in my position would—I chug the rest of the liquid in my glass and order another when the waitress passes by.

"Look, Tessa, I don't know if you know everything that happened with me and Cade . . ."

Shaking my head, I say, "Nope. He never told me anything."

"Yeah, well, I was Jason in that scenario. I had my head up my ass. I loved Cade, but I didn't think it was enough." She stares into her glass before she asks quietly, "Do you love Jason?"

Do I love him? More than my next breath. I love his quiet but steady presence at night after Haley's in bed and the house is silent and still. I love when he grumbles about drinking wine with me because it's a *girlie* drink but does it anyway because I ask him to. I love when he lets me sleep in and takes my little girl on a donut run, then plays with her for hours in the snow. When he plays dress-up and has tea parties and grumbles only a little when she wants to try out her bright pink nail polish on his toes. I love how he made me feel alive, made me feel like so much more than just a mom, how he made me feel like *myself*.

I swipe at the tears in my eyes before I look back up at Winter, echoing what she said. "Sometimes love isn't enough."

She pauses for a minute, then shakes her head. "It's everything, Tessa. Just give him a chance . . ."

I snort and gratefully accept the refilled drink the waitress sets in front of me, taking a long swallow. Give him a chance to what? Because from where I'm sitting, alone at a club and getting drunk just to forget him, there's no one around to give a chance to.

THIRTY-TWO

jason

Cade's words have haunted me for the last several days, spinning over and over in my mind until they're all I can hear. *You'd rather have it be all with them and nothing with Tessa instead of the other way around?*

Why didn't I ever think of it like that before? This whole time I was ready to give up something that made me happy, some*one* who made me happy, to spend my life being nothing more than a puppet for two people who don't give a shit about me. It took too long for me to get here, but I finally am. I don't know what the future is going to bring, what kind of life I'll lead, but I don't care. As long as I have Tessa and Haley with me, I don't care, because they're all that matters. They're exactly the kind of family my grandpa always told me was out there . . . the kind he always told me meant everything. The kind he warned me not to turn my back on. He wasn't ever talking about my parents . . . He was telling me I could find it for myself, if I only looked.

I found it . . . found *them* . . . and I almost let it slip right through my fingers.

I pull my car into the circular drive, stopping in front of the valet my parents hired. The party is already well under way, no other cars coming in behind me, so I pocket my keys and tell the guy I'll be right back. What I have in mind isn't going to take very long.

I make my way into my parents' house, taking satisfaction in the looks thrown my way when my parents' snooty colleagues and acquaintances notice my less-than-black-tie attire. I probably should've waited for a more opportune time. Should've come by when there weren't three hundred witnesses, but I never was one for doing what's expected of me, what's appropriate.

I twist my way through the throngs of people, looking for my parents. Finally, I find them by the fireplace, drinks in hand, fake smiles plastered on their faces, and thank fuck this isn't going to be my life anymore.

My mom is the first to notice me when I'm a few feet away, a gasp leaving her lips as her eyes grow wide. She grips my father by his forearm, and he turns to take me in, his eyes hardening.

"Jason," he says, his voice as hard as stone. "We've let everyone know you weren't feeling well. No need to put in face time. Everyone understands." The men and women standing around my parents shoot glances my way, obviously taking in my appearance—jeans and a hoodie don't exactly scream couture.

"Not sick, Dad, though I'm sure that was an easier excuse than the truth."

"Jason," my mom says warningly, her eyes darting around to her friends. "Maybe we can talk about this somewhere private?"

"Actually, I think here is just fine."

My father leans closer to me, his voice pitched low, but I know everyone around us still hears. "Take a minute to think about how you're acting. This isn't how someone of your status in the company should behave."

"Well it's a good thing I'm not working at the company, then."

"Semantics. As of January second, you will be there shadowing me to eventually take over, and that doesn't excuse any unruly behavior beforehand."

"No, I don't think you understand. I'm not going to be *anything* to the company. I'm not doing it." I step closer to my parents, looking them both in the eyes and finally laying it on the line. "It was never what I wanted, and if either of you had listened for two goddamn seconds to anything I said, you'd know that. You ruined everything good that Grandpa made of that company. You tore it all to shreds, and I want nothing to do with it. Find someone else to run the company, because it's not going to be me."

My father's face is beet red now, his eyes wild, and I know if there weren't all these people around, his temper would've exploded by now. His voice is low and controlled, but I can tell by his stance, by the set of his shoulders that he's feeling anything but. "You don't know what you're doing, Jason. Think very hard about what you're about to walk away from."

And by the look in his eyes, I know he's talking about more than just the job. He's talking about everything, them included.

And for once, I don't care. For once, I don't let a sense of obligation or the words of my grandfather keep me from doing what I've wanted to for years. Not when I know what's waiting for me outside these walls. Not after I realized my real family isn't bound to me by blood, but by something else entirely.

"I've already thought about it. And that's what makes this so easy."

AS SOON AS I leave my parents', I go to the one place that's always been more of a home than mine ever was. I don't even care what kind of wrath I'm going to incur from Cade. I have to see Tessa, explain what happened, tell her what a mistake I made, how stupid I was, and hope she'll forgive me.

Hope she'll take me back.

Tessa's car isn't in the driveway, and instead an older model Accord with Illinois plates is in its place. Hoping Tessa just let Cade borrow her car and she's actually inside, I go to the front door and knock quietly, knowing Haley's probably asleep because of how late it is. When the door swings open, it isn't Tessa who answers. Instead, her brother stands there, arms crossed, looking at me with a raised eyebrow.

"It took you a long time to pull your head out of your ass."

"Yeah, well, I was always a little slow on the uptake."

He moves to the side and lets me in. After I shrug out of my coat and take off my shoes, I follow behind him, looking for signs of Tessa along the way but coming up empty. Cade leads me to the kitchen, where Adam's perched at a stool.

"Hey, man," I say.

He tips his chin in my direction. "Finally pulled your head out of your ass, huh?"

"Yeah, yeah, I get it. I was an idiot. Took me a while, but I'm here. Now where's Tess?"

"You were a little too slow. She's not here," Cade says.

"Where is she?"

"I think she went out with that dentist again," Cade says casually, like he's not turning my whole fucking world upside down. Like he's not stabbing me in the heart a hundred times.

Adam chokes on his beer and shakes his head at Cade while I sink onto the stool next to Adam.

"Fuck. *Fuck*." I slam my hand down on the counter. "She's already out on a *date*?" The thought of that boring-ass guy with his hands on Tessa makes my fists clench on the island, and I have to force myself to stay here, to not go after her and tear through every possible place she might be.

It's her choice.

She thought I didn't want her, that she was nothing more than a hookup for me, and I let her think it. I deserve every bit of this.

"Don't be an asshole, Cade," Adam mutters.

Cade's leaning against the counter across from us, his arms crossed and eyes narrowed on me. "I'm gonna be an asshole until he tells me why he came here," he says to Adam, but he's looking directly at me.

I shake my head, taking a deep breath. Whether or not she's out with someone else, that doesn't change what I came here to do. What I *will* do if she gives me the chance. "I get where you're coming from, and I'm glad Tess has you to look out for her. But I don't give a fuck if you're my best friend or not, you don't deserve to hear it before she does."

He's quiet for a minute, studying me. Finally, he says, "You gonna break her heart again?"

"I hope not. I have to get her back first."

"That's *if* she'll take you back. You've got a lot of groveling to do." He walks to the fridge and pulls out two beers, handing one to me. "You can start tonight. Her, Paige, and Winter should be back soon."

His words take a minute to sink in, and when they do, it feels like a dozen cars have been lifted off my chest. "You're an asshole."

"Yeah, well, you're the guy who broke my baby sister's heart. I'd say we're still nowhere near even."

"Fair enough."

"So since you're here for her, can I assume you got your shit settled with your parents?"

"If by that you mean I no longer have any shit with them, then yeah."

Adam's eyebrows shoot up. "You walked away?"

"Yeah. Told them I didn't want any part of the company. And I did it in front of basically everyone who means anything to them. They had their holiday party tonight. I'm afraid there's no way for them to smooth this over. And they made it perfectly clear that if I did this, I'd be cut off from it all. I expect there'll be an eviction notice on my door any day now."

"Shit, man, what the hell are you going to do?" Adam asks.

"I've got a few ideas. I've got a call into the design firm I interned with during the summers. My mentor always said to call him if I ever wanted a job, so I'm hoping he wasn't blowing smoke up my ass. If he wasn't and I can actually get him to hire me, I'm not going to be making anything, really, to start, but it'll be something. And it'll be mine. And now that I've graduated— thanks to my parents' ultimatum—" I offer with a wry smile, "I actually have access to the trust fund my grandpa left me. It's not huge, but it's enough to resurrect the foundation my dad squashed." The satisfaction from that thought alone is priceless.

"You know they're totally going to shit a brick when they realize they can't control you anymore. That you don't need them," Adam says with a smile on his face.

I mirror it. "It's great, right?"

AFTER AN HOUR, we finally hear a car pull up, then a few minutes later, there's shuffling at the front door, then high-pitched giggles, at least one of which I recognize. Keys scrape in the lock, but it doesn't ever catch. Finally, Cade goes over and opens the door to find Winter and Paige trying to support a still-giggling Tessa. Paige's face is flushed red, her eyes a little glassy, and I have no idea how she's helping to hold Tessa up, because it's clear she's closer to drunk than just tipsy.

Tessa's arms are around Winter's and Paige's necks, her cheeks flushed, her hair a mess. She's wearing my favorite pair of jeans—the ones that hang so low on her hips, I can see the dimples at the base of her spine, and I sort of want to kill every fucker who got to look at her tonight.

"What the hell?" Cade asks as he shuts the door, looking among the three girls as Winter tries to tug everyone inside.

She rolls her eyes. "You try wrangling these two when they don't want to go anywhere. I'm just lucky I got them out before they started doing body shots."

"Hey, I'm not that bad," Paige protests as she wobbles along, Tessa's arm still wrapped around her neck. "I said *one* more shot, that's it!"

"Um, that was four shots ago," Winter says as she slips out from under Tessa's arm and takes off her coat. "You might want to get that one to bed." She tips her head in Tessa's direction. "She's gonna be hurting in the morning."

"Got it," Paige says, offering a salute. Or what I assume is supposed to be a salute. "Getting this one to bed." She tucks her arm farther under Tessa and starts dragging her in the direction of the kitchen—the opposite way of the bedrooms—when I finally step in. Tessa's eyes are drooping, looking like she's about thirty seconds from passing out, and Paige sure as hell isn't going to be able to hold her up when she does.

"I got her."

Paige squeaks when I lift Tessa into my arms and turn away. "Hey!" She comes around and points a finger right in my face, bumping it against my nose. "You're not supposed to be here. No penises tonight! That's the rule."

"Yeah, well, sorry. Nothing I can do about that."

She huffs and crosses her arms, glaring at me. "I hope she pukes on you."

"She probably hopes she pukes on me, too. I'm sure she'll call you tomorrow and let you know all about it," I say over my shoulder as I walk around her. "Adam, can you make sure Paige gets home okay?"

Paige is putting up a fight, arguing about her ability to get herself home just fine, while I head down the hallway and into Tessa's room. She's totally out, her head resting on my chest, eyes closed and mouth hanging open, and I hate that she's probably not even going to remember this in the morning.

Gently, I set her on the bed before I start the task of getting her out of her jacket and shoes. Even though I know she won't be very comfortable, I leave her in her jeans and shirt and move her under the blankets. She shifts, her eyes fluttering open, and she blinks at me, then heaves a sigh.

"I knew you'd come. Always . . . every night in my dreams." Her words are slurred together, but I can still understand them, and each word sends a punch to my gut. "Can't get a break from you. Just want a break . . ."

I reach up and brush her hair back from her face, and her eyes flutter closed. There are a thousand things I want to say, a thousand apologies I want to give, but she deserves better than me just suddenly showing up to say I'm sorry. She deserves everything she thought I'd never give her.

She deserves the happily ever after she's been dreaming about as long as I've known her.

I get her a glass of water and some Advil and set both on her bedside table. Then I grab a pen and one of the Post-it notes she keeps on top of the stack of magazines by her bed, writing three short words on it and sticking it on her nightstand, hoping she'll trust me enough one last time to give me this, even though I don't deserve it.

THIRTY-THREE

tessa

I've dropped my comb four times, had to mix up more color solution twice because I underestimated what I'd need, and called a long-time client by the wrong name—all in the last seven hours. My brain just isn't in it. And, if I'm being honest, it hasn't been in it. Not for the last two weeks.

That's how long it's been since I woke up with the mother of all hangovers, still in my clothes from the night before, smelling like stale bar. That's how long it's been since I rolled over and saw the water and Advil on my nightstand waiting for me. Since I saw the bright pink note with three words scribbled in Jason's handwriting.

Wait for me.

What the hell does that even mean? Wait for him for what? To come around? To grow up? To stop holding my heart prisoner? Because he has it. He has it under lock and key, completely vulnerable to him. And I hate it and I love it; I want it to stop and I want it to go on forever.

According to Paige, Jason helped me to my room that night from what she could recall, though she wasn't much better off than I was. And Cade wouldn't tell me what Jason was doing there in the first place. All I have to go on is that tiny Post-it note that's been like a weight in my pocket every day since he left it.

When the salon closes for the night, I walk with the other girls out to our cars. I let mine warm up for a minute before I head home, calling Paige on the way since she was watching Haley for me tonight.

"Hey, girlie," she answers. "How was work?"

"Long. How was the terror?"

Paige laughs. "Awesome, as always. She crashed, though. Probably all that candy I fed her for dinner. She can just stay the night here and I'll bring her by in the morning."

"No, that's okay. I can come get her."

"Why? You'll just have to get her all bundled up to go outside and then she'll be crabby because you woke her up. It's no big deal. She's sprawled out in her princess sleeping bag, anyway."

"You're sure?"

"Definitely. Enjoy your night off. Go have some fun."

I snort and shake my head, navigating my car into my driveway. "Yeah, you know me. Living it up, watching reruns of *How I Met Your Mother* until I fall asleep before eleven."

"I wouldn't count on it. Call me tomorrow."

Before I can decipher her cryptic statement, the line goes dead, and I shrug, slipping my phone in my pocket. Quickly, I make my way through the back door, turning on the light inside and unwrapping my scarf before I slip out of my coat. When my boots are off,

I don't even take time to change, instead heading straight for the kitchen. I pull a glass from the cupboard and open the fridge for some wine. I reach in to grab it, intent on pouring myself a healthy serving, since I have nowhere to be tonight and no little girl I'm in charge of, but something catches my eye. There, stuck to the side of the bottle, is a bright pink Post-it note, just like the one Jason left me his note on a couple weeks ago. Just like the one he used to give me his key all those weeks ago.

With shaking hands, I pluck it from the bottle, my eyes roving over the words several times before they actually register.

I'll give up my beer and drink wine every night if that's what you want.

I shut the fridge, my eyebrows furrowed. When did he leave this? I try to think back to the last few nights, if the note was there and I somehow missed it, but I haven't had a glass of wine since last weekend. I turn around, bracing myself on the counter when a flash of pink catches my eye. On the coffeemaker is another note.

I'll do the early-morning donut run so you and Haley can have your Saturday morning ritual uninterrupted.

My lips twitch in the corner, my hand going to my heart as I glance up and notice another note stuck to the sliding glass door. My heart speeding up, I hold my breath and walk over to it, plucking it off the glass and reading the words Jason's written.

I'll take Haley out every time she wants to play in the snow. Because I love it, and because you don't.

I spin around, my eyes darting to every surface I can see. I spot another flash of pink over on the TV, and with quick steps, make my way to it.

I'll watch 10 Things I Hate About You *for the hundredth time just because it's your favorite and I love watching you watch it.*

By the time I make it to my bedroom, having scoured every other space in the house, I've collected a dozen more. They've ranged from silly—*I'll let Haley paint my toenails whenever she wants (as long as she doesn't tell Cade)*—to sweet—*I'll take you out dancing whenever you want, just say the word.* My heart is pounding, threatening to jump out of my throat, and those butterflies that have been dormant for a few weeks are finally waking up from their slumber and fluttering around.

One last note—the only one in my bedroom—is on my nightstand, in the same location as the one from a couple weeks ago. The one where he asked me to wait for him. I lean over to read it.

Sorry it took me so long.

Directly below the words is an address I don't know, and when I peel the note from my side table, a glint of metal underneath it catches my eye. Pressing my lips together, I pick it up, noticing the shape is different from the last key Jason gave me, but even still, my stomach dips and swirls, memories assaulting me of the last time I used a key he gave me.

With shaky hands, I sit back on my bed and pull my phone from my pocket to dial Paige.

"Why are you calling me?"

"What kind of way is that to answer the phone?" I ask, my voice about three octaves higher than it usually is.

"Why are you freaking out? No, never mind. I know the answer to that. Why aren't you on your way to where you need to be?"

"What the hell?" I ask, my mouth dropping open. "How do you know I need to be anywhere?"

"Um, Haley's with me tonight, isn't she?"

I narrow my eyes, suspicion creeping in. "Paige . . ."

"No, don't do that. Don't second-guess. Don't think about all the shit that happened in the past. Look at what's happening now. *Right now.* Don't think, Tess. Don't plan. Don't take the smartest path. Just jump."

The line's dead before I can even summon up a word to respond with, but everything Paige said rings through my head. And for once, I don't overthink it. I don't worry about what waits at the end, what the possible outcome could be.

I grab my keys, slip into my coat, and drive.

I PULL UP in front of a modest single-story house in a decent neighborhood not too far from home. It's hard to see because it's so dark out, but a porch light shines brightly, illuminating the house numbers that match the ones written on Jason's note. I have no idea whose house this is, who I'm going to see. If this is just another piece of the puzzle Jason's set out for me or if this is the final destination. With shaking hands, I shut off the car and open the door before heading up the front path. Once under the beam of light on the porch, I notice another pink note stuck to the door, just below a small arched window.

Use your key.

I pull the key from my pocket, fitting it into the lock and twisting the handle. When I push through the door, it isn't at all what I expected. The house is barren, no furniture to speak of and only a handful of lights shining. I close the door behind me and notice a hall closet directly in front of me, another note stuck to the folding door.

Open me.

I pause for only a moment before I do as the note says, finding the closet empty, save for a small pink coat and matching snow pants, boots set out below them. There's another note stuck to the hanger, so I peel it off and read.

In case it snows and Haley doesn't have all her stuff with her.

Despite how nervous I am, how wary I am, I can't stop the small smile from creeping over my lips. I step back and turn to walk into the living room. A single floor lamp plugged into an outlet is the only thing in the space. On the wall directly behind it is another note, and I walk over to it, my stomach a churning mess of nerves.

Blue, yellow, or gray walls, do you think?

I glance around the house, pieces of the puzzle Jason's set out for me slowly clicking into place. Stepping back, I turn around and follow the light pouring from the kitchen. Nothing clutters the counter, though there are appliances in place, and a flash of pink catches my eye on the older, ivory refrigerator.

You know what to do.

Assuming it's a repeat of the hall closet, I pull open the door and see only two things inside—a bottle of my favorite wine and a six-pack of Jason's favorite beer.

I don't know what any of this means, but despite this, excitement is bubbling inside me, bursting under my skin like tiny firecrackers, and I need to see more. Closing the fridge, I walk out of the kitchen and look down the long hallway to what I assume are the bedrooms. The corridor is dim, only a tiny sliver of light coming from one of the rooms. With tentative steps, I follow the path down toward the light and push open the mostly closed door.

It's another empty room, the overhead light shining harshly down on what looks like a child's barn and a wooden horse stable. Walking quickly to it, I squat down to take in the intricate details. The stable is filled with three ponies, and a doll who looks remarkably like Haley is standing next to one.

A pop of pink on the roof of the barn catches my eye, and I realize it's another note. With shaky fingers, I peel it off the structure and bring it closer to read.

My renter's agreement frowns on having an actual Shetland pony in the backyard. Think Haley has a sense of humor?

Tears fill my eyes as I breathe out a laugh.

"I know it's bare, but I thought maybe she'd want to help decorate it herself."

Jason's voice startles me, and I push up to stand and spin around to face him. His hair is sticking up every which direction, like he's been nervously tugging at it all night, his eyes bright and a little wild, and I didn't realize just how much it would affect me to see him after all this time. My heart skips a beat, my mouth going dry, and I want to go to him. To fall in his arms and feel his breath against my lips, feel his hands on my waist, feel them cupping my face. I want to cross through this door and *be* with him, but it's not that simple. A few Post-it notes, while lovely and romantic, aren't going to cut it. All of this has been sweet, but I don't know what any of it means. Not really.

And I need him to tell me.

"I'm glad you found my notes."

I lift them up, all of them I've collected, even the ones from my house. "What do they mean?"

He takes tentative steps toward me until he's so close I can feel his breath against my face. "They mean I'm an idiot for thinking I could be okay not having you and Haley in my life."

"But what you said . . . What you told your mom—"

"Was to get her off my back. To keep you and Haley safe from them."

Shaking my head, I say, "I don't understand."

"Thanksgiving night when we were at my parents', Charles insinuated it was time for me to settle down to appease the partners. The night my mom was at my apartment, when you came by, she confirmed they wanted it to be with you. They wanted to use you and Haley to make me look better—to make the *company* look better." He swallows and his eyes harden, his jaw clenching. "I wasn't about to let them use you for anything."

"So you, what?"

"I lied to her. And then when you overheard everything, I didn't correct your assumption because I knew they'd always find a way to control something, to use you or Haley for their advantage, and I couldn't let them do that."

I shake my head, wanting to believe him, but still not understanding how anything's different now than it was before. "Then what changed?"

"I walked away," he says with a shrug, like he didn't completely rewrite the path of his life with those three words.

"You *what*?"

"I walked. I'm done." Hesitantly, he reaches out to take my hand, and I let him, needing the physical touch as much as he seems to. "The night I left you the note, I went to their house and resigned in front of three hundred of their closest friends and colleagues. It's safe to say I'm no longer welcome there."

"Jason . . ." With the hand not encased in his, I reach up and rest my fingers on his chest, searching his eyes for any kind of regret at his decision. But his gaze is clear. "What are you going to do now?"

"I got a job."

I snap my head back, looking at him with wide eyes. "You did?"

"Yep, with the firm I interned for. Entry level, but it pays enough to rent this place, so I'm calling that a win."

"What about . . . what about your apartment? Or—"

"It's gone. All of it's gone. Everything they ever gave me is gone. I have this little house that's not furnished and my tiny paycheck and the trust from my grandpa that I plan to use to start up the Elise Montgomery Foundation again. It's going to be nothing but hard work for a while—as I try to make a name for myself at the firm, and as I get the foundation up and running again—but that's okay. I'm up for it if you're by my side. I'm starting fresh, and I want you with me while I do it. I never thought I wanted this, Tess. I never thought I'd be the guy who watched chick flicks and drank wine and played tea parties, but I am. But only if it's for you. Only for you." He brings his hands up to cup my face, his thumb brushing over my bottom lip. "Say yes. Please, say yes."

His voice is pleading, like everything he has hinges on my answer. Like his whole world will crumble if I say no. I think about those weeks of bliss with Jason, making me laugh and live and love. Reminding me that everything doesn't need to be so serious, that it's okay to take things one day at a time. That it's okay to fall in love with someone who doesn't fit the perfect mold if they make you happy.

And I say the only thing I can. "Yes."

EPILOGUE

"Gotta put the horses away, shorty. It's bedtime."

Haley looks up at me from her perch on the floor in front of the barn and stable I got her last year for Christmas—the gift she got about three weeks late—and pouts. "Five more minutes?"

"You asked that fifteen minutes ago."

"Aww, come on, Jay!" she whines.

"Nope, not gonna work this time. Get in your fancy bed."

"It is pretty fancy, huh?" She smiles at me and gets off the floor to jump into her bed. One that's piled high with ruffled and feathered pillows and a whole lot of other shit I think looks ridiculous and don't even understand what the hell their purpose is, but she had a ball picking it all out for her new room. Whatever she wanted—within reason . . . I am on a fixed budget now. That was my motto. Still is.

"Can you read this one?" She grabs a book from the table next to her bed. "But read it like a pirate!"

I settle next to her and lean back against the four dozen pillows stacked up behind us, then proceed to do just as she asked. Halfway through, Tessa pokes her head in, smiles when I look up at her, and tips her head in the direction of the bathroom before slipping out of the room. Which brings a smile to my face, because I know exactly where she's going—this is our nightly routine in motion.

It's been almost a year since I moved into this place, since I begged Tessa to give me another chance. And now that Cade and Winter have moved back into the house he and Tessa shared, Tessa and Haley spend most nights here with me.

Can't complain about that.

By the time I've finished Haley's story, she's asleep against my side. Carefully, I pull myself away from her and get her tucked in before I slip out of her room and head straight for the bathroom, already tugging my shirt over my head. I'm half hard by the time I get into the bathroom and see Tessa lying in the tub, the mass of bubbles covering the parts of her I want to see.

"Hey," she says, smiling up at me. "She put up a fight?"

"Nothing a pirate disguised as a prince couldn't fix." I pop the buttons on my jeans and shove them down my legs. "How come we can never take showers together? All these bubble baths are fucking with my masculinity."

Tessa snorts, looking pointedly at my cock when I drop my boxers to the floor. Raising an eyebrow, she says, "Yeah, looks like it."

Unrepentant at my reaction to her, I shrug, which earns me a smile. She sits up and lets me slip in behind her, and I love this torture she puts me through. Brushing up against me when she sits back, her spine to my chest. Grabbing my hands and entwining our fingers, resting them on her bare legs. Forcing me to listen to her breathy sighs when I wash her back. Because I know I'll get to dry her off and take her to our bedroom and spend all night kissing and licking and sucking on all the parts of her the bubbles are hiding.

She rests her head against my shoulder while my lips brush against the curve of hers. It's quiet, only the sound of the bubbles popping, but eventually she breaks the silence. "How was work?"

"Good. I pitched my idea for the Nelson site and they loved it. Roberts named me lead designer for it."

She tips her head back to me, a huge smile lighting up her face. "That's awesome! See, you were worried for nothing."

"Yeah, well. It was my biggest project yet."

"I know, but they realize exactly what kind of work you do. They'd be stupid not to choose you for something like that."

"Roberts also agreed to do a fund-raiser for the foundation. Help us get some name recognition out there again."

She's resting her head on my arm, and I can feel the puff of her cheek as she smiles. "I'm so proud of you for doing that. Your grandpa would be, too."

I have little doubt about that, because for once, I'm content in the life I'm leading now. I'm *happy*. And that's all he ever wanted for me.

A hush falls over the room as I run my hands up and down her bare arms, counting down the minutes until we can get out of the bath and do all the fun stuff I've been fantasizing about all day.

Instead of saying she's done, like I was hoping she would, she asks, "Do you ever wonder what would've happened if you'd gone to work for your parents?"

I still behind her, my lips pausing against her skin, my fingers tightening around hers. "No."

She glances back at me. "Never?"

With a shake of my head, I confirm, "Never." And it's true. While it's been hard, finding a job in my field, being shunned by my parents, I wouldn't change it. Because I know, without a doubt, if I'd gone to work for Montgomery International, I wouldn't have Haley and Tessa, and they're worth every sacrifice I could've made. They're worth *everything*. "I wasn't ever happy in that life, Tess."

"And you are now? With us? Even with them out of your life?"

Happy doesn't even begin to scratch the surface. It's a single star as compared to the whole galaxy. But I know she needs to hear that I am, that I don't think I made a mistake doing what I did. That I don't regret it, choosing her and Haley over my parents. And I don't. Not for a single second.

My parents made their choice that day so long ago, when I made my intentions clear—that I wasn't going to be a part of the company. That I was going to live my life finally for myself. They cut me out of their lives without a backward glance, and after twenty-four years of hanging on so tightly to something that wasn't good for me in the first place, I've finally learned to let go. And I'm more content because of it.

I lean in and press my lips to hers, lingering for a minute and trying to infuse everything I feel for her into it. Trying to show her without words how much I love her, but I know sometimes she needs the words, too. I kiss the corner of her mouth and across her jaw until my lips rest at her ear. "Yes, I'm happy. I'll even be happy tonight when you put on your favorite movie again. And tomorrow night when you pour me a glass of wine. And next Saturday when I have to get up at the ass-crack of dawn to get donuts because I'm an idiot and started a ritual I'm never going to live down. Love does crazy things to a guy."

I press my lips to her ear and pull back to see her looking at me, a huge smile on her face, and I'm hit once again by how right this feels. Why I was never struck with that panic at being with her, why I didn't try to get away, why I never wanted to flee . . .

She's it for me. She and Haley are it—my family, the kind I've always wanted. The kind my grandpa always talked about. They're the home I desperately sought the entirety of my life.

Now that I've finally found it, I'm never letting them go.